T0385157

The Search for Othella Savage

Foday is from Sierra Leone and lives in Scotland where he works as a teacher. He studied English Language and Literature at Fourah Bay College and worked as a teacher and lecturer before moving to the UK. His short story, *Amie Samba*, was shortlisted for the 2019 Bristol Short Story Prize, and he has also had stories longlisted, shortlisted or highly commended for the Bridport, Seán Ó Faoláin, Mo Siewcharran, Brick Lane, Commonwealth, Morley, Bloody Scotland and Queen Mary Wasafiri writing competitions. *The Search for Othella Savage* won the 2022 Mo Siewcharran Prize.

The Search for Othella Savage

FODAY MANNAH

QUERCUS

First published in Great Britain in 2025 by

QUERCUS

Quercus Editions Limited
Carmelite House
50 Victoria Embankment
London EC4Y 0DZ

An Hachette UK company

The authorised representative in the EEA is Hachette Ireland,
8 Castlecourt Centre, Dublin 15, D15 XTP3,
Ireland (email: info@hbgi.ie)

A CIP catalogue record for this book is available
from the British Library

HB ISBN 978 1 52943 706 5
EBOOK ISBN 978 1 52943 705 8

1

Typeset by CC Book Production
Printed and bound in Great Britain by Clays Ltd, Elcograf S.p.A

Papers used by Quercus are from well-managed forests and other responsible sources.

Dedicated to the memory of my parents:
Foday Korma and Josephine Agnes.
Thanks for everything and deepest appreciation
for showing me the way.

'It was impossible for devils to live in men; men do as they please and the devil has nothing to do with it'

MONGO BETI

Scotland

CHAPTER 1

Trawling through her phone provided entertainment on nights when Hawa's insomnia was at its angriest. She started with WhatsApp, where the bright '32' in the top left corner of the screen showed the number of unread messages she had.

She first clicked on *The Queens of Sheba*, a group chat for former members of one of the university social clubs she had joined. One of their members – Zainab Zubairu – was seriously ill, and there was a plea asking for queens to contribute money to help with her medical bills. A colleague on the ground in Sierra Leone had posted a picture of Zainab, a crumpled heap in a frayed hospital bed. Her emaciated frame shocked Hawa, who remembered Zainab from university as a lithe athlete with the legs of an impala. Beneath the picture was an update on her condition – the doctor had diagnosed typhoid fever and had placed her on an intravenous drip. The queen who had uploaded the picture was suggesting they pool money to enable them to transfer Zainab to a private clinic at Hill Station, dismissing the government hospital as a *useless den of incompetence full of bastard-dog doctors*.

Another queen had posted a video of a married government minister from back home who had been caught in a guest house with a young side chick mistress. The side chick had secretly filmed him, his wrinkled penis slumped beneath his distended stomach as he tottered around the shabby room in a drunken haze.

Giggling, Hawa next clicked on another group chat titled *Ramat's Wedding*. Ramat – Hawa's younger sister – had been enveloped by a man who worked for a Chinese diamond-mining firm in Sierra Leone. She was due to get married in December and had hastily thrown together a WhatsApp group whilst also bombarding Hawa with endless personal messages featuring lists of what would be required for the big day.

Moving on from the wedding group, Hawa went straight to Ramat's direct messages, which numbered sixteen. Her sister had decided to change the colour of the bridesmaids' dresses from maroon to 'sand' and hoped that Hawa had not already purchased the maroon ones she had suggested just last month. Hawa scrolled through the pictures of the new collection of sand-coloured outfits collated from various corners of the internet. Her sister's final message was a personal prayer, asking that God grant Hawa the financial strength and fortitude to fulfil the responsibilities of the wedding.

Sucking her teeth, Hawa moved on. There was one new message from her friend Othella:

Stella Kowa found in the boot of her car.
She's barely alive!!! Police investigating. Mad!

Gasping, Hawa sat up and switched on the bedside lamp, propping her pillow against her headboard to form a cushion for her back. She knew Stella Kowa from various Sierra Leonean social events she had attended since arriving in Scotland – she was the custodian of a high voice, which she used to lead the choir in church. She had disappeared about ten days ago, and prayers were being offered regularly for her safe return. Now she had been found in the boot of her car.

The time on Hawa's phone read 3.25 a.m., a nagging reminder that her early shift at the hotel was now only a few hours away. Sighing, she moved on to Spotify. Othella, after reading an article in some magazine, had suggested that listening to falling rain was a must if Hawa wished to overcome her insomnia. A search revealed a long list, and she settled on a two-hour segment titled 'Relaxing Rain Sounds for Deep Sleep'. Switching off the lamp, she returned the pillow to its prone position. She laid the phone face down next to her head and turned onto her stomach.

The news about Stella Kowa in the boot of her car would further complicate her attempts to sleep.

CHAPTER 2

It was Othella who had suggested that Hawa try working as a chambermaid. She had described it as a doddle – minimal human contact and, therefore, much preferable to waiting tables. After all, how hard could it be to change a few bedspreads?

After a couple of shifts, Hawa realised that Othella's description of the job had been a case of false advertising, like teeth-whitening toothpaste and strap-on contraptions designed to develop abdominal muscles.

To compensate for her restless nights, Hawa began sneak-sleeping in the rooms she cleaned. She put the guests into categories, like assigning animal groups to kindergarten children. Hyena guests partied through the night – cackling creatures who returned to their rooms at dead hours, often expressing incredulity that there was no hot food available to them. They were the type who left used condoms on the floor and slept in, meaning their rooms could only be cleaned in the afternoons.

Then there were the Meerkat guests – loud invaders with scuttling children who left plastic toys scattered across their rooms. Meerkats were mostly in town for sightseeing and therefore proliferated during school holidays, their kids often entertaining themselves by screech-racing along the corridors.

The sneak-sleep-friendly rooms belonged to the Giraffe guests: pristine types who were in town for some random conference. Giraffe guests generally exhibited the alertness of people who had consumed coffee through their eyes. They left their rooms early, sheathed in sharp suits and swinging laminated identification badges, presenting Hawa with prime real estate within which to nap.

Hawa's last room for the day straddled two categories – Hyena messy but Giraffe empty.

The bed was dishevelled – duvet on floor, pillows flung. The squat fridge had been left open, an assortment of bottles strewn on the floor, a red rivulet from one of them staining the carpet like a stab wound. A large handbag, for which some hapless reptile must have been sacrificed, was capsized at the foot of the bed, its contents scattered.

Shaking her head, Hawa dumped the discarded alcohol bottles in the black bag attached to her cart. She then dropped to her knees and salvaged the items jettisoned from the handbag. Next, she yanked the bedspread off, reuniting it with the duvet on the floor. She did the same with the pillowcases. She yawned again. And then checked her phone again.

There was a new message from Othella:

Stella taken to Royal Infirmary. Police say she was in car boot for four days! Imagine that in this Scottish cold!

Shocked, Hawa sat on the bed and read the message again, her hand covering her mouth in disbelief. Shaking her head, she composed herself and set an alarm for ten minutes. She shuffled over and picked up the embossed DO NOT DISTURB sign, gold writing on a deep blue background. Opening the door, she glanced both ways, like a prewarned child, before crossing a busy street. Finding the corridor deserted, she hung the sign, shut the door and pulled the curtains closed. Kicking off her shoes, she tiptoed to the bed and sprawled.

Hawa had been down for four minutes when she heard a faint noise coming from the bathroom. Her eyes flashed open, and she sat up. Slithering off the bed, she cocked her head to one side, her ears straining for more sound. Hearing further movement, she mouthed, 'Oh God!' and quickly pulled on her shoes. She scuttled across the room to reopen the wine-coloured curtains, readmitting the grey light outside, which had now been joined by slanting rain. She then crept to the bathroom door.

'Housekeeping! Is anybody there?'

The reply was garbled and faint.

Hesitantly, Hawa pushed the door open.

She was met with the sight of a woman lying on her back on the floor, a pillow under her head. The woman was wearing a loose T-shirt that reached to her knees. Her skin was the shade of a burnished wooden carving, and even her apparent distress could not douse her beauty, her hair spread out, stark against the white of the pillow.

'Oh my God! Are you OK? Can you hear me? What's wrong? Are you hurt?'

Hawa dropped to her knees and prodded the woman with a finger.

The floor woman stirred, her eyes fluttering, askew fake eyelashes moving like palm trees in the wind.

'Are you OK? Are you hurt? Don't move! I'll call reception, and they'll get us an ambulance. Are you in pain? Can I move you? Of course I can't. Silly! Did you drink something? Are you cold?'

'I like the cold. Helps me cope with the hammering in my head,' the woman mumbled.

Leaving her prostrate, Hawa dashed into the room, removed a clean white bathrobe from her cart, and hurried back into the bathroom. The woman was by this time on all fours, like a baby learning to crawl, her flowing weave a curtain covering her face.

Hawa helped her to her feet and assisted her into the robe. The woman's scent was a cocktail of contradictions: expensive perfume meets alcohol with an undercurrent of stale sweat. Hawa guided her towards the bed and allowed her to collapse, releasing her a couple of seconds too early. The woman flopped like a stringless marionette, the mattress embracing her and muffling the impact. The palm-tree eyelashes fluttered open, and she smiled up.

'I'm fine. Just need some coffee,' she mumbled.

Hawa made a black cup, deciding that the woman's condition did not require sugar or milk, glancing over to confirm that she was not an apparition and was still on the bed. By this time, the woman had hoisted herself into a sitting position. Her weave cascaded down the white of the bath-robe, lending her a Cleopatra look.

Hawa brought the steaming cup over, realising as she walked that she should not have filled it to the brim. The woman took the coffee, her hands trembling slightly. Dark droplets splashed onto the white dressing gown, spreading into stains on impact. She smiled at her clumsiness and looked up.

'Who are you?'

'Hawa.'

'Where you from?'

'Sierra Leone.'

'Light-skinned girl from Sierra?'

Her accent was American and sounded like someone Hawa had heard on one sitcom or another. To test the temperature of the coffee, the woman extended a designer tongue, stained cerulean blue and decorated with a glittering piercing. It shot straight back into her mouth upon contact with the black liquid.

'Still hot, Hawa. So, what's a sista like you doing in Scotland?'

'University.'

'What you studying?'

'Politics with law.'

'Why you studying law?'

'Studying politics. The law is just an add-on so my father can boast to people back home.'

The woman on the bed disguised her lack of under-standing with a trilling laugh, the cup of coffee in danger of spilling again as she shook.

'In that ugly uniform, you definitely don't look like a lawyer!'

Hawa knew the uniform was ugly. Even Othella had joked that it wasn't the type of chambermaid's dress to feature in adult movies. This one was the standard spare garment foisted on agency staff: custard-yellow with a clumsy black collar and squat stripes around the arms. It had belonged to some woman named Nancy – vestiges of her perfume trapped in the folds and her name embroidered on the chest.

The woman on the bed raised the cup again, her tongue's previous encounter with the hot liquid advising caution. 'Hey, what happened to the sugar?' she laughed, holding the cup out to Hawa, who accepted it with both hands like an athlete receiving a trophy.

As Hawa moved across to modify the coffee, the woman on the bed continued to talk, her voice gaining strength with every uttered syllable.

'You heard of Lauryn Hill?'

Hawa confirmed she had.

'I'm here in Edinburgh for a winter tribute tour. Hip-hop and R&B. I do Lauryn Hill songs. Our final performance was last night, and we had a heavy wrap party, if you know what I mean. Always have to ask if people know Lauryn Hill because folk our age are often more into the likes of Drake, Billie Eilish and Malaika. You down with Malaika?'

'Yeah – I bought *Radical Solutions* last month,' Hawa replied, a light rising in her eyes at the mention of the artiste. The album had been an awakening for Hawa, forever on repeat in her headphones. She had, by this time, returned with the updated coffee.

The woman on the bed laughed, the sound rising from her stomach before becoming trapped in her throat, transitioning into a cough. She spluttered, holding a hand out to Hawa to indicate that she was fine.

'I sang background vocals on that album. Actually spent late nights in the studio working on beats and lyrics with Malaika.'

Hawa was overwhelmed by the celebrity-by-proxy situation. She remembered the *Guardian* review, which she had memorised to appear current during discussions in the students' union canteen. The paper had awarded *Radical Solutions* five stars: *Malaika's seismic debut album is a unique fusion of reggae and hip-hop that speaks to the complexities of contemporary global race relations.*

'So, you're a Malaika fan? That's cool,' the woman continued, invading her reverie.

Hawa smiled, straightening the tea and coffee sachets on the side table for something to do.

'Who does your hair, Hawa?' the woman asked, her consumption of the coffee having moved from sips to deep slurps. 'I like the look of those braids. Do you have hairdressers here in Scotland who do Black hair?'

'My friend Othella, from back home, has always done mine. She also lives in Edinburgh.'

'I've never been to Africa, but I am *from* there,' the woman mused. 'Watched this show when I was recording with Malaika. Oprah was dropping knowledge about how she's from Africa because some doctor tested her DNA. And so Malaika did a test, and the results said that her ancestors were slaves from The Gambia! Imagine that; Malaika born and bred in Bayonne, New Jersey but her people originally from Africa! After that, I set up a blog to celebrate my African roots. My blog name and Instagram is Songhai Sista – after the great African Empire. I try to dig down into my African roots. You could help me drop deep content on my blog, Hawa, seeing as how you're an original sista from Africa!'

Laughing in confusion, Hawa then explained how the rules stipulated that she couldn't clean a room whilst a guest was in it.

'Girl, forget the rules,' replied the woman on the bed. 'Tell you what, Hawa, you tidy the room while I throw down in the shower.' She struggled off the bed, closing the robe around her, her coffee cup abandoned upside down on the mattress.

The woman moved into the bathroom and Hawa heard the sound of running water. Then the woman began to sing, her voice in perfect pitch. Hawa smiled and shook her head as she recognised the lyrics from Malaika's *Radical Solutions*. She began her clean-up, going back and forth from her cart, and soon had the room looking presentable.

The woman emerged from the bathroom draped in a large white towel, with an equally large towel wrapped around her head, turban-style. She winked and gave a thumbs up to Hawa, who smiled back and moved into the bathroom to start her clean-up. They continued their conversation from the separate rooms, whilst Hawa cleaned the shower, changed the toilet roll, stacked clean towels and polished the mirror.

She checked the bathroom one last time before bringing out the rubbish bin, which she emptied into the black bag attached to her cart. Turning, she faced the woman, who was now wearing a sleek pair of black skinny jeans and a black Wu-Tang Clan hoodie. She had also applied bright red lipstick, her mouth reminding Hawa of a big cat in an Attenborough documentary.

The woman was holding a black drawstring silk bag adorned with gold lettering. She held it out to Hawa, in the manner of one handing over a birthday present.

'For you, my African sista. For making me a magic coffee that helped clear up my migraine. And for cleaning my room. You are a size six, just like me; I can read feet,' she laughed.

As if in a trance, Hawa moved forward and took the bag. She undid the drawstring and pulled out a sleek pair of dust-brown high-heeled shoes. She gasped and looked at the woman.

'No way can I accept these!' Hawa protested, her eyes startled. 'They look expensive!'

'Yes, you will take them,' the woman laughed. 'Got loads more – and they'll be happier with you. They ordered flesh-coloured shoes for us background singers whilst on tour in Japan with Malaika last year. Only problem, not all flesh is the same colour. Your skin's light, so you take them. I sure won't be wearing them!'

Taking the bag from her, the woman moved towards the linen cart, placing the shoes underneath a stack of towels.

'Nobody has to see them. They're your colour, though!'

Defeated, Hawa smiled and pushed her cart to the door. The woman's voice interrupted her as she was halfway out of the room.

'Why don't you find out if your girl Othella is free some-time soon to hook up my hair? And then we can go out. Tour's over, and we return to the States next Thursday, so I don't have to wear this scratchy weave anymore. I hear Edinburgh has some lit nightspots. Do you know any place that drops tight tunes? Somewhere that plays reggae, rap, R&B?'

'I don't go out often, but there are a few places we could try,' Hawa replied. 'The Bongo Club on Cowgate, perhaps? Or Lulu's and The Shanghai, which are both on George Street.' She was speaking on autopilot, remembering the places Othella had taken her when she'd first arrived in Edinburgh.

'Fab, then!' the woman replied, moving up to Hawa and patting her on the shoulder. 'My name is Anaka Hart, by the way – no relation to the comedian, though,' she giggled. 'Let's exchange digits. Hopefully your girl can do my hair soon. And then we can find time to explore your city!'

CHAPTER 3

When she got home, Hawa took the shoes out of their bag and held them next to her face in the bathroom mirror. They indeed were a match for her colour, which was something she often had to explain. She was not biracial but rather possessed the light skin common to her Fula people.

She next placed the shoes on her bed, stark against the dark background of her dyed *gara* bedspread. She took a couple of pictures and sent them to Othella on WhatsApp, with a message:

> *Look what I got while working today! American lady who gave them to me wants you to do her hair when you're free. Name's Anaka Hart. She's also into African culture and stuff, so you'll like her.* 😊 *xoxo.*

Othella responded almost instantly with an emoji of her head exploding, followed by four love hearts and a confirmation that she would be able to do Anaka's hair in a couple of days.

★

Anaka came for Hawa just after midday. She was wearing faded jeans that disappeared into Dr. Martens boots, and a long puffa jacket over a red jumper that featured the head of a black panther. Dismissing the taxi that had brought her along, she walked with Hawa from Longstone along the canal to Othella's flat in Baberton. They climbed the four flights of stairs, which were dominated by a strong smell of bleach.

Othella's door was half open, strident Afrobeats music wafting into the hall. Having fallen out with the Nigerian lady who had allowed her to rent a chair in a salon on Gorgie Road, Othella had simply converted her living room into a makeshift space to do hair.

In this pursuit, she had positioned a couple of black leather dining chairs in front of a long mirror from a charity shop. Above the mirror, Othella had arranged numerous black-and-white pictures of African icons. A large off-white leather couch, strewn with packets of synthetic hair in various shades, sat next to a sleek wide-screen television, which had been connected to speakers situated at the room's cardinal points. Flamboyantly attired artistes executed elaborate dance steps on the screen.

A black glass coffee table rested on an ash-coloured rug in the centre of the room, its surface covered with tubs of hair pomade, relaxing creams, pairs of scissors and a set of red plastic combs.

In front of the mirror stood Othella, oiling the furrows between the flowing black and purple braids of a striking teenage girl. Since their high school days, Hawa had always admired Othella's ability to hold and command any room she was in. Her skin was a deep mahogany, and she was wearing white jeans paired with an incandescent blouse with intricate patterns. During their boarding school days, Othella had been nicknamed 'Unopposed', a reference to the fact that no other pupil had stood against her for the position of sixth-form senior prefect.

Beyond Othella's stunning looks was an insightful intelligence and serrated wit, which had seen her achieve a first-class honours degree before moving to Scotland to complete a postgraduate degree in international conflict and cooperation. Othella had put off returning home – much to the chagrin of her university lecturer mother – preferring instead to stay in Edinburgh to *do hair while she found herself.* Hawa had always joked that Othella was a perfect advertisement for her side trade – her hair was always resplendent, and today it was arranged in tight dreadlock-styled twists.

Othella clouded them in embraces, excitement pouring out of her. 'Ah, my sister Hawa! I have not seen your face for two whole weeks! You live so close to me that if you put your hand out of your window, it will touch my door! And yet you only bring your mosquito legs to my house when you want me to make your hair long and nice like a mermaid.'

Othella continued, turning her eyes to Anaka. 'Is this our American sister who sings with superstars? Welcome, Anaka, and apologies for the scattered condition of this flat! Hawa, this is your house, so give Anaka something to eat and drink. There is rice and crain crain in the fridge. I also made some ginger beer the other day; it has lime juice and the kick of fire, but you'll like it! And whilst you're in there, flip the kettle for me. I will need hot water soon for this little woman's hair.'

Pleasantries over, Hawa dumped a box of hair on the floor, creating space for Anaka to nestle on the leather couch, after which she disappeared into the kitchen to carry out Othella's orders on refreshments. Over the droning microwave, she could hear the two women chatting like old friends, and she marvelled at Othella's uncanny ability to make people feel at home. The rice heated, she dished it onto a blue glass plate, pouring the homemade ginger beer into a matching glass. Placing the items on a tray, she carried it to Anaka, settling it gently on her lap.

'This is way too much for me!' the American protested, her eyes warm at the attention. 'Remember, I have to stay slim for singing and performing,' she laughed.

'That's an African portion for a special visitor. Eat what you can and leave the rest for me,' Othella said as she left the room. She returned presently with a bowl of boiling water which she held underneath the head of the girl, whose hair was now almost done. Gathering the girl's braids in a loose fist, she dipped the edges into the boiling water, the heat sealing the tips to prevent them from unravelling.

'You are now gorgeous, like a hybrid Beyoncé and Rihanna,' Othella joked, the girl dissolving into giggles at the compliment. 'Go to the kitchen and make yourself some food. Your father will be here to collect you soon. And remember the novel I gave you. Look for knowledge beyond Snapchat and Instagram!' A smile almost rupturing her face, the girl made her way to the kitchen, pausing in the hall to take selfies, pivoting and pirouetting her head to a variety of angles.

'Her name is Mandipa, and her father is a doctor from Zimbabwe who lives over the bridge in Dunfermline,' Othella explained, sitting next to Anaka on the couch. 'But he has sat down in marriage with a Scottish woman who knows nothing about our hair. Our brothers are always quick to choose milkshake women over their hot chocolate sisters!'

The three women dissolved into laughter at Othella's metaphors, their conversation flowing until the doctor arrived to collect his daughter, paying Othella in cash from a thin wallet whilst enthusiastically discussing the African icons on the wall.

Before Mandipa left, Anaka asked her father if it would be OK to take pictures of her intricate braids, explaining that she wanted to post the images on her Songhai Sista blog. 'I've seen quality braids back in the States, but this is on a whole other level, Othella!'

Once Mandipa had departed with her father, Othella turned her attention to Anaka, positioning her on one of the dining room chairs in front of the mirror. 'Did some of the heavy lifting yesterday,' Anaka explained, meeting Othella's eyes in the mirror. 'Took off my weave. Also washed and dried my hair.'

'Ace!' replied Othella. 'That will definitely save some time.'

'So, what about this whole Stella Kowa situation?' Hawa asked, her voice shedding the lightness of a few seconds previously. 'Any more updates?'

'I did not want to talk about Stella when that little girl was here,' Othella replied. 'But it is a bloody serious situation. Stella is suffering from serious hypothermia and has so far been unable to speak. She is too sick to receive visitors just now, but we should go see her sometime next week. She will need our support!'

Realising that Anaka would need background information on the situation, Othella relayed further details, her voice measured. 'Stella Kowa is from our Sierra Leone and sings in the church that I often attend. She's a nurse who lives in Granton. She did not turn up for a shift and her workmates raised the alarm. The police came to the church to ask questions. That was over two weeks ago. And then, yesterday, they found her car at an industrial estate in Dalgety Bay. She was in the boot, barely alive. She was taken to the Royal Infirmary and she's very weak!'

CHAPTER 4

They agreed to explore a few Edinburgh nightspots, Hawa and Anaka returning to Baberton in a taxi to collect Othella later that evening. From the car park, Hawa sent Othella a text to inform her that they were downstairs and ready.

'She's probably vetting outfits,' Hawa laughed. 'Even in school, we were late for classes almost every morning – even though it was simply a case of wearing the same uniform.'

'I get it,' replied Anaka, her teeth flashing white in the taxi's interior gloom. 'A girl has to look her best.' Othella had replaced Anaka's weave with flowing braids of a deep brown colour that reached just below her shoulders.

Five minutes later, there was still no Othella. Hawa checked her phone; the text she had sent had not been read. Deciding to pay the driver – who had begun to mildly complain that Saturdays were his busiest days – they left the taxi and headed to the entrance of the flats. The smell of bleach in the stairwell was, if anything, stronger than earlier in the day, and Hawa wondered if some fastidious tenant took responsibility for mopping at regular intervals.

Othella's front door was ajar again, but there was no music playing inside. Looking more closely, Hawa saw that the wood was shattered and splintered around the lock. Gasping, she clutched Anaka's arm and peered into the flat, her eyes startled.

'We're here, Othella. Have you been practising karate on your door?' The concern in Hawa's voice climbed over her joke. Anaka stepped slightly ahead of her, and they shuffled into the living room, their faces taut. The white leather couch seemed undisturbed – if anything, the number of packets of synthetic hair on it had increased from that morning.

The black glass coffee table had been shattered, though – shards of glass scattered among spilled hair creams and lotions that had congealed into an ugly mess on the grey rug. The red plastic combs were also scattered across the room, their stark colour calling out like miniature beacons.

Shouting out her name, Hawa kept trying Othella's number, the phone ringing out on each occasion, followed by Othella's voice wishing her a fine day and instructing her to leave a message. In the background, she could hear Anaka going through the rooms of the flat, calling out to Othella, her American accent suddenly sounding discordant.

'She's not here!' Anaka blurted out, returning to the living room. 'What do you want to do, Hawa? You think you should call the cops? This does not look good,' she added, her eyes surveying the chaos of the living room.

Two police officers arrived fifteen minutes later – a man and a woman – their radios uttering esoteric squawks at regular intervals.

'We came to pick up my friend Othella for a night out.

We were here with her earlier today,' Hawa explained, her voice sounding as if it belonged to someone else. In a daze, she felt Anaka's hand on her shoulder.

'So, how exactly do you know Othella?' the female officer, who had introduced herself as PC Stewart, asked in a measured voice that reminded Hawa of a headmistress.

'We grew up together back in Sierra Leone and attended the same schools and university. She's my closest friend here in Edinburgh.'

'When did you last see her?' PC Stewart continued, her partner, PC Borthwick, by this time having left them to wander through the flat.

'Earlier today. She does hair and I brought Anaka here to get hers done.'

'And what time would you say you left after she had done Anaka's hair?'

'Just after five. We agreed to pick her up for a night out. She didn't answer my texts and calls, so I came up.'

'Apart from you, Hawa, does Othella have any other relatives or close acquaintances here in Scotland?'

'Not really. We mix occasionally with a few other friends from back home and the other Africans who attend Othella's church. She used to share this place with a girl named Jattu, also from Sierra Leone.'

'Does Othella own a car?'

'No.'

'Did Othella seem stressed, nervous or unhappy when you saw her earlier today?'

'The exact opposite, officer. She was bubbly, gave us food, danced to music from her TV and did Anaka's hair.'

'We'll start making enquiries immediately. The door and the state of the living room are obvious causes for concern,' PC Stewart explained, leading the way out of the kitchen. 'Officer Borthwick and I will start with the neighbours to see if they heard or saw anything. I would also like you to give me the contact details of anyone Othella is close to in Scotland. Can you please also keep an eye on social media for us and inform us if anything with regards to her location pops up? We're going to have to seal off the flat. Officer Borthwick will take some further details from you. I'll also need a recent picture of Othella, and since she has no family here in Scotland, I was wondering if you, Hawa, could possibly be a point of contact for now?'

By this time, they were standing outside the flat.

'Wasn't the lady found in the boot of her car in Dalgety Bay also from Sierra Leone?' Officer Borthwick said to his partner in a low voice.

'Yes, she is. Her name is Stella Kowa,' replied Hawa, before PC Stewart could answer.

'And you know this Stella Kowa?' Borthwick asked.

'Yes. She led the choir in Othella's church. Do you think the same person could have done this?'

'Let's stay calm and not get ahead of ourselves. We have your details, and we'll be in touch with any updates,' PC Stewart said, her eyes supportive.

They abandoned the night out. Anaka returned to her hotel, demanding that Hawa keep her updated on any news. With her insomnia on steroids after Othella's disappearance, Hawa decided to scroll through her phone, hoping that her friend's social media might offer a clue to her whereabouts. Othella's last Instagram post was from four days ago, highlighting a couple of novels she had bought in Waterstones. Facebook was similarly arid – Othella's last post was from her birthday on 14 May, a general smiley message thanking everyone who had wished her well. She moved on to Othella's last message on WhatsApp, the terse line beneath her name reading *last seen today at 18.07.*

CHAPTER 5

Hawa had known Othella since she had arrived from the United Kingdom to join her primary school in class seven. Othella – who had been born in Glasgow – was an only child whose parents had returned home to Sierra Leone *to serve the country* after a couple of decades abroad. Her mother, Dr Zaydah Savage, had accepted a position as a lecturer in Black Literature at Fourah Bay College, whilst her father had taken a keen interest in the politics of the ruling party. Until he lost his life in a harrowing road accident involving a speeding convoy whilst campaigning during national elections.

Othella returned to Scotland after they graduated from university, whilst Hawa spent a couple of years eking out a living as a teacher of history and English at an all-girls Catholic school in Brookfields. And then she received a Commonwealth Scholarship to pursue a postgraduate degree in Scotland. She had been delighted to learn that Othella had completed the very same degree a year earlier and was still in Edinburgh.

Their reunion had been warm and raucous, largely involving long nights through which they laughed over memories of their youth. Hawa's induction into the life of Scotland had included Othella taking her to several Edinburgh nightclubs, the V&A Museum in Dundee and, finally, to the church at the bottom of Leith Walk, an establishment that worshipped under the auspices of Pastor Ronald Ranka, who was, as Othella put it, *a true man of God from our own Sierra Leone!*

Pastor Ranka, on hearing that Hawa was a fellow Sierra Leonean newly arrived in Edinburgh, had pointed out that there was an empty room in a flat he owned in Longstone. The rent was £600 a month, which, split three ways, was a negligible expense, even for a student with limited funds. Hawa had been slightly unnerved by Pastor Ranka's transformation from an animated presence at the pulpit, who a mere ten minutes previously had been delivering a hectoring rant about the damnation vented upon the people of Sodom and Gomorrah, to a landlord angling for a paying tenant.

Upon learning who her parents were and where her home town was, the pastor remarked that he knew Hawa's stepmother well, gushing that she was an esteemed member of the church's chapter back in Sierra Leone; it was, therefore, his responsibility to make sure Hawa landed softly in Scotland. Moving on, he had introduced Hawa to Elijah Foot-Patrol and Santa, the two men currently living in the flat, both of whom were also from back home. Both were wearing suits and garish ties, Santa's outfit a size too small for a man of his girth. Elijah Foot-Patrol was tall with a shaved head, his movements reminding Hawa of a cane rat. Both men hurried over when the pastor beckoned, shaking

Hawa's hand warmly and expressing excitement at having *a beautiful sister in Christ* to share the flat with.

Santa had driven them all back to the flat straight after church in a rusty black Volkswagen Golf, Elijah Foot-Patrol explaining their names to a bemused Hawa on the way.

'He is Santa because he is fat and is the chef of the house,' he had laughed. 'Santa cooks like a woman and works in restaurants. He can imitate any food you can imagine – even White people's food! And he can get you a clean and proper job as a waitress if you want, my sister!'

As if picking up a baton in a relay race, Santa spoke next, the steering wheel resting across his ample stomach. 'Don't listen to this man's big talk, my sister! He is like a radio with new batteries. We call him Elijah Foot-Patrol to distinguish him from another Elijah, who was also from back home and who used to live here before being deported. But since this Elijah does not own a car, we call him Elijah Foot-Patrol.'

Both of the men dissolved into laughter, their geniality putting Hawa at ease.

Hawa had lived with them since, each tenant having a room as their fiefdom, whilst the kitchen, bathroom and living room were shared. Her room was cramped and stuffy, with just a single small window that looked out onto the building's car park, three storeys below. Scrawlings in the disjointed hand of a child covering sections of the walls suggested that a little person had occupied the room at some point.

Although the flat was shabby and sparse, it suited a student for whom the month always seemed longer than the money she made. Another benefit was her proximity to Othella, who lived in another of Pastor Ranka's flats at Baberton, a fifteen-minute walk along the canal path.

Pastor Ranka had asked Hawa if she would consider assuming a more active role in the church. She had declined, stressing that her studies required her full attention, though her position would possibly change once she graduated.

CHAPTER 6

Hawa decided that the best place to begin her search for Othella was the Lion Mountain Church. Since her initial visit with Othella when she'd first arrived in Scotland, she had only been a few more times, explaining to a deeply dismayed Santa and Elijah Foot-Patrol that Sundays were key if she was to stay abreast of her studies. Othella, meanwhile, had been more liberal with Hawa's lack of enthusiasm for the church.

'I know you've never been super-keen on Christianity, Hawa, but believe me when I tell you that the church is involved in good programmes to help our people back home. I understand the pressures of working and studying in this country, so I will open your eyes to what we do at Lion Mountain once you graduate,' she had explained.

Santa was delighted when Hawa asked if she could come to church with them, launching into praise for the virtues of the pastor, his eyes wide with enthusiasm. 'You returning to church with us is news that carries sunshine with it, my sister! Like I have always said, Pastor Ronald Ranka is a true man of divine discernment who goes above and beyond to help Africans in this White people's country. My mother is a big elder in Lion Mountain back home in Sierra Leone, and as soon as I got here to Scotland and introduced myself to Pastor Ranka, he found me a place to lay my head in one of his flats within two weeks! And the rent we pay is very small! This means I have more money to send over to my mother who is not very well, whilst helping with the payment of school fees for my younger sisters. And so, I am very grateful! And whilst there, we will pray for the safe return of our sister Othella.'

On Sunday, Santa, as was customary, rose early, the sounds of his hymns waking Hawa, who had fallen into a shallow sleep at around 3.30 a.m., her mind still whirring with thoughts of what could have possibly happened to Othella. She had been in text contact with Anaka Hart, and the American had surprised her by stating that she would love to come to church as well.

Hawa showered quickly, settling on a loose floral dress she had bought in a charity shop in Morningside. Charity shopping had been another lesson from Othella during Hawa's early days in Edinburgh.

'But you do not just go to every single charity shop,' Othella had explained, deep knowledge dancing in her eyes. 'You visit the charity shops in the wealthier areas of the city. You know the Armani jacket you say you like very much? I bought it in a Morningside charity shop for just £35. I checked the price of the same jacket online and it's going for £240!'

Smiling sadly at the memory, Hawa checked her phone again, hoping that perhaps Othella had suddenly resurfaced, and replied to one of her numerous messages. There was nothing. Sighing, she dressed quickly.

Santa and Elijah Foot-Patrol were already waiting for her when she emerged from her bedroom fifteen minutes later. Elijah Foot-Patrol was eating a plate of leftover lasagne Santa had brought home from one of his chef shifts. Both men were in their customary suits, Santa's threatening to disintegrate at the seams whenever he moved.

Taking Hawa's appearance as his cue, Elijah Foot-Patrol wolfed down the rest of the food and gulped down a glass of water, before disappearing into the bathroom from where he emerged swilling mouthwash, which he kept in his mouth as they descended the stairs to the car park. Once outside, he spat the mouthwash into a cluster of grass, turning to compliment Hawa's dress in the same movement.

They picked Anaka up from her hotel, the American emerging from the foyer in a black tuxedo-style jacket and sleek pinstriped trousers. Smiling, she climbed into the back of the car, her perfume dominating the cramped space. Squeezing Hawa's knee, she drawled out a greeting. The men in the front of the vehicle were unable to conceal their glee at going to church with someone as glamorous as Anaka.

The Lion Mountain Church met in a narrow hall located in a dark brick building that nestled between the bottom of Leith Walk and Constitution Street. Santa managed to squeeze the vehicle into a space on the opposite side of the street, a few yards ahead of a bus stop. Descending from the car, Elijah Foot-Patrol led the way in, a thick brown Bible clutched in his hand.

The church hall was three-quarters full when they walked in. Hawa had always joked that stepping through the doors was like stepping back into Sierra Leone, with the over-whelmingly Black congregation mostly dressed in clothes that spoke to the fashions back home. Straight-backed orange plastic chairs were arranged in neat rows on dark laminate flooring. There was a raised stage at the front of the hall on which stood a thick wooden pulpit and a matching lectern. A swaying band and small choir were in the full throes of an uplifting song. A striking Black woman with high hair and large earrings led the singing, emphasising her lyrics by jabbing the air. The rest of the band were White, four men dressed in loose jeans and grey shirts. The lyrics of the hymns were projected onto a large white screen at the back of the stage.

Hawa, though she hadn't visited the church in a while, was still familiar with most of the congregation, and passed out waves and smiles of greetings to different sections of the hall, whilst Santa led the way to a line of chairs three rows from the front.

'Where is the pastor?' Anaka whispered during a lull at the end of a hymn.

'He always arrives late,' Hawa explained. 'Apparently, he travels from Broxburn and has to do an early morning service with a small group in Livingston before joining the Edinburgh branch of the church just after eleven. You'll know him when you see him.' Anaka squeezed her hand in reply, singing along with the choir, which had swept into the next hymn.

About ten minutes later, both Santa and Elijah Foot-Patrol

broke from the row, hurrying outside. 'They have gone to receive the pastor,' Hawa whispered to Anaka. They returned soon after, Elijah Foot-Patrol holding Pastor Ranka's Bible and a teal folder, whilst Santa carried his bag, which was made of brown leather. With the pastor was a tall White woman with flowing black hair, wearing a sky-blue trouser suit. She walked confidently, making her way to the empty front row, whilst Santa and Elijah Foot-Patrol scuttled onto the stage, laying out Pastor Ranka's Bible and other paraphernalia in preparation for his sermon. He had lagged behind his welcome party, distributing handshakes and hugs like alms, after which he also climbed onto the stage.

Pastor Ranka had always reminded Hawa of an exotic creature. He was a narrow man with an oval head and a stiff neck, his skin a shimmering dark brown. He was wearing a deep blue three-piece suit over a white shirt and a golden tie. He moved with an entitled confidence, smiling at the choir as he took his place at the pulpit, nodding along to the current hymn as he leafed through his Bible.

The hymn completed, the pastor commenced his sermon, the thrust of which concerned the darkness that continued to consume the female youth of today through social media, which promoted a culture of *promiscuity and perversion.*

'Why do our young daughters and sisters believe that being scantily clad whilst dancing to the music of the devil is the right road to follow? Why do our daughters believe that a culture of preening and posturing is to their benefit?' Pausing for effect, he surveyed the congregation, from whose ranks sporadic murmurs of concurrence arose.

The next phase of the service involved people in need of special prayers approaching the stage for the pastor to place his hands on them. Again, as though they were orchestrating a well-rehearsed production, Elijah Foot-Patrol and Santa, along with a smattering of other enthusiasts, hurried to the front of the hall to stand behind the people waiting for special prayers. Pastor Ranka made his way down the line, placing his hands on those who had come forward. A couple of them slumped backwards and were caught by appointed stewards standing behind them who then lowered them gently to the floor. Elijah Foot-Patrol was carrying a small bundle of purple cloths which he used to cover the worshippers who had collapsed to the floor, where they lay for a few minutes before groggily rising to their feet and returning to their seats.

The collection of tithe envelopes followed, after which Pastor Ranka offered his closing prayers and then moved on to announcements.

'Our hearts remain heavy at the disturbing news of the disappearance of one of our congregation, a fellow Sierra Leonean, Othella Savage, who went missing from her flat in Baberton. Othella is our own sister, and like a number of you here today, I helped find her accommodation, and she has always been an unflinching member of our church. We cast a prayer of light and positive energy, asking the Almighty to deliver her safely to us! We, however, say thank you to the Almighty for the safe return of our sister, Stella Kowa, who was found in the boot of her car. Were it not for the grace of God, our sister would have surely perished, and we thank the Almighty for delivering our Stella from the jaws of damnation. Like Jonah, who remained alive in the belly of a whale, our sister Stella was also protected and shielded from the darkness of death.'

He then shifted to lighter announcements, which included arrangements for a fitness walk to the Pentland Hills at the end of the month. The service over, the congregation shook hands and broke into clusters where conversations on life and family took prominence.

Hawa and Anaka were soon approached by a man named Jerry Holt, who lived in Bathgate and coordinated the fitness walks to the Pentlands that Pastor Ranka had mentioned. Jerry, who played the keyboard in the church's band, always brought jars of homemade jam to sell in church, which had led to him acquiring the moniker Jam Jerry, a title which elicited broad smiles from him. Jam Jerry was of slender build and moved with the agility of a professional athlete, his face framed by a thick brown beard. Hawa, out of politeness, bought another jar, complimenting him on the quality of the last batch, which remained unopened in the fridge at home.

'I was wondering if you had by any chance heard from Othella, Jerry. She always talks about your walks in the Pentlands,' Hawa asked, taking a step closer to him.

'Not a peep,' replied Jam Jerry. 'Actually, she never really liked the group walks, so we mostly went just the two of us. But the last time was a couple of months ago, now. Pouring with rain, so it was, but she enjoyed it. She did mention bringing you along, Hawa, so feel free to join for a wee walk whenever you're free. Definitely a worthwhile experience.'

Their discussion of where to purchase appropriate boots,

if Hawa ever considered going on a walk with him, and the specific nature of the fruit and preservatives used by Jam Jerry in his produce, was interrupted by the pastor, who was suddenly at their side, his eyes fixed on Anaka. His closeness carried with it his aftershave, his eyes curious and probing. At his elbow hovered Santa and Elijah Foot-Patrol.

'Santa tells me you are a first-time visitor to our humble church and that you are from America?' Pastor Ranka enquired, his voice engaging and melodious as he clasped Anaka's hand.

'That's right, sir,' Anaka replied with a half-smile. 'My name is Anaka. Anaka Hart. I met Hawa over here, and she introduced me to Othella. So I'm here to help pray for her safe return!'

The pastor's smile slipped as he released Anaka's hand. 'Our Lord moves in mysterious ways, my sister. I am sure our Othella will return to us soon. So, are you a sister in Christ also, Miss Anaka Hart?'

'My folk are devout Baptists from Atlanta, so I was raised in the church indeed, Mr Pastor. Started singing in church before using my skills in other forms of music,' Anaka replied, her eyes holding the pastor's.

'And then we must get you to share your gift with us in the near future, Sister Anaka. Our choir could always use a new voice. Where are you staying whilst in Scotland with us? I am sure Hawa here has told you that we help people out with affordable accommodation.'

'Currently at a hotel in Maybury, but I plan on moving out soon. I was thinking of staying in Edinburgh to relax a bit and get to know the city. Luckily, in Miss Barrie, I've found the perfect guide,' she finished, smiling at Hawa.

'Then we can find you a place to stay, no problem,' Pastor Ranka exclaimed, his eyes bright. 'Of course, you will have to pay something to stay there. But our rates are comparatively quite low. My aim is not to make a profit from our properties, but rather to provide assistance to fellow brethren. If you are interested, we can arrange something as early as tomorrow. And you can even share the new space with Miss Hawa over here. Hawa finishes university soon and has promised to take a greater interest in our church! We are always on the lookout for positive and enthusiastic young people to be vehicles for the transportation of our message of faith and charity for the less fortunate. I'm sure Hawa has nothing against Santa and Elijah Foot-Patrol but she would surely appreciate the opportunity to live in a testosterone-free environment if possible!'

Both Santa and Elijah Foot-Patrol buckled over in laughter at the pastor's joke, the latter slapping his thigh. Anaka thanked him, pointing out that the offer was very kind and that she would think about it. After that, the pastor moved away to talk to a family who were patiently waiting at the church's entrance, with Santa and Elijah Foot-Patrol following in his slipstream.

By the time Hawa and Anaka left the church, most of the worshippers were still outside engaged in warm conversations. They were just in time to see Pastor Ranka climb into the passenger seat of a high black BMW vehicle, the dark-haired lady in the powder-blue suit taking the driver's seat.

She nipped the vehicle into traffic, Pastor Ranka waving as they drove away.

'That's his wife,' explained Hawa. 'She is a human rights lawyer. She helps people from the church with immigration issues and seeking political asylum.'

Pastor Ranka arrived to pick up Anaka and Hawa a week later. The flat he had earmarked for them was in Balerno, an area he described as *very civilised and private*. 'And there are buses right into the city centre at regular intervals. The Lothian Bus number 44 is the one to get,' he explained as he turned the big BMW on to Lanark Road, leaving Hawa's old flat in Longstone behind. Anaka had come over earlier in the afternoon in a taxi, whilst Elijah Foot-Patrol and Santa were at work.

The flat Pastor Ranka drove them to was in a new development, with giant Cala Homes billboards advertising *dream accommodation for families*. He parked in a space in front of a large block, to the right of which stood a row of unfinished homes. Plastic sheeting fluttered in the breeze. Workmen in hard hats and fluorescent vests scurried about, the sounds of hammering and drilling punctuating the afternoon.

'We only purchased this one a month ago,' Pastor Ranka explained as he led them up a flight of stairs that still carried the smell of fresh paint, 'so you will be the first tenants, which should tell you how special you are to our ministry.'

Taking a set of keys out of his pocket, he unlocked the door to flat number 4. The smell of fresh paint was again prominent inside, a thick grey carpet underfoot. There were two bedrooms, each with a low double bed. The living room was snugly furnished with items Hawa recognised as coming from IKEA, whilst the kitchen housed a tall black fridge and a matching kettle, microwave and toaster.

'That's the tour over,' Pastor Ranka said, handing the keys to Hawa. 'The rent is only £400 a month, including utilities. You have a basic Sky package, and I believe the London branch of our church features regularly on channel 626. This is your home for as long as you want it, my sisters. Santa and Elijah can help you move, no problem. Take care, and we will talk later.'

He paused at the front door, removing his spectacles and blinking at Hawa. 'I know you are worried about Othella, which is one of the reasons I brought you here, Hawa – so you can see that you are not alone in this struggle. God scripts things and has His reasons for everything in this life. Look, for example, how He saved Stella Kowa's life? She is now safe in hospital, and you should visit her if possible. In times of trauma and turmoil, human company is like a warm blanket. Santa can drive you to the hospital, no problem, if you are free.'

And then he was gone, his aftershave lingering as Anaka and Hawa further explored the flat.

Santa and Elijah Foot-Patrol helped them move into the new flat, making a couple of trips in the Volkswagen, which were enough to ferry Hawa's meagre belongings from Longstone to Balerno. Anaka checked out of her hotel, arriving in a taxi with a single suitcase and a couple of holdalls, which contained the accoutrements of her trade.

The men stayed for around forty-five minutes, helping the

ladies settle in whilst purring over the pristine nature of the flat. 'Certain people are placed on this earth to open the way for the less fortunate!' Elijah Foot-Patrol gushed, as he tested the water pressure in the shower. 'Pastor Ronald Ranka truly holds no value for material possessions and willingly shares his fortunes with his congregation! Can you imagine what a place like this would cost to rent at full price?'

CHAPTER 7

Santa arrived the next day to take them to the Royal Infirmary to visit Stella Kowa. Hawa had cancelled her shift at the hotel, explaining to Lesley, the breezily efficient lady who ran the temp agency, that she was moving house and would be taking the week off. 'One of the advantages of working for agencies,' she had explained to Anaka as the American made her way through the full English breakfast Hawa had prepared earlier that morning, 'is that you get to choose your own shifts and arrange a work schedule that suits you. Perfect for someone like me, whose availability is dictated by university commitments.'

Once ready, they descended to Santa's car, which was, as usual, dominated by the smell of a collage of foods. Santa talked work as they travelled, searching for an appropriate radio channel before eventually settling on Capital FM, whose animated DJ introduced each song with a dramatic flourish and unfunny jokes.

'Have you spoken to Othella's mother back home?' he suddenly asked as they joined the bypass at Wester Hailes.

'I called her the day Othella disappeared,' Hawa replied, slightly jarred by the question. 'She was quite worried, especially when I explained the state of Othella's flat. But then she calmed down slightly, saying that mothers are subliminally connected to their children, and that she believed that her daughter was safe and well. Then she spent the rest of the time grilling me on what good novels I had read recently.'

'Why is she asking you about books when her child is missing?' Anaka asked, her eyes puzzled.

'She was our Black Literature lecturer back home,' Hawa replied with a light smile. 'Whenever I went to visit Othella at her house, we would spend time discussing Alice Walker, Langston Hughes and Toni Morrison.'

With the bypass quiet in the early afternoon, they were at the hospital within fifteen minutes, Santa grumbling at the fact that they had to pay for parking. 'If I did not have you two with me, I would have simply found a nearby residential estate to leave the car,' he chuckled.

From the hospital foyer, a narrow receptionist directed them to ward seven, where they would find Stella Kowa. They took the lift up, Santa humming a hymn as they ascended. Ward seven was subdued when they arrived. A smiling nurse offered to take them to see Stella.

'She's doing very well — we're happy with her progress,' the nurse explained. 'Dr O'Hara was with her earlier on and was delighted to see that she's much more lucid now. I think there's already a visitor with her, so you might have to play it by ear. Strictly speaking, she's only allowed three people at a time in her condition.'

Stella Kowa had been placed in a rectangular enclosure of high white screens. She was much smaller than when Hawa

44

had last seen her, her harrowing ordeal having shorn her of weight. She looked tired, but her eyes lit up when she saw Hawa. Tubes snaked out of her arm, whilst a console to her side displayed red numbers and beeped from time to time. There was an ashy tinge to Stella's complexion, and her head was swathed in a thick tan-coloured bandage.

The other visitor turned out to be the pastor's wife, who was dressed in an identical suit to the one she had worn to church the previous Sunday, the only difference being that this one was grey. She rose from a straight-backed chair when she saw the new arrivals, releasing Stella's hand from her grasp. Passing out whispered greetings and smiles, she expressed particular joy at seeing Anaka again, stressing that she was looking forward to hearing her sing in church in the near future.

'I didn't get the opportunity to chat with you on Sunday. My name is Amanda. I am Pastor Ranka's wife. I work as a lawyer during the week. I had a meeting at the Scottish Parliament today to discuss the rights of immigrants, so I thought I'd pop by and see how our Stella was getting on,' she explained, her eyes bright. 'I was just about to leave, and now I won't feel too guilty about departing, since you are here to keep her company.'

Picking up a designer handbag that had been balanced on the low cabinet next to Stella's bed, she exchanged hugs with them all, asking that Santa walk with her, as she had something to discuss with him regarding the upcoming fitness walk to the Pentlands.

The two of them away, Hawa settled on the chair vacated by Amanda, Anaka pulling up one on the other side of the bed. 'This is Anaka. She's from America but is our good friend. How are you, Stella? Seeing you on this bed today is a blessing that has no measure or definition,' Hawa continued, tears in her eyes.

'It was not my time to leave this world,' Stella Kowa replied, her voice faint and reedy. 'I was going to work one day and was in the car park scraping ice off my windscreen. I don't remember anything else, except waking up in here. Sometimes I remember smelling lemons, but I don't know why.' She paused, reaching for Hawa's hand. 'The doctors say that there is a big cut at the back of my head and that somebody must have hit me with something blunt and heavy. But I remember nothing, Hawa.'

'God is good indeed,' Hawa continued. 'Please do not worry about anything, Stella, and know that we are all here to support you.'

'How is your friend Othella doing?' Stella asked, her eyes vague.

Hawa paused before continuing, deciding on the spur of the moment not to tell Stella that Othella had disappeared. 'She's fine but working today. Otherwise, she would be here with us to see you.'

'Othella invited me to Pastor Ranka's house in Broxburn last month. It was the third time she had invited me to one of these functions, and I was surprised that you weren't there, Hawa. It is only the women from the congregation who come, together with some of our sisters who live in Glasgow. And we talk to men about the church. The only other man from our country was big Khalil.'

Their conversation was interrupted by the arrival of a

shuffling nurse, different from the one who had led them in. Her presence filled the rectangular space, pointing out that the visitors had outstayed their allocated time, and that they had to leave since Stella must be allowed to rest.

CHAPTER 8

Santa dropped Hawa and Anaka back at Balerno, explaining that he had promised to go shopping for a new bed with Elijah Foot-Patrol. 'Elijah is superstitious and believes that sleeping on a single bed is the reason why he has been unable to find a woman,' Santa chuckled. 'Apparently, there's a place at Newbridge that sells cheap double beds, and Elijah wants us to go have a look.'

Back in the flat, Hawa mulled over what they had learned from Stella Kowa, thinking aloud, her voice mildly bitter. 'You think somebody is your close friend, but then you wake up one day and realise that you don't really know who they are. Othella, who shared everything with me from a young age, went to meetings at Pastor Ranka's house with other women. But why? If only Stella had been able to tell us a bit more before that pencil of a nurse interrupted!'

Anaka kicked off her shoes, collapsing onto the couch. 'When I worked with Malaika in Philly, she always memorised sayings to repeat in her interviews to sound deep and sensitive. She used to quote this Márquez writer dude who said that everyone has three lives: a public life, a private life and a secret life. So don't be upset, Hawa. You're just finding out about Othella's secret life. Maybe she didn't tell you because she knows how deep you are into your studying.'

'But one thing that Stella said stuck out,' Hawa replied. 'She mentioned that Khalil was also at these functions. Why would Khalil be at Ranka's house, when he never ever even comes to church? He is a Muslim who fasts during Ramadan.'

'Who is this Khalil, anyway?' Anaka asked.

'He's also from Sierra Leone. He was training as a nurse, but then he dropped out. He currently works as a bouncer at a spot called Sing City. It's a karaoke club.'

Anaka's eyes lit up, a smile covering her face. 'Then let's check out Sing City, Hawa,' she said, hopping in excitement. 'We can have a little fun and then talk with this Khalil! Perhaps he can help us track down Othella.'

There was a queue snaking outside Sing City when they arrived. A pair of bouncers wearing expressions that looked like they had been manufactured in the same factory let them in with curt nods when it was their turn. As they squeezed past, Hawa asked one of them where Khalil was tonight. He replied that Khalil would be on door duty after eleven, instantly turning his attention back to the queue.

Once inside, they entered one of the themed spaces, The Hollywood Room, managing to find a table underneath a clutch of fake plants. To the left of their table was a bevy of women out on a hen do, the bride swathed in a giant silver sash and her friends around her in similarly sized scarlet sashes. A frazzled waitress, who looked young enough to still be in high school, received their drink orders once they had sat down, and soon returned with glasses and bottles perched on a deep wooden tray.

The women of the hen party had by this time thrown themselves into the karaoke, taking turns to screech songs, alcohol rendering their voices hopelessly out of tune. The bride sang last, and cheered on by the entire room, managed to produce a decent rendition of Eurythmics' 'Sweet Dreams'.

'This is a cool spot, Hawa,' Anaka offered, her eyes shimmering in excitement as they travelled around the bar, the bright strobing lights casting her face in a fascinating glow. 'We should sign up for a song or two whilst we wait for Khalil to turn up. Don't worry if you can't sing, Hawa – sass and attitude is all you need! I've worked with loads of fellow background singers who have frogs in their throats but have been on world tours with some of the most lit pop stars.'

'I've only ever sung in the shower,' Hawa laughed in reply. 'No way am I ready for a stage in front of other people.'

Laughing, Anaka left her to sign up, strutting across the busy space to chat to the DJ, who was ensconced in a little raised booth close to a low ramp that led to the toilets. Hawa observed their discussion, smiling at the ease with which Anaka held herself, the DJ at one point throwing his head back in laughter at a joke she must have shared. Anaka returned to the table soon after, stopping off at the bar to buy a couple of cocktails, which she plonked on their table.

'That's me all signed up to croon. I'm on after another song from our bridal party friends.'

When her turn came, she was introduced by the DJ, his voice carrying through the venue.

'Next, we have the lovely Anaka Hart, who is joining us today to sing "Killing Me Softly". Give her a wee hand as she comes forward! Anaka, ladies and gentlemen!' Winking, Anaka disengaged herself from her leather jacket, which she dropped in Hawa's lap, then strode to the stage, accompanied by a smattering of applause.

And then she sang, her voice reducing the room to hushed respect. Anaka's voice was silk, and Hawa sat motionless as she listened, not even daring to take a sip from her drink whilst the American sang, total concentration a requirement.

The bar exploded when Anaka brought the song to an end, her smile wide and white as the patrons cheered and whistled. Still smiling, she returned to their table, hugging Hawa like a long-lost relative and scooping up her cocktail as she settled into her chair.

Impressed by Anaka's presence and voice, the hen party staggered over to offer praise and congratulations, the bride declaring in a drunken haze that she wanted Anaka to sing at her wedding reception, the fact that it was a mere week away not being a problem. They spent the rest of the evening with the hen party, taking turns to sing, Anaka holding the venue in her palm as she produced flawless renditions of a couple more songs.

They all traipsed out of the karaoke spot just after 1 a.m., when the lights were switched on. The bride-to-be was draped over Anaka, insisting that she was dead serious about her singing at her wedding. Anaka eventually agreed, only then being released by the bride, who tottered off to join her friends.

Outside was busy with mini clusters debating whether

to go home or to continue the revelry in other nightspots. Holding Anaka's arm, Hawa nodded to the two bouncers who had replaced the ones who had let them in earlier in the evening. She did not need to point out Khalil; the other was a White man with sharp blond hair in a ponytail.

Khalil was built like a heavyweight boxer and was a full head taller than his fellow bouncer. He was wearing black jeans and a matching black jacket with a bright orange logo on the back that claimed allegiance to some security firm. Hawa walked up to him, tapping him on the shoulder. Khalil turned, his expression shifting from the stern professionalism of dealing with rowdy patrons to one of pleasure. He enveloped Hawa in a tight hug, his voice a bellow.

'Hawa herself! Were you inside there? So happy to see you!'

'Arrived earlier and asked the other bouncers where you were. But they said you were on the door for the later shift. And so we were inside enjoying the singing. This is my friend, Anaka Hart. She's a singer from America who was here for a show. But she liked Edinburgh so much she stayed – we're just checking out some spots.'

Khalil shook Anaka's hand, asking what their plans were for the rest of the night. 'We just might head home,' Hawa replied, turning to eye Anaka to see if it was OK with her.

'How are you getting home?' Khalil asked, his eyes wandering over a couple of chaps whose conversation was going from passionate to slightly confrontational.

'We might just get a taxi or see if there's any night buses about,' Hawa replied, pulling her jacket around her.

'I can drive you home no problem,' Khalil offered. 'My

car's parked just across the road – you can sit in it and wait for me. Just need another twenty minutes to clear this place out and shut down for the night.' Before they could respond to his offer, he had extracted a bunch of keys from his pocket, clicking open a deep red Mercedes that was parked outside a busy kebab shop. As Hawa hesitated, Khalil smiled, passing on the keys to Anaka who took them, returning his smile. Placing an arm round Hawa's shoulders, she led the way to the car.

CHAPTER 9

Hawa spent the next day putting the finishing touches to her dissertation, which was due at the end of the month. She had written her thesis on the contagion theory in relation to conflicts, analysing how civil war had spread from neighbouring Liberia to her own Sierra Leone in the early nineties. She had printed off a final copy of the dissertation at the university library, which she now went through with a green highlighter, marking the odd error that she then amended on her laptop. After carrying out a final check on her bibliography, she attached the document to an email and sent it to her supervisor.

Anaka was still asleep. After their visit to Sing City, Khalil had driven them home and come up to the flat for a cup of coffee. Once settled, Hawa had broached the subject of Khalil being at Pastor Ranka's house in Broxburn, where Othella and other ladies had apparently also gathered.

'Yes, it's true, I do work for your pastor once in a while. He knows that I follow Islam and as such will never be a part of his church. However, he asks me to provide security at his house for a big function once in a while.'

'What kind of functions?' Hawa asked.

'The pastor holds charity events for important donors. He lives in a place called The Badgers, which is in Broxburn, and he has a big, big house.'

'What did providing security involve?'

'I think it's just for show really, because all I do is stand outside and welcome the guests whilst directing them where to park their cars. Pastor Ranka instructs me to wear dark suits like you see in the movies. They are strange events, but he pays me good money and so I do it. Very easy work with plenty of food to eat and lots of happy people.'

'Did you see Othella at any of these functions?'

'Several times. But there was that one occasion when she left early. I could hear people giving speeches and then Othella came out and said she was going to walk all the way back to Edinburgh. Pastor Ranka followed and tried to talk to her, but she just kept walking. Pastor Ranka then asked me to drive after her and make sure she got home OK. After gentle words from me, she agreed to get into my car, and I took her home. But she did not speak all the way back to Edinburgh.'

'Who else did you know at the function, Khalil?'

'Most of the young sisters here from Sierra Leone were there, and some other women from other African countries. There was that Abigail girl from Ghana, the tall one who lives at Craigmillar. I thought it was a prayer meeting for the female members of your church. But there were also many men in big-time cars at the functions. Often, I could hear cheering and loud clapping. Everybody always seemed to be in a fine mood, except your friend Othella on that one occasion when she walked out.'

Khalil had left their flat just after 3 a.m., asking that Hawa and Anaka please come back to Sing City in the future.

Anaka emerged from her room just after noon, traipsing into the kitchen from where Hawa heard the kettle click. Anaka trundled out of the kitchen five minutes later with a couple of cups of lemon tea, one of which she settled on the table beside Hawa, who was scrolling through online clothing stores. Observing her, Anaka's eyes lit up. She asked what Hawa was looking for.

'Bridesmaids' dresses for my sister Ramat's wedding in December,' Hawa chuckled, as she enlarged a billowing tan-coloured outfit.

'But why are you buying her things for her wedding?'

'The burden of the one who lives overseas,' Hawa replied, a sad smile tugging at the corners of her mouth. 'People back home believe that those of us who live in the White man's country usually have access to unlimited stashes of money. We receive requests for help almost every day. But since Ramat is my very own sister who slept in the same womb as me, and not a distant potato-leaf relative, I will do all in my power to try and help.'

'Heavy stuff, Hawa. How do you manage to pay for all this back home responsibility?'

'You can never respond in one blow, Anaka. You try to work some extra shifts and then see if you can buy one bridesmaid dress at a time. So far, I got three from a sale in Debenhams.'

'And how many bridesmaids does your sister have?'

'She initially said twelve, but I talked her down to six,' Hawa laughed. 'Come, I'll show you what I've got so far.'

She led the way through to her bedroom, hauling out a box that she had placed at the back of her wardrobe when they moved in. Anaka held the dresses up, expressing admiration at their cut and colour.

'And of course, I have the shoes that you gave to me, which will be perfect to wear on Ramat's big day. You should come to Sierra Leone with me for the wedding!' Hawa finished, her eyes bright at the prospect.

Anaka seemed initially uncertain; her forehead lined in slight creases as she pondered the offer. 'Won't I need a visa to enter your country? Isn't that expensive?'

'You pay for your visa on arrival these days. And that besides, you're beautiful and American and so my airport people will let you in with open arms and a red carpet. And you did say that you needed to unwind after heavy touring and stuff. Believe me, Anaka, my people will treat you like a queen,' Hawa giggled as she returned the wedding outfits to their cardboard box.

Their conversation was interrupted by the loud vibrating of her phone, which she had left on the cabinet next to her bed. 'It's Santa,' Hawa exclaimed as she scooped it up. The expression on her face went from mild pleasure to deep alarm once she answered, her eyes widening as she raised her free hand to her mouth. Dropping the phone on the bed, she turned to face Anaka.

'Stella died about an hour ago in hospital. The police are now treating it as murder.'

CHAPTER 10

Hawa had accepted a shift at the hotel the following day and so left Anaka in the flat. She had brushed away Hawa's concerns at leaving her alone, insisting that she would just catch a number 44 bus into Edinburgh to do some *touristy stuff*. 'Don't worry about me. Just go make some paper and I'll see you later.'

On the bus to work, Hawa checked her phone. Somebody had already added her to a WhatsApp group titled *Kasankay for Stella Kowa*, inviting friends from all over the world to contribute money to send her body back to her mother in Sierra Leone for burial. The group's administrator was a woman in London who claimed to be Stella's aunt. She said that she would be in Edinburgh by the weekend, whilst providing bank details for funeral contributions from people in the UK. There was also information for people who wished to make contributions on the ground in Sierra Leone and in North America.

The group chat had been deluged with tributes to Stella, with friends and relatives offering glowing memories. Hawa, who had only known her loosely, was moved by the heartfelt remembrances, with pictures showing Stella in school uniform, at weddings and at a variety of other social functions through the years.

The shift at the hotel was a blur, with the rooms on her floor being drama-free – most probably inhabited by Giraffe guests. One of the other chambermaids was off with food poisoning, the supervisor pleading that Hawa and another woman cover the absence by agreeing to stay an hour longer than their designated shift.

Hawa checked the WhatsApp group in honour of Stella Kowa again when her shift finished. The number of messages had now risen to 428. Donations had continued to roll in from friends and family across the globe and the total was currently over £3,000. In addition to the numerous pledges of financial support was a string of Bible verses and prayers, predominantly asking that Stella rest in peace. There was also an update on the condition of Stella's mother in Sierra Leone, who was so distraught at the untimely death of her only daughter that she had collapsed and had to be rushed to hospital.

Anaka was splayed on the couch when Hawa arrived home, a deep purple blanket covering her to the chin. She had lit lavender-scented candles, which she had placed on the low stools at the corners of the living room, lending the space a sombre glow. The television was tuned to some random music channel, though the volume was muted and the artistes dancing on-screen looked strange without the accompaniment of music. The American stirred when she heard Hawa come in, opening her eyes whilst managing a tired wave as she stretched out, her feet ensconced in thick pink socks escaping the bottom of the blanket.

Sitting next to her on the couch, Hawa brought her up to speed on the arrangements for Stella Kowa's funeral and the plan to transport her body to Sierra Leone. 'Stella is from Kenema, which is in the east of the country, and her mother has asked that they bury her in her family's compound. They said that they would not be happy if their child were to be laid to rest in a strange country away from her people. And so we have been asked to contribute money for her *kasankay*.'

'This is so creepy! It doesn't feel real,' Anaka replied, pulling the blanket back over her feet. 'We were at her hospital bed just the other day and now she's gone. And what's *kasankay*?'

'*Kasankay* is the material in which the dead are wrapped before they are buried. But these days, contributions for *kasankay* in our country refer to any money presented to the family of the deceased to help with the costs of the funeral, irrespective of religion. And you're so right about Stella; she seemed well and good and spoke to us very clearly. How could her condition have gone downhill so quickly?'

Not having eaten, and wanting to take their minds off Stella Kowa's death, Hawa went into the kitchen to make groundnut soup with rice. Anaka trundled in to watch her, asking Hawa more questions about the food she was preparing and the funeral rites and practices in Sierra Leone. Leaving the kitchen, Anaka returned with her laptop, a sleek rose-gold Apple MacBook, which she settled on a worktop to type up Hawa's explanation of the concept of *kasankay*, along with the recipe for the groundnut soup.

'This is perfect for my blog, Hawa – thanks again for dropping such deep knowledge!'

Anaka insisted on tidying the kitchen after the meal whilst Hawa returned to her phone for updates. Stella's aunty from London had arrived in Edinburgh and would be staying at a hotel at Haymarket. Pastor Ranka had been made an administrator for the WhatsApp group and had declared that the church would take responsibility for flying Stella's body back to Sierra Leone once it was released. There was also going to be a vigil in a week's time to which all people who had known Stella were invited.

The following morning, Hawa received a phone call from a police officer who introduced herself as Detective Inspector Cynthia McKeown. She had been assigned the Stella Kowa case and wanted to come round to talk to Hawa, who expressed surprise at the request since she had only had a peripheral relationship with Stella.

When the police arrived, Hawa offered them tea. McKeown accepted but her partner, a tall man with thick brown hair, declined. Anaka was yet to emerge from her room, having stayed up through the night to edit and post entries on Songhai Sista and catch up on episodes of a popular Netflix show she had fallen behind on whilst touring.

Detective Inspector Cynthia McKeown was slender and elegant, her presence filling the room with an authoritative aura. She had tastefully arranged blonde hair that rested just beneath her shoulders and was wearing black narrow-framed glasses. Smiling, she settled on the couch next to her partner, whom she introduced as Detective Paul Brady.

She took a couple of sips of her tea, the light smile on her face straightening into a stiff line of officialdom. 'Have you heard from or seen Othella Savage since you reported her missing?'

'No. No contact whatsoever,' replied Hawa, slightly puzzled at the question.

'And you have seen nothing from her on social media?'

'Nothing. Her platforms remain cold.'

'I am sure you've already heard about the death of Stella Kowa?'

'Yes. I got the news a couple of days ago. We are all still quite shaken.'

'Do you have any suspicions as to who would hold a grudge against her, or perhaps even Othella Savage?'

'Not really.' Hesitating at first, Hawa related her discussion with Stella Kowa in hospital, leaving out what she had learned from Khalil, the nightclub bouncer, knowing that, due to his shaky immigration situation, he would most definitely not welcome any scrutiny from the police.

McKeown nodded, her expression stiff. Tossing her head, she asked her next question. 'Apparently, your friend Othella had a flatmate. Do you know where we can find her?'

'Her name is Jattu. Yes, she shared a flat with Othella, but she was frequently away when I visited. Not sure where she is currently.'

'Do you know Jattu's surname?'

Hawa knew Jattu's surname was Sesay, but instinctively did not supply it, once again heeding the unspoken code of immigrants treading carefully when it involved the police. 'No,' she replied, dropping her eyes to the carpet.

Sensing Hawa's hesitation, McKeown probed further, a smile offered in support. 'Helping us with information is vital, Hawa, if we are to find out who is responsible for the death of Stella Kowa, and whether the disappearance of your friend, Othella Savage, is connected. We do not aim to cause undue distress – our job is solving crimes.'

Hawa smiled sadly. 'I have already told you everything I know, but of course, I will pass on anything else I find out.'

'It's gone beyond just finding your friend,' Detective McKeown explained, taking another sip of her tea. 'Stella Kowa's death is now the key priority, which is not to say that Othella's disappearance is less important – my colleagues are still on the case. However, Stella's unfortunate death now means that whoever hit her over the head and locked her in her car boot could be looking at a charge of murder. And, without wanting to unduly alarm you, I am concerned for Othella, who could also be in danger. It's imperative that we find her as soon as possible.'

CHAPTER 11

The vigil for Stella Kowa was held in the Leith Community Centre. Pastor Ranka had suggested the venue as they would need a bigger space to accommodate all those expected to attend to honour Stella Kowa.

They had settled on a Thursday evening, with Stella's body due to be flown home to Sierra Leone the following Monday. Santa and Elijah Foot-Patrol arrived to drive Hawa and Anaka to the vigil, both of them in their church suits, whilst the women chose dark dresses and low shoes.

The hall was heaving when they arrived, with almost every person from Sierra Leone currently living in Scotland in attendance. Hawa even recognised a wizened woman whom they all called Aunty Marie, who often explained how she had come to the United Kingdom in the sixties by ship. Blue plastic chairs had been arranged around tables in the manner of a wedding reception, with loose clusters of people gathered in whispered conversations, and Santa managed to secure four seats to the left of the raised stage. Already sitting at the table was a couple who introduced themselves as Mr and Mrs Musakambeva, from Zimbabwe. They lived in Kirkcaldy and had established a care company in the Fife area, explaining how Stella had worked several shifts for them in the past. Also at the table was Lesley Liberton, the proprietor of Hawa's temp agency, who, according to the WhatsApp group, had donated £300 towards Stella's *kasankay* fund. She exchanged sad smiles with Hawa, accompanied by a friendly wave.

Stella's London aunty sat on the stage, clothed in a wide ash-coloured Africana gown, the neck and sleeves of which were embroidered with silver thread. Behind her, a couple of enlarged pictures of Stella had been mounted on flip-chart boards. One featured a young version of her in her St Joseph's Convent school uniform, whilst the other was of her graduating nursing school, resplendent in a dark gown, her carefree smile jumping out of the picture.

Clutched in the hand of Stella's aunty was a large white handkerchief, which she used to dab her eyes intermittently, her distress palpable. Leaving their table, Hawa climbed the steps to the stage, crouching to the level of the London aunt's chair.

'My name is Hawa Barrie, and I just want to express my sympathy for Stella's passing. Take heart, Aunty – and may God grant the family strength and peace in this difficult time.' Nodding, the London aunty clasped Hawa's hand, mumbling thanks. Hawa moved away, giving way to the queue of people waiting behind her to offer their condolences. Joining the aunty on the stage were Pastor Ranka and his wife Amanda, heads bowed as they shared a whispered conversation.

The programme started about twenty minutes later. The church's choir was in attendance, delivering powerful songs in between tribute speeches. Stella's London aunty spoke first, struggling to control her distress as she delivered a heartfelt celebration of her niece, her eyes liquid.

'When this Stella child arrived in London, she stayed with me in Lewisham for two whole years. She came to this country and wanted to be an accountant because she had studied economics back home in Sierra Leone. But I advised her and told her that there are no accountant jobs for Black people arriving from Africa in this country. That is why I told her to study nursing, and we filled out her application to study in this Scotland.' The London aunty paused, the hall reduced to a reverential hush as she continued. 'Every time this Stella child came to London, she still stayed in my house and cooked cassava leaves for my family. She was a child with good home training who carried respect for her elders on her head. Stella left Sierra Leone after the war to escape the suffering. In this country, she was supposed to be safe. But somebody with Satan in their hearts decided to take her from us and . . .' At this point, the London aunty broke down. The pastor and his wife rushed to her side and gently ushered her back to her seat.

Pastor Ranka spoke next, delivering a convoluted speech on the nature of evil and how faith was the only true solace through darkness. He pledged the church's *unflinching support* to Stella's family, stressing that his ministry had taken responsibility for flying the body back to Sierra Leone.

The choir then delivered a closing hymn, after which the attendees were invited to help themselves to a buffet that had been spread on tables at the far side of the hall. People had by this time broken from their tables to mingle. Hawa and Anaka spent time chatting to a group of nurses still in uniform who had worked with Stella. It was one of them who had raised the alarm when Stella failed to show for work, and her eyes were red-rimmed as she spoke of the sweet nature of their now-departed colleague.

Not being in the mood for the food on offer Anaka and Hawa helped themselves to bottles of water, whilst Santa and Elijah Foot-Patrol, as was customary, hurried over to the stage to join Pastor Ranka, who was deep in conversation with Stella's London aunty, his arm on her shoulder.

Just outside the door of the main hall, in the foyer, Hawa noticed Detective Inspector McKeown. She had shed her dark work clothes and was instead wearing a navy-blue dress that reached just below her knees. She was in the midst of an overflow of guests who had made their way out of the hall, seemingly just another person who had known Stella and had turned up to pay their respects.

'You're here?' Hawa said once she reached her side, noticing the officer's perfume, which had been absent when they had met in an official capacity.

'Indeed, I am, Hawa. Just thought I'd come to get a better feel for the case. Something tells me that Stella Kowa's death was not random and that whoever locked her in her car boot is somebody known to her.'

'And you think that person might be here right now?'

'It's a distinct possibility. But with so many people here, it's a needle-in-a-haystack hunch. Nice tributes for Stella, though. I've been here since the start, and hearing about her life helped me get to know her a bit as a person.'

'And will that help you find who locked her in the boot? Surely, you should have been able to uncover something by now!'

'I know you're upset, Hawa, but it's not that straightforward. We have a few lines of enquiry that we're following. But these things take time.' Anaka had now joined them, nodding curtly at the detective as she enquired with her eyes if Hawa was OK.

'Santa's looking for you, Hawa,' Anaka said, her eyes not leaving Detective McKeown, who moved off into the hall to join the queue for the buffet. 'Says he wants to take us home because he's working early tomorrow.'

CHAPTER 12

Prompted by Detective Inspector Cynthia McKeown's enquiries, Hawa decided to try to contact Jattu Sesay, Othella's old flatmate. The number she had for Jattu had apparently been disconnected, a monotonous voice informing her that it was no longer available.

She had got to know Jattu loosely through Othella, though she was rarely around when Hawa visited their flat, thanks to the many shifts she worked for Lesley's Links and a variety of nursing agencies. Jattu had always been warm and amenable, occasionally helping Othella wash customers' hair over the tub in their cramped bathroom, whilst entertaining them with ribald jokes and outlandish anecdotes.

Resorting to Facebook Messenger, Hawa sent Jattu a couple of lines enquiring after her health and asking for her new phone number. Jattu replied almost instantly, saying that she was fine and well, her message accompanied by numerous smiling faces, beneath which was her number.

Storing the details in her phone, Hawa created a new contact, doing the same on WhatsApp, where Jattu's profile picture turned out to be a svelte biracial child eating ice cream.

How are you doing my sister? How's Glasgow?

Glasgow is good Hawa! No drama and now married to a nice white man who treats me with respect. I am his African Queen. 😊 😊 😊

So happy for you Jattu! And I see you also have a son? Fine and healthy boy-child!

God takes the glory my sister. His name is Tyler, and he is my world. After all the prayers and holy water, God finally placed a boy-child in my stomach. Have a birthday for him this weekend and you should come. Live in Bearsden.

Thanks my sister. Would love to come but was wondering if you have seen or heard from Othella? Flat empty and things broken. Stella Kowa is also dead, so I'm very worried! 🙁

I heard my sister! What kind of wahala has decided to come down on our sisters in this faraway country? Come to Tyler's party and we will talk. Party is on Saturday at 3. God bless my sister xxx.

Anaka insisted on accompanying Hawa to Glasgow to see Jattu.

And when he heard that Jattu was hosting a birthday party for her son, Santa offered to take them in his wheezing Volkswagen, his eyes shining at the prospect. 'That Jattu woman knows how to play magic with pots! And that is why I always carry a Tupperware container in my car for leftovers.'

'Sierra Leonean children's parties are not your usual parties,' Hawa explained to Anaka as she dished some jollof rice she had made into a large foil tray. 'These occasions are just opportunities for us all to keep company because we are far away from home. And so, a child's party or a wedding or a graduation party usually takes the same format – everybody from our community is invited to enjoy loud music and plenty of food, with everyone bringing a dish. My heart is not happy to go to this party, but if Jattu helps us find Othella, then it will be worthwhile.'

Before leaving, Anaka took a few pictures of the rich jollof rice for her blog.

The party was in full swing when they arrived, Santa gabbling in excitement at the size of Jattu's house, to one side of which sat a massive double garage with white doors. A large black Range Rover with furrowed wheels and tinted windows was parked in the drive, its personalised number plate mixing the JAT from Jattu's name with a sequence of numbers.

Callum, Jattu's husband, greeted them at the door, taking their jackets as he bleated about roadworks on the M8 and the weather. He was a broad Scotsman who worked in finance, his thick grey hair in harmony with a matching beard. He led them through to a big space just off the main living room, dominated by an oversized pool table, where clusters of guests were settled on wide chairs. Knowing most of the people from previous social occasions, Hawa and Santa passed out greetings, pausing to introduce Anaka.

Pleasantries over, they sought out Jattu, finding her in the ample kitchen, with its high island of black marble covered with trays of food. Jattu, who was snug-shaped, was swathed in a flowing Africana gown made from *oku lappa* material that swept all the way to the ground.

Jattu's son, Tyler, balanced on a stool by the island as his mother cleaned his face with a wet wipe. When she was finished, the child jumped down to join his friends waiting at the kitchen door, all of them whooping like hyenas as they hurtled into the wide garden at the side of the house, in the middle of which was a giant trampoline.

Raising her head, Jattu saw Hawa, her face breaking into a smile.

'So, my child's birthday made my sister Hawa finally set foot in my new house! This is Glasgow and it is not far from your Edinburgh at all, my sister. We are alone and far away from our people back home, and so we must stay in contact and hold each other with both hands.'

'University and work have swallowed me,' Hawa replied, her eyes alight. 'But I do ask after you whenever I see Othella. You're in my head always and it is so good to see you rising so well in life,' she continued, settling the tray of jollof rice they had brought onto the island, before dropping into Jattu's embrace. She then introduced Anaka, who also received a tight hug from Jattu. Santa's greeting involved lifting Jattu clean off her feet in joy, twirling her around as she squealed in mock terror.

'This is your house, my people, and there is plenty-plenty

food to eat!' Jattu declared, once Santa had set her back on the ground. 'Have whatever you want. Callum, my husband, is in the dining room and can serve you drinks, no problem. We will cut the cake soon and the children will be picked up by their parents at six. But us adults can stay to keep company and chew gossip.'

They had the conversation in a cosy room which Jattu introduced as Callum's study, a space which he used to work from home. By this time, the guests had all left, leaving Santa with Callum in the living room, watching *Top Gear* on a huge wall-mounted television.

Tyler, who was battling sleep, had welded himself to his mother, simpering as she carried him on her hip. She settled on the lush carpet in the study, her son eventually falling asleep on her chest, his mouth open in oblivion.

'So, Othella has disappeared,' she started, her voice low to avoid waking her slumbering child. 'You must find her quickly, Hawa. Lion Mountain Church is a dark place.'

Startled, Hawa spread her hands in confusion. 'But Lion Mountain is led by your own Pastor Ranka who rents us cheap rooms to stay in? Is he not a man of God who is always there to help us?'

Jattu scoffed before replying, Tyler stirring slightly, as if jarred by his mother's anger. 'That's the surface image, Hawa. Perfume smells nice, but that does not mean you can drink it. How can a man from our poor country have more than six flats in a White man's country like Scotland? And you notice how most of the flats are rented to us young ladies? The flats you and Othella have in Longstone

73

and Baberton are small-time, my sister. Do you know that Pastor Ranka also has flats in Morningside, Barnton and Blackhall, the rich areas of Edinburgh? His brother is Cecil Ranka – that big-man politician from back home who steals government money through crooked contracts. It was he who helped the pastor buy all these flats. That's where his real business takes place, Hawa.'

'And what business would that be?' drawled Anaka, leaning forward, her eyes serious.

'This is Scotland, my sisters. There are not a lot of Black women here. And so many men see us as a fantasy. This is the pastor's big scheme. African girls from the church stay in these flats almost for free, but only if you are willing to work as church ambassadors!'

'What is a church ambassador?' Hawa asked, her voice low and unsteady.

'Pastor Ranka says his dream is to make the church a powerful international organisation. And so he has to build connections with donors from all over the world. The church ambassadors are responsible for keeping these donors happy. I was an ambassador,' Jattu replied, wiping a trail of drool from her son's cheek.

'Ah, Jattu, this is a big story that cannot be true,' Hawa replied.

'I swear on the life of this angel child lying on my chest,' Jattu replied, her eyes filled with sadness. 'Remember when I stayed with Othella at Baberton, I used to tell you people that I worked night shifts for the Scottish Nursing Guild for good money? Not all those shifts were genuine. I spent time at one of Pastor Ranka's flats in a little town called Linlithgow, where I worked as an ambassador. It is not always sex. Sometimes, we travel abroad and go on dates with these donors.' Jattu paused in her explanation to slightly move her son, whose weight had caused one of her legs to cramp.

'When I was back in Sierra Leone, one of the Lion Mountain preachers declared that Satan had placed a stone in my stomach, which was why I would never get pregnant,' Jattu continued. 'For three years, I sat down in marriage with a man who beat me and then left me because I could not produce a child. And even when I came to this country, I again joined Lion Mountain, believing that special prayers could put life into my womb. But Pastor Ranka said he had a dark dream in which demons poured cement into my stomach and as such I would never have a child! But then I met Callum, and this strong child sleeping on my chest climbed into my stomach. It was then that I realised that the pastor and his people chew and vomit lies in their church!'

'I had no idea of the suffering you saw before God gave you Tyler,' Hawa replied, settling her empty wine glass on Callum's wide desk.

'So how does this drama involve Othella, then?' Anaka asked.

'Othella was the chief church ambassador. In fact, it was she who encouraged me to become one. She invited me to meetings and said that working as a church ambassador was good because the money raised helped our poor people back home. Pastor Ranka liked Othella because she was beautiful but also had a powerful brain that the men respected. When she spoke at the functions, the donors listened to her and were encouraged to contribute funds to the church. Othella was with me at the pastor's house in Broxburn for many of the meetings – a long time ago, even before you arrived in this country, Hawa. But since I married Callum and God put Tyler in my womb, I no longer go to those nonsense Lion Mountain functions. And let us not forget that Stella Kowa, who was found in her car boot, was also an ambassador! She and I even went down to London a few years ago to fundraise for the church.'

'When was the last time you heard from Othella?' Anaka asked, her voice low.

'I went to the flat a couple of months ago to collect some shoes and country-cloth bedspreads to give to Callum's mother – she says she likes the bright colours of our Sierra Leonean fabrics. Since I still have a key, I just popped by without telling Othella. But my key did not work. And when I texted Othella, she said she had changed the locks because she thought that the flat was no longer safe! And now she has disappeared.'

CHAPTER 13

After work the next day, Hawa FaceTimed Othella's mother, the connection to Sierra Leone for once strong and stable. Dr Zaydah Savage was resting on a wide sofa, her sturdy metal bookcase, which Hawa remembered well from her visits to the house, prominent behind her. Dr Savage was in essence an older version of Othella, having passed on her arresting elegance and attractiveness to her daughter.

Speaking calmly and often consulting a piece of paper on which she had written details of the police's investigations, Hawa explained the current situation to Dr Savage.

'The priority quite naturally seems to be finding out who locked Stella Kowa in her boot, especially as she is now dead, Aunty Zaydah. And so, even though I keep stressing that they increase their efforts to find Othella, they seem to think that's not a burning issue at the moment. The person in charge of the case is a Detective Inspector Cynthia McKeown, who seems genuine and competent. But even she keeps saying that her hands are tied, as the violent death of a woman connected to the church must remain their priority. And because Othella's passport is missing, they are considering the possibility that she may have left the country voluntarily.'

'Which to a certain extent is understandable,' Dr Savage replied, fanning herself with an old university prospectus as she spoke. 'My heart breaks for the parents of that Stella Kowa child. The qualifying-year students spent most of today's tutorial discussing the issue, which is rife on social media. I am worried about Othella. I continue to call and text her every day, with no reply so far. And I appreciate so much how you have stood up for her in Scotland with the police. I lived in the United Kingdom myself back in the day and know how dealings with the police can be complicated and heavy, especially for us Black people!'

They chatted for a few more minutes, Dr Savage again thanking Hawa for her efforts on the ground, whilst urging that they continue to pray for the safe return of Othella. 'It's like the poet Khalil Gilbran said, Miss Hawa: just because you give birth to a child does not mean they belong to you. God willing, Othella will find her way back to us in her own time.'

In her efforts to tame her insomnia, Hawa had moved on from listening to the sounds of falling rain suggested by Othella to creating a playlist of slow songs. She started with favourites from her youth, including ballads from Whitney Houston, Mariah Carey and Celine Dion. Anaka had laughed at her choices, suggesting that Hawa could do with listening to deeper Black music.

'But Whitney and Mariah are Black singers,' Hawa had argued back.

'Mariah and Whitney sing diluted pop music, Hawa. They got the pipes to croon with real range no doubt, but I prefer the old-school divas. If you're seeking ballads to drop you to sleep, then try some real vintage soul sounds from Aretha or Nina Simone or Billie Holiday. I studied their style to help with my singing when I started out.'

Before Hawa could respond, Anaka had tuned in to You-Tube on the television, and they spent the evening listening to the singers she had suggested, Hawa adding the tracks she liked to her sleep playlist.

Later on, whilst Hawa waited for reluctant sleep to arrive, she turned over in her mind the messages she had just read on her phone. The arrangements for her sister's wedding continued to gather pace, and a hall at the Brookfields Hotel had been booked for 19 December. But Ramat was deeply upset because a couple of their aunties from their late mother's family had said that they would not be attending the wedding. This was because Ramat's man had, in their stern opinion, disrespected the family by living with their girl-child in sin without formally introducing himself in a traditional laying of kola nuts ceremony. Hawa had sent her sister a voice note, promising that she would talk the aunties round in due course. They were more likely to listen to her since she lived overseas and was therefore given a higher status in the family's hierarchy.

Hawa also spent time on Facebook, which was awash with congratulatory messages for The Leone Stars, her country's national football team, who had managed to qualify for the Africa Cup of Nations for the first time in twenty-five years. She clicked on a video which featured a horde of shirtless youth hurtling through the centre of Freetown, belting out songs hailing their footballing heroes. Another video featured the bloated president, swathed in an elaborate white gown, proclaiming that the national team would receive all necessary support.

She was woken by the sound of music creeping under her door. A glance at her phone told her it was 9.43. She could hear the strains of Anaka rapping. Smiling, she yawned and stretched, then rose to join the American in the kitchen. She was deep into the lyrics of a *fabulous female emcee named Rapsody*, who she explained was *a conscious sista who will never get the credit she deserves since female rappers these days think that fame can only be achieved by wearing skimpy outfits and shaking their behinds!*

'But Rapsody is a different class,' Anaka explained, her voice bright and warm. 'She released a whole album dedicated to celebrating Black women like Nina Simone, Oprah, Michelle Obama and Afeni Shakur! Now that's impressive, Hawa. Rapsody's the best out there! I know I've worked with Malaika, but my dream is to collaborate with Rapsody!'

Laughing, Hawa flicked the kettle as she settled on a high stool, promising to check Rapsody out.

CHAPTER 14

Hawa received a text message from Pastor Ranka later that week, claiming that he had some important church business to discuss with her and Anaka. He arrived just when they had finished watching an episode of a drama set on a university campus. His wife, Amanda, was with him, Hawa pointing out to Anaka as they watched their arrival through the window that today she was driving a sleek black Tesla rather than their customary high BMW.

Hawa greeted them at the door, ushering them into the living room. Amanda was all smiles, expressing joy that this property had found its way to upstanding people like Hawa and Anaka. 'As you know, this is one of our more recent properties, and when I heard that it had been allocated to you two, I was consumed with joy. God has been kind to us and blessed us financially, and so it is only fitting that we extend the hand of kindness and charity to the less fortunate.'

They had by this time settled on the sofa, facing Hawa and Anaka, who were sitting on a couple of matching low chairs. 'Amanda speaks clean truth, and she has taken the words right out of my mouth,' the pastor added, flashing them a smile, his teeth perfectly aligned. 'Which is why we are here today, my sisters. Our ministry continues to grow, and we believe that it is time for you to take more responsibility by helping us raise funds for the church.'

As he spoke, Amanda reached into a plump black bag that she had brought with her, removing a stack of documents and brochures sheathed in a plastic folder. Rising, she handed a set to both Anaka and Hawa as Pastor Ranka droned on in the background.

The brochures were bright and slickly produced, highlighting the Lion Mountain Church's activities in Sierra Leone, which included a rehabilitation centre for war orphans and a planned vocational institute for teenage mothers. The pictures jumped off the pages and tugged at the heartstrings: smiling, dark-skinned children, their eyes full of hope and happiness as they ran about, sat in front of computer screens and swam in the sea at Lumley Beach.

'This is the core of our work back home, for which we need considerable funds, especially as we do not receive any help from the British or Sierra Leonean governments,' Amanda said, picking up from where her husband had paused, though Hawa found the words *back home* strange coming from the mouth of a White Scottish woman. 'The orphanage is full to capacity, and our centre has had to admit more children whose parents perished during the Ebola epidemic,' Amanda continued, her eyes gentle and moving. 'So we'll be holding a fundraising function this Friday at our house in Broxburn, with many donors who can aid our noble cause. You, Hawa, and the lovely Anaka can help us by serving as church ambassadors.'

The phrase jolted both Hawa and Anaka, remembering what they had heard from Jattu in Glasgow. Staying calm, they tried not to look at each other, their eyes remaining fixed on Amanda.

'What do church ambassadors do?' Anaka asked, her voice level.

'Nothing much, Miss Anaka. They just meet donors and explain the fabulous work we do back in Sierra Leone,' Amanda explained, her eyes warm. 'We usually host drinks receptions where the pastor, the church ambassadors and I can deliver speeches and presentations on the brilliant work we continue to do. And since Hawa and yourself have shown a deep respect for our church and are both ladies of faith, we believe that you can help us deliver this worthy message. We've considered asking you to work as an ambassador for a while now, Hawa, but we thought you needed time for your studies.'

'We will be delighted to help and feel honoured that you have chosen us,' Hawa said, her voice faux enthusiastic. 'I have finished university and will be free right up to December, when I plan on going home for my sister's wedding.'

'I'm free for now, too, until I either decide to go home to the States, or take up Hawa's invitation to visit Sierra Leone,' Anaka added.

'We will give you a wee allowance to buy clothes for your role as church ambassadors,' the pastor said. 'You can pick out clothes to your taste. Amanda will take your bank details to transfer your allowance, and we will send a car to pick you up on Friday evening.'

CHAPTER 15

A taxi picked them up from the Balerno flat at 7.30, the driver whistling to himself as they drove along Long Dalmahoy Road. They stopped at the rail crossing at Kirknewton to allow a thundering train to pass. The driver paused his whistling to explain how a stupid teenage driver had nearly died after ignoring the lowering barriers to dart over a similar crossing at Kingsknowe just last week. 'The laddie was just in front of me and didnae pay attention to the crossing. The eejit just nipped across and the train clipped his motor's backside! Lucky to survive, so he was. And the toerag didnae even stop! Just drove his motor off while we had to stay behind and talk to the police!'

Expressing horror at the driver's story, Hawa chatted to him till they arrived in Broxburn, learning amongst other things that he intended getting out of the taxi trade as *Uber bastards have ruined the whole bleeding business.*

Hawa knew West Lothian mainly through car trips with Santa to the big shopping centre in Livingston. As they travelled, she explained to Anaka how Livingston, which was very close to Broxburn, was a town of roundabouts, and how Santa had once spent twenty-five minutes trying to untangle himself before eventually finding his way on to the A71 back to Edinburgh after they had been to a Boxing Day sale at the Livingston Centre.

Taking a left turn at a roundabout, the taxi turned down a road that featured neat houses and plush gardens. A few more turns through similar residential streets took them to The Badgers Estate, which hosted even more ornate houses. Reading the street names, Othella noticed the taxi turn into Badger Park, stopping at a tall townhouse. Four cars were parked in the drive, Anaka and Hawa recognising the BMW that Amanda usually favoured.

Thanking the taxi driver, they alighted from the vehicle, relaxing when they saw Khalil looking smart in a black tuxedo over a black shirt and tie. Unlike at Sing City, Khalil gave them cold eyes, nodding curtly before turning his attention to a White couple who had arrived in a black Jaguar. Confused at the snub, Hawa took Anaka's hand for support, leading the way to the front door.

Just inside, a smiling young Black woman with auburn-coloured braids stood balancing drinks on a silver tray. Hawa recognised the girl as Aisha, also from Sierra Leone, who had arrived from London about four months ago. She had been stunned by her youth and striking attractiveness when they met at a wedding reception when Aisha first arrived in Scotland. Aisha had explained that she was a member of Lion Mountain's London chapter and had been brought up to Scotland by Pastor Ranka because there were apparently more opportunities up north. She was inter-ested in working as many shifts as possible, and had spent the evening bombarding Hawa, Othella and anybody else who gave her their ears with questions about where to find work, storing the details of numerous temp agencies in her phone, her mouth overflowing with thanks. Smiling, Hawa asked how Aisha was settling into life in Scotland, pausing to introduce Anaka.

The options on Aisha's tray were cranberry juice, sparkling water and fruit punch, which she offered them in a low, musical voice. Choosing a cranberry juice and a fruit punch respectively, Anaka and Hawa wandered into a spacious living room that featured big African-themed carvings and towering bookshelves made from wood of a similar shade to the carvings.

People were scattered across the living room, deep in conversation. In the midst of one of the groups was Amanda, wearing the same cut of trouser suit she usually favoured, although today's edition was scarlet red. Her eyes caught Anaka and Hawa across the room, a wide smile appearing on her face as she made her way over to them.

'You arrived safely. So delighted to have you here. I've just been explaining our ministry's work to a few donors who are new to us.' Dropping her voice, she asked if they had received the clothing allowance she had transferred to their bank accounts the previous day. She then positioned herself between the two ladies, arms round their shoulders, and led them into the midst of people she had left.

The guests were neatly dressed and polite, and introduced themselves as being interested in charity and particularly impressed by the work the Lion Mountain Church continued to do to improve the lives of the less fortunate in Sierra Leone. The most animated among them was a man who introduced himself as Dr McAllister, who lived in Rosyth. Upon hearing that Hawa was studying international conflict and cooperation, he latched himself on to her, chopping the air as he spoke, his breath heavy with whisky fumes.

'The current Tory government continues to promote xenophobic policies designed to turn our backs on the lives of the less fortunate. They even decided to downgrade Dfid, which did such great work in tackling poverty and deprivation in countries like yours! I worked with Dfid in Ghana for three years at the helm of innumerable projects that made a real difference. And now the government has decided to cut the foreign aid budget! Tone deaf and selfish to the extreme!'

'An unfortunate development,' replied Hawa, nodding as she sipped her drink. 'I applied to work for Dfid myself when I was back home but was unsuccessful. Their projects are commendable and well documented.'

'I know they say that international development is dead,' continued Dr McAllister, ejecting more fumes at Hawa, 'but surely, we as a rich Western society should be encouraged to do more for third-world nations like yours. Which is why I am here today!'

Hawa chatted some more with the man, their discussion eventually moving on to strategies to counter government corruption in the developing world. To her side, Anaka was standing between two men in dark suits, their eyes on her as she moved her hands in animated explanation.

Aisha, who had offered them drinks at the entrance, now drifted into the room, accompanied by another woman who was similarly attired in a black skirt and white shirt, and they travelled through the guests with shy smiles, offering them canapés from smart trays.

Soon after, Pastor Ranka entered the room, the guests bursting into applause as he took a position in front of a whiteboard on one of the walls. With Amanda by his side, he talked them through the slides on the screen, delivering a passionate spiel on Lion Mountain's mission back home and how donations from donors – several of whom were with them today – continued to make a marked difference in the lives of the *needy and deprived.*

'Our church ambassadors are here with us today and are willing to discuss all aspects of our church's mission with guests. Those of you who have attended these fundraising events before will be familiar with the format.'

He paused, and Amanda slipped her hand into his and kissed him on the cheek before picking up the explanation of the evening's proceedings. 'If you are new, then you need not worry, as our church ambassadors can provide you with information on how to donate money and the strides we continue to make with regards to battling poverty back in Sierra Leone. The evening will be very informal, with the objective of making all guests feel relaxed and welcome. Our ambassadors can show you around the house, where there are plenty of private spaces for discussions.'

Anaka and Hawa dithered, unsure what to do, but Amanda was soon at their side, a forced smile on her face. 'This is it, ladies. No pressure. Just take guests to any room in the house and explain to them the details we discussed yesterday. Focus especially on the Ebola epidemic and the need for funds to expand the orphanage. I heard you talking to Dr

McAllister earlier on about charity and deprivation, Hawa, so this should be a walk in the park for you. You can do the same, Miss Anaka; just use that American charm and help them relax. We would also love you to sing at the end of the night, so think of something good. Anything that helps to put our guests at ease would be most welcome.'

Before they could digest their orders from Amanda, a portly man in a tweed jacket appeared at Anaka's side, smiling up at her. He extended his hand, leading the American out of the room. Hawa was left with the final guest, a tall man with a broad face that had experienced sunshine recently. He smiled at Hawa, exposing teeth that seemed too small for his mouth. 'I usually chat to ambassadors in the study,' the man said, extending his hand, three of the fingers of which were adorned with gold rings.

Hawa took the tall man's hand, his palm reminding her of oiled meat. His movements suggested he was familiar with the house, as he led Hawa up a flight of steps that opened into a hallway of grey walls and smart potted plants. The study was at the far end, the tall man ushering her through.

The room was a space of black wood and leather, featuring plush chairs around an imposing mahogany table. Bookcases stretched across the walls, which were in the same shade of grey as the hallway outside. At one end of the room there was a huge tank through which a variety of tropical fish swam, their bright colours lit up by an ornate lighting feature suspended above the water.

'You can sit if you want,' the tall man said, his voice tinged with a slight gruffness. 'My name is Gerald. Gerald

Carmichael. Some ambassadors prefer to sit on the table, but whatever suits you will be fine.'

Hawa, her heart racing, sat on one of the chairs furthest from the tall man, noticing how the carpet swallowed the heels of her shoes.

'Would you like something to drink?' Carmichael asked, already striding across to a trolley in the far corner of the room.

Hawa accepted an orange juice, which he brought over in a slender glass, his hand resting briefly on her exposed shoulder as he set the drink down on an octagonal coaster on the desk. He then poured himself a generous draught of whisky, placing his glass on a matching coaster, before lifting one of the leather chairs on the other side of the table and placing it next to Hawa. Taking the arms of her chair, he swivelled it until she was directly facing him.

'So, have you worked as an ambassador for long? I don't remember seeing you at one of these functions before?'

'It's my first time. Pastor Ranka told me about the good work Lion Mountain continues to do back home, so I thought it was only right that I also lend a hand,' Hawa replied.

'Are you from Sierra Leone, too? Most of the ambassadors come from Sierra Leone, although a few others I've been with were from other African countries. There were even a couple from the Caribbean a few months ago. Lovely ladies with such musical accents and beautiful dark skin!' He paused to take another sip of his drink, inching his chair closer to Hawa's. 'Would you like me to massage your feet? Or I could probably just suck your toes if you prefer?' Carmichael smirked, his hand descending to one of Hawa's feet before she had time to contemplate the offer. He removed her left shoe, resting her foot on his chair between his legs, which were spread apart. 'You're wearing tights? Always difficult to massage feet through tights. Of course, we could simply rip them if you prefer?' He leered, exposing his miniature teeth, which reminded Hawa of a rodent. Before she could reply, Carmichael had thrust his finger into the sole of her left tight, ripping it apart, after which he proceeded to clumsily knead her exposed toes.

Startled, Hawa yanked her foot back, searching for her shoe on the carpet. 'My feet are fine. And I don't like massages, to be honest. Anyway, were we not supposed to be chatting about charity programmes and donations for the church?'

The man scoffed, and his eyes suddenly hardened. 'You don't need words to secure donations. We simply transfer funds as per usual, which as far as I know goes a long way towards improving the lives of your people back in Africa. This part of the evening is to relax and unwind.'

'I'm just finding out how these evenings work,' Hawa replied, pushing her chair back slightly, the movement compromised by the thickness of the carpet.

The man softened, his rodent teeth exposed again. 'We don't have to do anything here. Not everything has to happen tonight. Would you prefer to go for a meal with me? Or you could visit me at my house. I live in Stirling, a place called Bridge of Allan. You'd like it. We could arrange something.'

'That sounds much better,' Hawa replied, rising from the chair. 'If you give me your details, we can find a time.'

'Sounds like a plan then,' the man said, rising to the trolley, where he made himself another drink. 'Pastor Ranka has always stressed that all our interactions with his ambassadors should remain civil and consensual. He wouldn't want another situation like what happened with that Shakespeare Girl!'

Her heart quickening, Hawa picked up her glass and walked over to Carmichael, her sudden proximity softening his expression. 'That's an interesting nickname – Shakespeare Girl.' She false-smiled. 'Who was she and what happened?'

'She had a name from a Shakespeare play and she liked to use big words, so we donors called her Shakespeare Girl. She usually spoke at these fundraisers. And then she attacked one of the donors. Stabbed him in the neck with a broken bottle in one of the rooms. Then she stormed out, and we never saw her again. Blood everywhere. The donor said she was crazy and randomly attacked him. He spoke with some kind of foreign accent, and he didn't come to any more fundraisers after that. Don't blame the poor bastard. I wouldn't come back if some crazy bint stabbed me in the neck! Pastor Ranka said it was an accident and that there was no need to involve the police. Anyway, enough depressing talk about Shakespeare Girl. Let's focus on making plans for you to come visit me in lovely Stirling! I'll nip to the toilet and then we can sort something out!' Placing his glass on the trolley, he patted Hawa's cheek before shuffling out of the room, humming a tune as he left.

Alone, Hawa moved behind the big desk, trying the top drawer, which was locked. The second drawer slid open, revealing a bunch of receipts for meals and hotels, beneath which was a clutch of brochures from previous years high-lighting Lion Mountain's charitable endeavours in Sierra Leone.

Settled beneath the brochures was a pile of photocopies of numerous passports. Working swiftly, Hawa laid them out on the desk. Extracting her phone from her clutch bag, she took photographs of the photocopies. The passports all belonged to women, and the majority were Sierra Leonean ones, similar to hers, with one from Liberia.

When she had finished, she returned the papers to the drawer before rising and walking over to the fish tank.

Khalil offered to drive them back to Edinburgh at the end of the night, his eyes still hard and hostile. Mainly because she wanted to get to the bottom of his animosity, Hawa agreed, and Khalil once more gave them the keys to his car, which was parked halfway down the street in front of a small children's playground. As they waited, Hawa moved from the back into the driver's seat, switching on the engine and turning on the heating, before settling on a radio station.

'What happened to you upstairs?' Anaka asked from the back seat, her face illuminated by the light of her phone as she examined something on the screen.

'Man in the blue suit made me a drink and tried to massage my feet. He even ripped my tights! Think he wanted to have sex with me right there in the study if I'd let him!' Hawa replied, her voice bitter and charged with emotion. 'At least now we know that what Jattu told us is true. What about you? What happened when you went to your private room?'

'Now that's no joke! Why the hell did he rip your tights? You OK? He didn't assault you, did he, Hawa?' Anaka asked, raising her eyes from her phone and placing her hand on Hawa's shoulder in support.

'The bastard ripped the section around my toes. Claimed he wanted to massage my feet, and I honestly felt like kicking him in the face. Told him I didn't want a massage, and he said we could go to his place in the future. No worries, Anaka – I stopped the creep before he did anything. How about you?'

'Went into a downstairs room with that short man. He told me he was going to France next week and wanted me to accompany him to Paris. Said he's recently divorced and that he'll pay and all that, and all I had to do was say yes.'

'I also found out that Othella must have attacked one of those donors,' Hawa said as she slipped through the space between the fronts seats to join Anaka in the back. 'Foot-massage creep said they called her Shakespeare Girl, and that she stabbed somebody with a broken bottle.'

Khalil joined them presently, bringing with him the smell of aftershave and some takeaway mini quiches he had wrapped in a snug foil bundle. Without uttering a word, he tossed the food parcel onto the passenger seat and climbed in. Engaging gear, he drove off, only talking to them when they had passed the luxury car village at Newbridge.

'You, Hawa, are a person who does not listen to advice and instead you like to play with fire! Why did you come to this place today? When you asked me all those questions about my job for your pastor, I had no idea that you planned to step foot in his house! This is not a business to play around with.

That man might pray to God in his church, but there are things that happen in that house that are no joking matter!'

'But I need to find out where Othella is, and if her disappearance is linked to the death of Stella Kowa,' Hawa replied, leaning forward in her seat. 'This is Scotland and not Sierra Leone, my brother. Here, the police are much more straightforward and cannot be bribed to throw water on hot issues. If you know anything, you should help us! My head is not completely empty about what happens to women who are ambassadors, but we need strong evidence if we are to prove anything.'

Khalil scoffed before replying, his voice hard. 'I cannot help you, Hawa. My job is to provide security and sometimes drive people home. Pastor Ranka deliberately chose me because he knows I am a Muslim man who does not believe in your Christianity business. I work for him because it is an opportunity to make money. I am building a house for my mother back home, and construction materials like cement and zinc continue to climb in price. I do not have the brain for book learning in this country like you, Hawa, and when I tried to study their nursing, the education did not make sense to me. And so I can only use my size to make money. These people see a big Black man and believe I am strong. At work, they call me Mike Tyson and give me many shifts to stand at the door as a security man!'

They stopped at a traffic light, Khalil laughing lightly at the nickname before continuing. 'My papers are still not in order to stay in this country, especially as I am no longer studying nursing. But Amanda, the pastor's wife, has the brain of a sense-bird and speaks legality as easily as drinking water. She can help a poor immigrant like me get the red book, which means I can stay in this country for as long as I want to. If I stay in line with these people, they will make sure that my affairs do not end up in the gutter. I speak to my mother every week, my sister Hawa. In Sierra Leone today, hunger and suffering are human beings who lie down in bed with people. There is hardly any electricity or running water. Salaries do not get paid! But here in Scotland, although I do not have a big status, I am still able to make a little money every month.'

'What's a red book?' Anaka asked, her voice low.

'British passport,' Hawa replied. 'It's actually burgundy in colour, and changed to blue recently, but to us it's the red book. Getting it is the ultimate dream of many immigrants here.'

Nodding at Hawa's explanation of the power of the red book, Khalil continued to outline his views on Pastor Ranka and his wife's influence until they reached Balerno. This time he declined their offer to come up to the flat for a cup of coffee.

CHAPTER 16

With her finances boosted by the money Amanda had transferred for the church ambassador clothing allowance, Hawa explained to Anaka that it was time to put her car through its MOT. 'One of the chefs at work was giving away an old banger a few months ago and so the African in me volunteered to accept it,' she said as they descended the stairs to the car park. 'It doesn't have an MOT certificate, which means it is illegal to drive it. But Santa brought it over from Longstone at night to avoid the police,' she laughed, leading the way over to a battered white 2008 Mini Cooper with a soft black roof that had been invaded by splotches of green mould.

The car had a musty smell, typical of stale air, with takeaway menus and a couple of paperbacks littering the back seat. The engine spluttered before roaring into life, and Hawa eased it out of the car park, inviting Anaka to rummage through the collection of CDs that were stacked in the dusty glove compartment.

'You never told me you had a ride, Hawa. It looks like a little toy car – nothing like the big four-wheeled truck I drive back home.' Anaka laughed. 'It's a bit beat down, but it runs smoothly no doubt. And it's got a solid sound system, which is always a bonus!'

'I had to have a car, Anaka,' Hawa laughed. 'When I worked as a teacher in Sierra Leone, only the head teacher had one, which meant you either walked to work or travelled by uncomfortable public poda podas.'

'Poda podas? What are they?'

'Oh, they're these overcrowded minibuses driven by guys who don't care much for safety or the rules of the road – but almost everyone uses them for convenience. When I got here, Othella told me about Auto Trader and Gumtree and showed me cars that literally cost as little as £50. Haven't really needed to drive it though, because public transport in Edinburgh is quite good.'

Hawa had no shifts the following day and so spent the morning looking for information on the women whose passports she had photographed on her phone in Pastor Ranka's study. Anaka had risen to join her, managing to look alluring even in baggy pyjamas, sleep having left her braids straggly and scattered. Hawa made breakfast, squeezing lemon juice into their porridge, explaining to an impressed Anaka that her Fula people often did the same to the rice pap they ate in the evenings after fasting during the month of Ramadan.

They sat next to each other on the couch, Hawa's laptop open in front of them. Checking the pictures of the passports on her phone, they used Facebook and Instagram to search for the women, hoping to make contact and perhaps get more information on their connection to Pastor Ranka and the roles they played in his church.

The first passport belonged to Aisha Brewah, the young waitress who had served them beverages and canapés.

The second belonged to a girl named Alberta Rogers. Hawa's search revealed two women with that name, both of them Black. The one who matched the picture apparently now lived in Sweden, with multiple photos on her Facebook profile showing her with her husband and twin girls at a theme park.

Hawa sent her a friend request and a direct message, introducing herself as a woman from Sierra Leone seeking information on life in Sweden as she was going there for a short holiday.

Next was the Liberian passport, belonging to a woman named Naomi Wreh. Facebook and Instagram pictures told Hawa that she worked as a waitress at Rumbidzai's Room, a restaurant on Dalry Road here in Edinburgh.

The final document belonged to a woman named Kumba Matturi. Their searches on social media only located one person with that name – a teenage girl whose pictures mostly showed her in school uniform.

'Don't think that's her,' Hawa said, her eyes travelling between the image on her phone and the Facebook profile on her laptop.

'We should go for a meal at that Rumbidzai's Room restaurant where the Naomi Wreh girl works,' Anaka offered, rising from the couch to stretch. 'I do love a meal out and it would be a chance for us to talk with her and see if she can fill us in on the whole Othella situation.'

They collected Hawa's car the next day. The mechanic, a lovely man named Ronnie, who had taken the car for a wash and valet before handing it over, took great pains to explain how important it was that Hawa took the vehicle for a service once a year. Happy to no longer have to rely on public transport or lifts from Santa, Hawa drove to Rumbidzai's Room later that evening. Among the wires associated with her trade, Anaka found an aux cable, which she used to connect her phone to the car's music system, choosing a Spotify playlist that she had titled *Haunting Slow*.

When they arrived, a svelte and attractive Black woman welcomed them, introducing herself as Rumbidzai, the owner. From her head flowed an elegant weave the colour of tea with too much milk. She wore a sleeveless figure-hugging electric-blue dress with miniature black half-moons around the throat.

The restaurant was half full when they arrived, Rumbidzai assuring them that their lack of a reservation was not a problem, since they were rarely busy on weekdays. Handing them two stiffly laminated menus, she led them to a table in the far corner with a vase of plastic flowers. On the wall behind the bar hung a massive Zimbabwean flag which had been positioned over an imposing silver clock, whose numerals were fashioned from pieces of cutlery. The other walls displayed striking African and Caribbean paintings. Rumbidzai explained that the restaurant had been opened by her and her husband Franco, who was from The Bahamas. 'The food we cook here is an Afro-Caribbean fusion that speaks to both our backgrounds,' she said, her voiced laced with pride.

Once they were settled, a waiter in tight black trousers took their drink orders. They each asked for a small white wine. Hawa said with a laugh that her people back home would be mildly alarmed at how much alcohol she had started to consume since meeting Anaka.

'Do girls not drink much in Sierra Leone?' Anaka asked as she took a sip.

'A fair amount. It's just that my Fula people are quite conservative, being predominantly Islamic. And so drinking is an absolute taboo, usually.'

'Drinking goes with my line of work,' Anaka replied as she peered at the menu. 'You perform at so many concert venues and mix with so many happy people who're throwing down and having fun that you learn to just swim in the booze. I never drank in high school. I was a good Christian girl who sang in church and all that. Only started when I enrolled in college.'

'You never mentioned you went to uni,' Hawa replied, startled.

'Only one semester, so it doesn't really count. Enrolled to study music at Clayton State back in Atlanta. It was fun until me and a couple of others on the course decided that you couldn't really study music in laptops, books and lecture theatres. We dropped out and formed a group. We called ourselves Soul. Cut a couple of tracks and produced a decent demo. Made some waves in a few low-level clubs and on local FM stations but nothing major. One day this dude asked me if I'd like to sing background for the launch of some teenage pop princess. Did that a few times and made decent money as a session singer. Cut a couple of tracks, which really didn't come to much. I called myself Heart – a play on my surname.'

Anaka's reminiscences were interrupted by the return of

the tight-trousered waiter, enquiring if they were ready to order. Having decided to skip starters and go straight to mains, Anaka settled for Cajun beef and spiced rice, whilst Hawa asked for sadza with oxtail, which Rumbidzai had recommended as the *ultimate Zimbabwean meal*. Their orders taken, Anaka continued her story, Hawa fascinated by this glimpse into the life of her American friend.

'Then I was in a relationship with this dude named Bilal who was semi-big in the music business. Guy with dread-locks who made my heart melt.' Anaka laughed at the memory. 'He hooked me up with Malaika, who took me on her US tour. Had to break up with Bilal, though – he had other priorities. But *Radical Solutions* blew up and the record company said she had to ride the wave and do a world tour. We played Tokyo, Germany, Brazil, Mexico, Canada. Finished in early February and returned to the States. But then I got signed up by a company who heard me singing Lauryn Hill songs in a local club. And that's how I ended up in Edinburgh, where you found me laid low by one of my migraines on the bathroom floor in the hotel after our wrap party.'

As they continued to chat, Anaka shared more of herself, her anecdotes reducing Hawa to a mixture of awe, aston-ishment and loud laughter. Rumbidzai herself brought over their plates, and before she started her meal, Anaka took pictures of the dishes to post on Songhai Sista.

Anaka and Hawa expressed deep satisfaction at the quality of the food, which was well seasoned with an engaging hint of spice, and they decided to order dessert, both settling on sturdy chunks of zebra cake. Rumbidzai arrived again to clear their dessert plates away, beaming when Anaka and Hawa gushed over the quality of the food and the service. 'We loved every minute of tonight,' Hawa said, smiling up at her. 'We were told about this place by your waitress, Naomi Wreh. But I see she's not here today,' she added, eyeing Rumbidzai closely.

At the mention of Naomi, Rumbidzai's smile dissipated. 'Naomi from Liberia? Oh yes, she used to be such a reliable and brilliant waitress. But she has not been in for a whole week, and my phone calls are not being answered. Are you friends with her?'

'Absolutely,' Hawa lied. 'Her country is right next door to my Sierra Leone, and we used to hang out occasionally. But I heard she moved house, and I don't have her new address.'

'Oh, not to worry,' Rumbidzai replied. 'I have all the employees' addresses, and I was thinking of going to check on her, anyway. I'll write it down for you, so you can give me one less thing to do.' Disappearing behind a counter at the front of the restaurant, Rumbidzai typed into a laptop, then wrote Naomi's address on a bright green Post-it note, which she handed to Hawa. Anaka paid the bill with a sleek black credit card, Rumbidzai's smile widening at the generous tip.

'Come back anytime, my sisters,' she offered as she followed Hawa and Anaka to the door, exchanging hugs with them as they stepped into the chilly night.

It was late when they left the restaurant, so they drove to Naomi Wreh's place the next day. Rumbidzai had written down her address in neat, slanted writing.

The turning for Forrester Park Avenue where Naomi Wreh lived was right by a high school. Her building was a dull brown rectangular structure behind a low white wooden fence. Glancing up at the building, Hawa calculated the numbers, explaining to Anaka that flat E must be on the top floor as she parked between a white Sky Television van and a blue Toyota.

The front door to the block was open, a child's buggy positioned under the stairs in the entrance hall. Climbing to flat E, they knocked nervously, Hawa having decided on a cover story about an initiative to collect second-hand clothes and shoes if Naomi were to answer. There was silence from inside, with the sound of soft music coming from flat F opposite. A few more knocks yielded no result, their efforts suddenly interrupted by the door of flat F jerking open.

A small, middle-aged White woman with greying hair stared out at them, her eyes hostile and suspicious. Clutched to the woman's chest was a tiny dog that began to bark and snarl, revealing sharp, serrated teeth. Hissing, the woman lowered the dog to the floor, ushering it back into the flat and pulling the door closed behind it. 'Goan wheest yourself, Baxter. He's not usually like that. Just a wee busybody, so he is! Are yous looking for the coloured lassie who lives in there?'

'Yes, we are,' replied Hawa, smiling down at the woman. 'Her name's Naomi and we just wanted to make sure she's OK.'

'Havnae see her since last week. She's usually singing along to church music, which upsets my wee Baxter. But she's a lovely lassie. Just havnae seen her since last week.'

'Thanks for that, we'll see if she's somewhere else.' Hawa smiled, trying to raise her voice above Baxter's barking, which continued to sound from beyond the door.

'And her bin doonstairs hasnae been emptied either and is beginning to smell a wee bit. Was gonnae move it to the street so the binmen could empty it, but didnae want to touch other folk's bins if you ken what I mean,' the woman continued, obviously pleased to have a chance of talking to other people, and therefore reluctant for them to go. 'I live here alone with wee Baxter, so I'm here all day. Been signed off from work with stress. The blue car doonstairs belongs to the coloured lassie. But she dosnae drive it that much.'

Thanking her again, they went down the stairs, absorbing the information that had been provided by Naomi's neighbour. When they got back outside, Hawa wheeled Naomi's bin into the street, the huge letter E painted on the side identifying it as hers.

'This her car then?' Anaka asked, running her hand over the side of the blue Toyota. 'Couldn't have driven it recently with that flat tyre,' she added as Hawa peered through the windows, a thick jacket and an empty New Balance trainers box resting on the back seat.

As they moved towards her car, Hawa absent-mindedly tried the driver's door of the Toyota, which was locked. Then she noticed that the boot was slightly open. Inserting both of her index fingers into the gap, she gently lifted it. Screaming, she jumped back in horror, colliding with Anaka, both collapsing on the soggy grass.

Lying in the boot was Naomi Wreh, her eyes fixed like glass marbles. She was wearing a baggy bottle-green T-shirt and a denim skirt, her tongue lolling out of her mouth like a limp pink rag. The tightness of the boot had left her knees bent at an unnatural angle and she had lost the shoe on one foot. Her skin had lost its rich dark lustre, replaced by a dull grey hue. Scattered around her were numerous multi-coloured tree-shaped air fresheners, their tangy, sweet smell reaching out of the open boot.

CHAPTER 17

From the back of the patrol car, Hawa observed the police cordoning off a large area, including 18 Forrester Park Avenue's front garden and the street where she had parked her car just ahead of Naomi Wreh's blue Toyota. Blue-and-white police tape stretched as far as the eye could see in both directions, winding around tree trunks, electricity poles and the wire fence that separated them from the railway line below.

The moments leading to her being ushered into the back of the police car remained clear in Hawa's mind, and she wondered why people in movies and novels often described traumatic events as occurring in a haze. She had called the police herself whilst Anaka had slumped back against the building's white fence, her knees pulled up to her chest as she uttered soft mewling noises.

A couple of police cars arrived soon after, followed by an ambulance and a plain white van. The first two officers had peered into the boot of the car, slipped on gloves and covered their boots in blue plastic bags, then started to stretch out their cordon. Anaka had been placed in the back of a separate police vehicle, watching, like Hawa, as more and more gawking neighbours continued to congregate on the margins of the cordon, phones out as they took videos and pictures.

The windows of the surrounding flats also framed people peering down on proceedings, as a forensics team in ghoulish white paper suits congregated around Naomi's car. Looking around, Hawa recognised the neighbour from flat F who had given them information on Naomi. She was at the entrance of the building, Baxter clutched to her chest, her lips moving in an animated monologue as she outlined some theory to a police officer who continued to remonstrate with her to return to her flat upstairs.

Next to arrive was the midnight-blue car Hawa remembered as belonging to Detective Inspector Cynthia McKeown, the one she had used to visit her at Balerno. McKeown was today accompanied by a different partner, a wiry balding man in a smart grey suit. Detective McKeown spoke with one of the police officers who had first arrived on the scene, his hands whirring animatedly as he emphasised some point. He spoke to her for a few minutes then pointed at Hawa in the back seat of the car. Detective McKeown nodded as she moved towards it, gesticulating at her partner as she walked. Opening the door, she slid in next to Hawa, admitting her faint perfume and the cold outside air, the internal light illuminating her features in the gathering gloom of dusk.

'Hello, Hawa. I know you must still be in shock, but I will have to take you down to the station for an interview since you and your friend discovered the body. Your friend will be taken to the station separately, where she'll also be interviewed. You are not under arrest, by the way. Please follow me.'

McKeown led the way over to the dark car she had arrived in, passing the vehicle in which Anaka had been placed. Hawa tapped the window with her fingernails to get Anaka's attention, the American reciprocating with a vacant stare, a sad half-smile tugging at the corners of her mouth.

'Please don't try to talk to your friend just now,' McKeown said quietly as she opened the back door of her vehicle, motioning Hawa inside.

As they drove away, Hawa noticed that the police were in the final stages of erecting a tarpaulin tent over Naomi Wreh's car.

She was driven to Corstorphine Police Station, round the corner from the PC World Othella had taken her to when she had needed to buy a laptop for her studies over a year ago. A uniformed female officer who looked young enough to be still in school got Hawa to sign a thick ledger, stating that her decision to come to the police station was voluntary. As she did so, McKeown briefly discussed sports shoes and nutrition with the policewoman, both of them having apparently signed up for the Edinburgh marathon next month.

McKeown led the way up a flight of stairs that led to a corridor of blue walls and grey doors. Halfway down the corridor, the detective opened one, and Hawa followed her through. Having watched several police series and movies, she expected the room to feature a metal table, cameras on the wall, a tape recorder and a one-way mirror. To her surprise, the first thing she saw was a desk on which was positioned a sleek black computer and little else. There were pictures on the walls, all nondescript and generic, paintings of random countryside settings and small animals. At the far side of the room was a burnt-orange couch that hosted a couple of matching plump cushions.

'Take a seat, Hawa. Would you like something to drink?' McKeown said as she removed her suit jacket, which she draped over the back of the swivel chair by the desk.

'I'll have a cup of coffee if that's not too much trouble,' Hawa replied, her voice low and steady.

'Milk and sugar?'

'Milk and half a teaspoon of sugar, please.'

'Would you like a biscuit, Hawa? I have some divine Highland shortbread.'

'No, thank you.'

'Motherwell is my team, as you might have guessed from the mugs. I grew up there and still go to watch them when time allows.' The detective smiled. 'Hence the matching couch.' She laughed then took a sip of the tea, her face turning serious as she faced Hawa, placing a snug miniature device on the couch between them. 'I will be recording this discussion, Hawa, so here goes. I spoke to my officers at Forrester Park Avenue, and they say you phoned to report a dead woman in the boot of a car. We have managed to identify the woman as one Naomi Wreh, originally from Liberia, who has lived in Scotland for the last three and a half years. We are still trying to establish how she died and who put her in the boot. Can you help us at all, Hawa?'

'We did not kill her!' Hawa blurted out, her voice assuming a shrill note.

'No, no, no, Hawa. You are not currently a suspect,'

Detective McKeown soothed, her hands spread in placation. 'Mrs Gillies, the neighbour who lives in flat F, said she observed you and your friend arrive in your car from her window. She said she gave you information about Naomi Wreh's disappearance. She said she also saw you open the boot. The coroner's report will, of course, tell us more about Naomi's unfortunate demise, but I am sure she wasn't killed today. We just need to know why you were at her flat.'

Hawa placed her shaking hands around the mug, the heat from the coffee travelling up her arms to the rest of her body. 'I saw a photocopy of her passport at Pastor Ronald Ranka's house,' she whispered, the trembling intensifying as she spoke. 'He invited us to be church ambassadors and my friend Anaka and I went to his house in Broxburn. I was in his study, and I came across several photocopies of passports belonging to women. I took pictures of them on my phone and started to contact them to see if they had heard from Othella.'

Without waiting for McKeown to reply, Hawa placed her mug on the floor, extracting her phone from her pocket.

Sliding closer to her, Detective McKeown peered at the pictures as Hawa flicked through them, stopping when they got to Naomi's, which she enlarged by tapping on the screen. 'I found out from Facebook that Naomi worked at Rumbidzai's Room on Dalry Road, so we went there for a meal. The owner confirmed that Naomi worked for her but had not shown up all week. She gave us her address, asking that we check on her, which is what we did. Nothing much has been done since Othella disappeared. A missing Black woman is never really a priority, so we just decided to try and do something ourselves.'

Sighing, McKeown apologised for the perceived slight and the apparent inactivity of her department. 'There are issues with resources and personnel, Hawa, but rest assured that I have taken a particular interest in this case. Women are absolutely much more likely to be targeted by violent crime and the colour of the victims' skin has in no way dictated my personal response to this harrowing affair. I continue to gather evidence, and these pictures you took will go a long way in helping us. But more worryingly, this is the second woman who has been murdered, with a third – your friend Othella – missing. Like I said, it's still early days, but the circumstances faced by both Stella Kowa and Naomi Wreh appear identical. They were both attacked and locked in their car boots. And on both occasions, the perpetrator filled the boots with air fresheners. We found 57 in the boot with Stella Kowa when we found her in Dalgety Bay, whilst officers on the scene today also report a large number in the boot of Naomi Wreh's car.'

'And all the more reason why I need to find Othella, detective. I might have forgotten to mention it, but Jattu told me that Othella changed the locks to her flat. Jattu says it was because Othella thought it was no longer safe. And her fears were brought to life, because somebody broke down her door and took her away.'

'We don't know that she has been taken away for sure, Hawa – I would advocate restraint and a bit of optimism. The fact that Othella changed the locks is vital information, no doubt, and it would have helped if we had known this earlier.' McKeown had by this time risen from the couch, her face lined and serious. 'My final piece of advice would be for you to absolutely desist from investigating these unfortunate events on your own, Hawa! Apart from complicating police procedure, you run the significant risk of placing the lives of you and your friend, Anaka Hart, in serious danger. Step back and allow the police to do what we are trained to do.'

Hawa was reunited with Anaka later that evening, McKeown instructing a police car to take them back to their flat in Balerno. Anaka had been interviewed by McKeown's partner, who had similarly tried to ascertain how they had found themselves at Naomi Wreh's flat.

Covering themselves with a blanket when they got home, they watched the television in the dark without really seeing the images, the volume turned down to a whisper. They went over the events of the day, both still in shock.

'Those eyes of hers as she lay in that trunk will stay in my head for a long time. Stayed in Scotland to unwind and have a bit of fun but never would have thought I'd get mixed up in this whole other level of crazy drama,' Anaka said, her eyes shimmering in the low light. 'Perhaps I should just go back home and clear my head of all this, Hawa!'

'Absolutely. If you feel you have to go, that's totally under-standable,' Hawa replied, her voice level. 'I need to see this to the end though, not just for Othella's sake, but also for the other women who have been cruelly taken from us. If someone set out to kill them, for whatever reason, then I need to at least see if I can help the police find out the truth.

Religion, where I come from, is presented as being full of light and goodness. But Pastor Ranka and his church, which we trusted, are obviously involved in something dark.'

Anaka must have tidied her room, Hawa thought, smiling at her snug, neat bed, the six pillows stacked like Jenga bricks. Not making her bed was a frequent lapse on her part, especially since Othella's disappearance, which had skewed several aspects of her everyday life. With sleep again evading her, she went through her phone, starting with Anaka's Songhai Sista posts, which featured all the pictures she had taken since she had met Hawa in the hotel room. Hawa smiled at the pictures of Mandipa's braids, remembering the light that had poured out of Othella as she had advised the teenager to read more novels as a means of broadening her mind. She then moved on to *The Queens of Sheba* WhatsApp group, which had good news on Zainab Zubairu: the money they had contributed for her healthcare had enabled her to be moved to the private hospital at Hill Station where she was responding to treatment. A picture from her latest hospital bed showed her smiling brightly, her eyes much more alive than in the one taken when she was in the government hospital a few weeks ago.

Ramat's wedding plans continued to soar, with the upset aunties who had previously declared that they would not be attending having agreed to at least reconsider. Ramat now wanted Hawa to see if she could source pens, key holders and towels featuring pictures of her and the groom, which could be given out as souvenirs on the big day.

Smiling sadly to herself, Hawa reflected how affairs back home often provided context and grounding amidst her troubles in the faraway country she found herself in.

CHAPTER 18

News of the deaths of Stella Kowa and Naomi Wreh exploded the next day. A couple of national papers carried garish headlines, proclaiming that two women had been murdered with a similar modus operandi, with their bodies abandoned in car boots and covered with air fresheners. One of the papers had glibly proclaimed that the murders were the work of a serial killer, colourfully dubbed *The Car Boot Killer*, who seemed to be targeting Black women.

Cynthia McKeown phoned Hawa to discuss the articles, sounding angry and upset. 'I wanted to check that you were OK, Hawa. Just seeing the stories myself and I am furious. Somebody in our department must have leaked the details of our investigation to the press. Though most of what they have written is utter garbage, they have printed snippets of information that are supposed to be confidential.'

'What confidential information? I thought that, as Othella's primary contact, I was up to speed with every step your department is taking.'

'It's a bit complex, Hawa, and we didn't want to alarm you or seed further panic. I would prefer to update you on the investigation in person rather than over the phone.'

At that moment, Anaka appeared at the door, holding up her phone with one of the articles displayed on the screen, whilst she mouthed, 'Have you seen this?' Nodding, Hawa mouthed back that she was talking to the police. Anaka stepped into the room, climbing onto the bed where she sat cross-legged, scrolling through her phone as she waited for Hawa to finish the call.

'Headquarters think we need to hold a press conference to allay the fears of the public whilst seeking to douse the sensationalist twaddle being peddled by the press,' Detective McKeown continued, her voice tinged with frustration. 'One of the papers has also mentioned your friend, Othella Savage, claiming that she's missing and is likely the killer's next victim. As Othella's primary contact, we might need you to appear with us to help raise the profile of her disappearance in the near future.'

'That's what I've been trying to get done for weeks. But the last time I phoned to express my dissatisfaction at the police's progress, I was told they were on it and that these things take time.'

'Things have obviously changed, Hawa. Remember that I'm on your side. I'll keep you posted on plans for our press conference and please, please do not allow the papers to bring you down. And try not to talk to any reporters, if possible, as I am sure they'll seek you out, especially if things continue to leak from our end.'

Hanging up, Hawa turned to Anaka, who thrust her phone forward. 'This article's saying more weird stuff about Stella and Naomi. Been reading it while you were talking, Hawa.'

★

They went to church on Sunday, Hawa driving them there in the wheezing Mini. The church, to their surprise, was heaving, with several people Hawa did not recognise in attendance. Unable to join the row close to the front they had occupied on their previous visits, they squeezed in next to a family three rows from the back. The choir was in full lusty voice as usual, the lyrics dancing on the screen at the front of the hall.

Once again, at the usual time, Santa and Elijah Foot-Patrol scurried out of the church to receive the pastor, smiling warmly at Hawa and Anaka as they scuttled past.

They returned presently without Pastor Ranka, accompanied instead by a White man wearing a smart grey suit over a blood-red shirt. The man wore thick glasses, and his face was adorned with a neat goatee beard that matched his brown hair. With him was Pastor Ranka's wife, Amanda, wearing one of her signature suits, this time in khaki brown. Amanda sat in her usual spot in the front row, whilst the man climbed onto the stage to stand in front of the lectern on which Santa had settled a thick red Bible.

Thanking the choir when they finished their latest song, the man on stage then introduced himself as Pastor Saul Steele. He was visiting from Lion Mountain's London branch and would be stepping in for Pastor Ranka, who was currently *battling demonic forces that seek to lay him low.*

'But a church is not a single person, my people,' Pastor Steele explained, jabbing the air for emphasis. 'Today, I am standing here in front of you, speaking in the same voice as Pastor Ranka who cannot be with us. The Lion Mountain

Church knows no background, race or colour, and we are united as one people in Christ Almighty.'

Pastor Steele then went on to discuss the murder of another sister, declaring that her sad and untimely demise was further evidence of the need for faith and heartfelt prayers. 'We pray that the police are guided in their search for the people responsible for the deaths of sisters Stella Kowa and Naomi Wreh. We also offer up prayers for their loved ones at this most difficult time, and our ministry will do everything to support the families.'

At the end of the service, people gathered in clusters outside the building, their conversations muted and subdued. Hawa led the way over to Santa and Elijah Foot-Patrol, who were leaning against Santa's Volkswagen, both of the men studying some detail on Santa's phone. Noticing Hawa and Anaka suddenly upon them, Santa thrust the phone into his pocket, fixing them with a nervous smile.

'I would have collected you to bring you to church, my sisters. But I did not hear from you this morning and assumed you were perhaps not coming to worship today,' he explained.

'We only decided to come at the last minute,' Hawa replied. 'Got my car fixed anyway, so no worries, Santa.'

'I heard how you and Anaka were the ones who found the dead body of sister Naomi. The police came to talk to me and Elijah also, asking stupid questions about the church and Pastor Ranka. They were quite hostile at times and acted as if they thought our church's hands were inside the deaths of sisters Naomi and Stella. But I shouted at them and told them that our ministry was clean.'

They were joined at this point by Amanda and Pastor Steele. Amanda was leading the new pastor around the clusters, getting him to meet the congregation and shake hands with them, and they both oozed charisma and charm as they passed from group to group.

'You still have not sung for us, Miss Anaka,' Amanda said as she hugged her and Hawa. Giving Santa and Elijah Foot-Patrol curt nods, she turned to Pastor Steele who was standing just behind her. 'You are, of course, familiar with Santa and Elijah who met you at the airport yesterday. This is Hawa Barrie and her friend Anaka Hart, who is visiting from America. They are both key members of the church and have recently been enlisted as church ambassadors, dedicated to advancing our charitable endeavours back in the home country. Hawa is doing a postgraduate degree in international conflict and cooperation at Stirling university, and as such has a unique perspective and skillset with regard to aid and development. We're hoping she can assume a leading role in our charity work in the future, either here in Scotland or back in Sierra Leone.'

Slightly flustered by Amanda's deep knowledge of her educational background, Hawa smiled in embarrassment, mumbling that she was flattered and would be happy to help in whatever capacity she could in the future. Introductions over, Pastor Steele shook their hands, insisting that they simply call him by his first name, Saul.

'It fills me with light and happiness to see the great work undertaken by the Edinburgh branch of the church,' he said, his arms spread in emphasis. 'I am fully aware of the darkness that afflicts us at the moment. We must not lose faith but remain strong and steadfast in the Lord!'

Detective Inspector Cynthia McKeown led the press conference from behind a wide table on which were arranged tape recorders, microphones and bottles of water. She was flanked on either side by a couple of male officers, their smart uniforms adorned with glinting buttons and epaulettes designating their rank.

Smartly dressed in a deep blue suit and white shirt, McKeown outlined the specifics of the case, her hair moving as though it had a life of its own whenever she turned her head. Reading from a script, she outlined the basics of the cases: two women had died after being abducted and locked in their car boots. The police investigation was ongoing, with several persons of interest having been interviewed. The briefing finished, the floor was thrown open to members of the press, their questions coming thick and fast.

'Is it credible to assume that a serial killer is currently operating in Edinburgh?'

'What are the police doing to allay the fears of Scotland's Black community, with evidence suggesting that their women are being targeted by this killer?'

'Can Police Scotland confirm the rumour that the murders are tied to the mysterious Lion Mountain Church both ladies attended?'

'Is it true that another woman, one Othella Savage, is also missing, and could be the serial killer's third victim?'

'Should women in general and Black women in particular be on high alert?'

'Could the murders be tied to ritual practices and dark traditions often prevalent in the African countries the murdered women are from?'

McKeown waded through the questions with admirable composure, her answers in the main vague and generic. She reiterated that police enquiries were continuing, whilst appealing to the press to steer clear of *wild and sensationalist conjecture*.

'Our main priority naturally remains bringing to justice the individual or individuals who have perpetrated these heinous and despicable crimes. But we must also remember the sensitive nature of these murders with especial regard to the families. We urge that restraint and due consideration be shown when discussing and reporting these sad and deeply unfortunate events.'

CHAPTER 19

Disillusioned by the scant attention given at the press conference to Othella's disappearance, Hawa and Anaka decided to intensify the search themselves. 'She's not going to make headlines unless you put her name out there,' Anaka pointed out as they drove home from a nearby Tesco. 'You're from Africa, Hawa, but in these here places, White folk even put out posters when their dogs and cats go missing. So, what's to stop us putting Othella's name out there to the public?'

When they arrived home, Hawa opened her laptop as Anaka put the groceries in the fridge. A quick Google search revealed several sites advertising free templates for missing people. Anaka by this time had joined her from the kitchen with two glasses of cranberry juice, one of which she settled on the floor next to Hawa's foot.

'Red seems to be the colour for these posters,' Hawa explained, scrolling through a range of examples – most contemporary, though a few would not have looked out of place in an old Western movie, advertising rewards for notorious bandits and highwaymen. 'We'll keep it simple – just a massive picture of Othella underneath a heading saying she's missing.'

'And the last place she was seen and who to contact if anybody sees her,' Anaka chipped in, squinting at the screen as Hawa manoeuvred fonts and images on the template, inserting Othella's name in bold red letters beneath the word 'missing' in block capitals. 'We're talking about a Black woman in Scotland, so she's going to be easy to spot, surely,' Anaka continued, sipping her cranberry juice as she moved from looking over Hawa's shoulder to nestling next to her on the couch.

'Next we need a picture,' Hawa continued, turning her attention to her phone, which had already compiled an Othella album. 'They say you should always opt for a recent photo in these things,' Hawa added, scrolling through the dozens she had, Anaka imploring her to slow down.

After careful deliberation, they settled on one taken a few months previously at an Independence Day celebration for members of the Kenyan community in Scotland. Hawa had taken it in the foyer of the hall where the function was held, and Othella's customary smile shone out of the picture, her hair in her trademark dreadlock twists. She had chosen to wear a sharp white shirt she had bought in the Lacoste store in Livingston, with its tiny green crocodile logo nestled in one corner. Hawa then added a brief description of what Othella had been wearing when they had last seen her, and details of whom to contact with information.

Pastor Ranka failed to turn up to church again the following Sunday. Pastor Saul Steele once more led the service. He explained that Ranka had returned to Sierra Leone on urgent business concerning the expansion of the church's orphanage to cater for the children who had been left orphaned by the recent Ebola epidemic.

Anaka finally sang at church, delivering a hauntingly brilliant a cappella version of *Amazing Grace*. The American was feted at the end of the service, worshippers praising her voice as a true gift from God. The other big topic of discussion was the poster for Othella, which Hawa had shared on her social media platforms and through the church's WhatsApp group, and people kept coming over to commend her initiative, whilst promising to further share.

Amanda was amongst those who praised Anaka's performance, and before she left in the high BMW, she turned to Hawa, her smile transitioning from warm to slightly forced.

'A slightly delicate business, Hawa, but we were wondering if you could possibly take responsibility for your friend Othella's things, which are still in the Baberton flat. As far as I know, the police have concluded their enquiries with regard to the property. Demand for accommodation continues to rise, and in the true spirit of the ministry, we would like to offer the space up to another deserving member of our brethren.' As she spoke, she reached into her handbag, made from expensive burgundy leather, and extracted a couple of keys, which she passed on to Hawa.

Hawa called Khalil, who said he would be delighted to help collect Othella's possessions. 'My car's a rust-bucket Mini that's only got two doors – not ideal for moving things, if you know what I mean,' Hawa laughed down the phone. 'There's no furniture, since that came with the flat, so it's mostly clothes, shoes and books, which should fit in the hall cupboard in the Balerno flat, no problem.'

Khalil promised to pick them up at around noon the next day, then paused before asking what Hawa thought of him taking Anaka on a date. 'Your American friend is a fine-fine girl with fire and spirit. And as you are my true Sierra Leonean sister, you should beat my drum and say good things about me to her. You know that I am a straightforward man who does not cultivate confusion in the lives of the women I go out with!'

Laughing, Hawa pointed out that it made more sense for Khalil to ask her out himself. Later, Anaka collapsed in laughter on the couch when Hawa relayed his exact words of self-recommendation.

'He is quite good-looking – no harm in hanging out with him for a drink or something,' Anaka said, smiling. 'Perhaps we could double-date or something. Come on now, Hawa; you can't tell me that there're no men sniffing after someone as fine as you?'

'Not at the moment. Too busy studying and working extra shifts to pay for Ramat's wedding,' Hawa laughed. 'Went on a couple of dates with a guy named Charlie on the course with me, but nothing serious. Also had a brief dalliance with a footballer from Ghana who plays for Hearts.'

'No way you dated a baller, Hawa! What happened? Why you no longer stepping out with him?'

'He's young,' Hawa laughed in reply, 'And rather full of himself. Seemed to think it was OK to have me as one of quite a few ladies in his life. And so, I put ice on things. I still see him occasionally for the odd meal. But enough about me, Anaka. You go out with Khalil if you want to. He's a decent guy, and since I've been in Edinburgh, all our interactions have been drama-free.'

As promised, Khalil drove them to Othella's flat the following day. He seemed nervous and ill at ease for once, which Hawa put down to his plan to ask Anaka out on a date.

When they arrived at Baberton, the stairwell once again dominated by the smell of bleach, Khalil offered to carry the plastic boxes they had brought with them up to the flat. Hawa used one of the keys Amanda had given her to gain access. The forced door they had encountered on their last visit had been replaced by a plain one of sand-coloured wood with a black handle.

The flat was eerily quiet when they entered. Hawa switched on the hall light before leading the way into the living room, which seemed much bigger now the broken black glass table had been taken away. The packets of synthetic hair had been placed neatly in a large cardboard box, on top of which was a Tesco plastic bag containing the tubs of hair products that had not been spilt. Khalil, without waiting for instructions from Hawa, picked up the box, muttering that he would just take it down to the car.

Shouting a thank you at his broad retreating back, Hawa made her way into Othella's bedroom, Anaka just behind her. The room was dominated by an imposing double bed, leaving just enough room to squeeze by to get to the window, which was covered by heavy floral curtains. Hawa yanked them open, admitting the dull early afternoon light from outside, opening the window in the same movement.

Then she went through the drawers of the bedside table, on top of which was a black lamp. First, she pulled out a plastic folder of photographs from Othella's young days back in Sierra Leone, with Hawa featuring in quite a few of them. There was also a collection of receipts for a range of transactions and another folder containing Othella's degree certificates.

The drawer beneath was full of Othella's underwear, whilst the bottom one hosted a range of odd items, including keychains, old greetings cards and invitations to weddings and other social functions. Working swiftly, Hawa emptied the drawers into a small cardboard box they had brought, Anaka by this time having opened the fitted wardrobe, revealing Othella's few belongings.

'She was never really into owning lots of clothes – another thing we have in common,' Hawa explained. 'Othella was a master at securing deals at sales and she also loved the odd charity-shop rummage.' At the bottom of the wardrobe, there was a black suitcase and a couple of large sports bags, which the women pulled out and placed on the bed. They packed Othella's clothes, then used a black bin bag to collect her shoes, finding some in the wardrobe and others stacked in a chaotic pile behind the door.

Khalil returned, insisting that he carry the heavy suitcase down to the car, whilst Anaka and Hawa took a sports bag each. A couple more trips up and down the stairs had Othella's belongings stacked in the boot and on half of the back seat of the old Mercedes.

Before leaving, they checked the other bedroom, which had been occupied by Jattu Sesay. The room was bare, except for the single bed on which Othella had piled a huge stack of her novels.

'Her books!' Hawa exclaimed. 'Oh, we cannot leave these here! These were her babies, and she was always buying new ones.' Shaking his head in bewilderment at Othella's obsession with *book-learning business*, Khalil nipped downstairs, explaining that he had more black bin bags for them in the car. Anaka followed him down with a heap of native country-cloth bed sheets, which Hawa had confirmed as being representative of Sierra Leone.

In their absence, Hawa leafed through the books, remembering Othella's habit of numbering them on their title pages, adding proverbs and quotations she considered relevant and meaningful.

The last things to go were the pictures of African icons in the living room. Hawa remembered how she had spent a day helping Othella to gather images from the internet, printing them on glossy card before placing them in cheap frames from ASDA. Othella said it was something she had seen in some fancy interior design magazine, laughing at the considerably cheaper version she had put together.

Anaka purred over the pictures as they stacked them in a cardboard box, saying that they would make for a great feature on her blog. 'But I only recognise two of them,' she complained, her eyes puzzled.

Laughing, Hawa promised she would tell her about the other icons when they got back to the Balerno flat.

Khalil arranged to pick Anaka up later that evening, the plan being that he would take her to a Moroccan restaurant in Tollcross. Filling the flat with her customary vivacity as she got ready, the American sought Hawa's advice on what to wear before settling on black skinny jeans and a sleeveless mustard-coloured blouse.

He arrived just after 8, smiling up at their window as Hawa waved down at him. Anaka gave her a hug before leaving, enveloping Hawa in her perfume and joking that she shouldn't wait up for her.

Realising how hungry she was after Anaka had left, Hawa microwaved some leftover rice and groundnut soup. Covering herself up to the chest with a blanket, she ate in front of the television, losing herself in a nature documentary on South American jaguars. An hour later, she unplugged her laptop in the bedroom and brought it through to the living room. Anaka must have made her bed again. Hawa smiled at the neat stacking of the pillows in the American's strange Jenga pattern.

Checking her university portal, she realised that their degrees had been released and that she had been awarded an MSc with Distinction in International Conflict and Cooperation. Throwing the blanket to the floor, she hit the YouTube link on the TV, selecting a song by a popular singer from back home, and danced around the room in light celebration. After a couple more tracks, her mood dipped again as the disappearance of Othella and the deaths of Stella Kowa and Naomi Wreh placed guilt in her head.

The fact that Othella's passport was missing still puzzled her, as it could mean that her friend had used it to travel abroad. She went through what she knew so far, opening up a document on her laptop to note her observations:

- *Lion Mountain Church has hands in a shady scheme that involves women working as ambassadors and providing pleasure for prospective donors.*
- *Othella was a major player in the church and attended Pastor Ronald Ranka's house in Broxburn, where she was involved in a violent altercation with a donor.*
- *Stella Kowa and Naomi Wreh were both church ambassadors before they were killed.*
- *Amanda, the pastor's wife, uses her legal influence to help vulnerable women with immigration issues; this puts them in her debt and makes them easy to exploit.*
- *Pastor Ranka has returned to Sierra Leone, most likely because the affairs of his church are under police scrutiny.*

Then she typed the names of the women connected to Pastor Ranka and the church:

- *Stella Kowa – Deceased*
- *Naomi Wreh – Deceased*
- *Aisha Brewah – Brought to Edinburgh by the pastor. Previously a member of Lion Mountain's London branch. Passport in drawer.*
- *Kumba Matturi – Passport in drawer.*
- *Alberta Rogers – Passport in drawer.*
- *Othella Savage – ???*

She saved the document and turned her attention back to the television, flipping channels until she stumbled upon a BBC Four documentary on the music of Motown. She hadn't switched on the living room lights, preferring instead to sit in the gloom, the light from the television casting dancing lights across the room. It was after one when the documentary finished, with still no sign of Anaka. The American's last texts had been pictures of her dessert from the restaurant and a selfie of her in the ladies' room, eyes happy and full of light.

Switching off the TV, Hawa went to bed, knowing it was an empty gesture as sleep was unlikely to come to her.

CHAPTER 20

Hawa could trace her insomnia back to when her father brought a new woman to their house. Hawa's mother had died in her early fifties, shredded by an aggressive cancer that their Sierra Leonean hospitals had been unable to combat. The elders of the family implored that she be taken to Ghana for treatment, but she lost her fight before the arrangements could be made. The funeral and period of mourning had been a blur, with Hawa and her sister Ramat leaving boarding school to return home.

About a year later, their father brought home his new wife, with a toddler in tow whom he introduced as Bintu, their sister. Unable to bring herself to call the strange woman 'Mama', as decreed by their father, Hawa had come up with a compromise which saw them addressing the new matriarch of their household as 'Aunty Theresa'.

It was from Aunty Theresa that Hawa first heard of Pastor Ronald Ranka, and his Lion Mountain ministry, which was then in its embryonic stages. A firm believer in the charismatic pastor's message, Aunty Theresa brought a puritanical fervour to their house, throwing down edicts on etiquette and behaviour: Hawa and Ramat, being girls, should be more domesticated, demonstrating *good home training*. This, according to Aunty Theresa, was vital if they were to become productive Christian women who would one day sit down in harmonious marriages with good husbands.

Evenings in the household were consumed by sprawling prayer meetings featuring animated members of the Lion Mountain Church who experienced visions through *the holy gift of divine discernment*. Watching films together on the large family television, which Hawa and Ramat loved so much, was now a thing of the past. Instead, Aunty Theresa's church people would attend in droves, taking turns to collapse to the floor of the living room, jerking and writhing spasmodically, then rising to narrate the visions they had seen.

One such vision had pictured Ramat with a suitcase at an airport, a revelation that had caused the gathered people to burst into loud applause, as this foretold of a journey to a White overseas countries, where prosperity and good fortune were assured. Another vision, however, had seen Hawa tied up with thick ropes whilst lying subdued on the ground. This was a *harbinger of darkness*, Aunty Theresa explained, fixing Hawa with a worried look. She had instructed her to fast for seven days, after which she was expected to travel to a local stream at the break of dawn on the eighth day to bathe, dousing herself in holy oils to blockade the darkness that had been seen in the vision.

Hawa had fasted for three days and then refused to continue, calling into question the veracity of visions seen by the Lion Mountain people. This had caused an uproar, with Aunty Theresa suggesting that living under the same roof as Hawa was to be in the presence of a dark rebelliousness that was unbecoming in one so young.

Hawa's father, who had been a devout Muslim, had strangely gone along with Aunty Theresa's religious changes to his household, often proclaiming that both religions worshipped the same God, anyway. He implored Hawa to complete the period of fasting, but she refused, insisting that she would prefer to accept whatever dark fate awaited her.

Aunty Theresa had also taken umbrage at Hawa's focus on education, sniffing and sneering at her stepdaughter's obsession with reading. She would often wake her and Ramat early every morning and send them to fetch water and chop firewood, rather than relying on the houseboys their father had always hired. Ramat accepted Aunty Theresa's regime with benign nonchalance, loosely following the orders handed down. Hawa, on the other hand, rebelled, which invariably led to confrontations with Aunty Theresa, usually when their father, a successful electrical engineer, was away at work.

Aunty Theresa would report Hawa's transgressions whilst in bed with their father at night, Hawa listening to her skewed version of events through the walls of their room, which was next door to the one she shared with her sister. At times, Ramat's light snoring would compromise her ability to hear what was being said about her, and she would nudge her sister to shift her position and halt the rasping sounds she produced as she slept.

Following these nocturnal briefings, her father would often storm into their room, hurling dark threats and insults at his daughters for being ungrateful and refusing to thank

God for giving them a pure and holy woman to care for them like a true mother though she had not carried them in her womb.

In time, Hawa took to sleeping very little at night, living under the threat of a constant cloud of anger and negativity. But a return to boarding school and then university reduced the altercations with Aunty Theresa, with Hawa often choosing to stay on campus or with friends during the holidays rather than come home. Ramat, being less academic, did not go to university, enrolling instead in a vocational institute whilst living at home.

Hawa left the family house when she graduated, renting a small two-bedroom place in Tengbeh Town, where she lived whilst she taught history and English at St Joseph's Convent school in Brookfields. She asked Ramat to live with her, leading Aunty Theresa to damn them both as children who had Satan in their hearts. Their father initially refused to speak to his daughters, towing Aunty Theresa's line of their being evil. The girls, however, took to visiting him at his office at Electricity House in the city centre, where he proudly showed them off to his workmates, gave them money and treated them to fried chicken from the Rooster Restaurant on the ground floor of the building.

And then Hawa secured the Commonwealth Scholarship to study in Scotland, to Aunty Theresa's stiff indifference and her father's secret elation. She had left Ramat in the flat at Tengbeh Town, sending money every month to help with rent and other expenses.

Her insomnia was therefore an inheritance she carried with her from her time with Aunty Theresa, and it had refused to shift even after she found herself in Scotland. Another legacy from her time with her stepmother was a secret dislike and suspicion for the Lion Mountain Church, which was the main reason she had refused to regularly attend their services when she arrived in Scotland.

CHAPTER 21

Police Scotland released the body of Naomi Wreh a week later. Unlike the local Sierra Leonean community, who had pulled together to send Stella Kowa's body back home to be buried, the Liberians on the ground in Scotland had settled for burying Naomi in Ratho. Her parents had apparently been killed during the civil war in Liberia, and she had come to Scotland on a refugee resettlement programme when she was a teenager.

A second police press conference confirmed that Naomi Wreh had been killed before being put in the boot of her car, the cause of death being blunt-force trauma to the head. They were therefore appealing for witnesses who had possibly seen something suspicious. Pictures of Naomi and her car were circulated, with the hope that memories could be nudged. There was also a CCTV snippet of her buying groceries at her local Scotmid, after which she was filmed walking down the road.

The church had once again agreed to fund the cost of the funeral, as Amanda confirmed after Pastor Saul Steele conducted the Sunday service in the continued absence of Pastor Ranka. Naomi Wreh was laid to rest with a clutch of church members in attendance. The ministry provided a minibus for mourners to attend the service, and Hawa had joined the group. Anaka chose to stay at home. They had sung a few hymns at the graveside, and an elderly lady named Joanne, who was also from Liberia, delivered a moving eulogy.

Detective Inspector McKeown called Hawa the following day, inviting her to the station for a chat.

'I have an early shift at the hotel tomorrow until two. I could come right over after that since your station is just a few minutes' walk away,' Hawa suggested.

'Perfect,' clipped the policewoman. 'Just ask for me at reception and I'll see you then. Nothing to worry about, but my superiors have finally decided to turn the spotlight on Othella.'

The shift the next day passed without incident. Finished, Hawa grabbed a plate of fish and chips from the staff canteen. Although she was agency staff, she worked at the hotel so often that the supervisors all insisted she eat in the canteen whenever she wanted. She changed out of the ugly yellow uniform into a pair of black skinny jeans and a night-blue turtleneck jumper that she had packed in her rucksack specifically to wear to the police station.

Jumping in her car, she was at the station in five minutes, finding the schoolgirl-looking policewoman from her last visit at the reception desk again when she arrived.

'Afternoon – how can I help you?' she asked, her voice matching her innocent, open face.

'I'm here to see Detective Inspector McKeown. She's expecting me.'

The young officer spoke into the phone, moving her hands in harmony with the brief conversation, her eyes never leaving Hawa. Placing the receiver down, she smiled, exposing perfect teeth. 'Detective McKeown is expecting you. She's up the stairs to the left, same as last time. She says you should know where to go.'

Thanking her, Hawa went up the single flight of stairs. Cynthia McKeown was waiting for her.

'Hi, Hawa, and thanks for coming. How's your day been? Apologies for asking you to come at such short notice.'

'Not a problem, detective. I was working round the corner, like I said yesterday.'

Smiling, McKeown led the way along the corridor to her office, then gestured for Hawa to sit on the couch before going over to make coffee, remembering her specifications from her last visit.

Settling down next to Hawa, McKeown fixed her with serious eyes. 'We continue to investigate the deaths of Stella Kowa and Naomi Wreh, although to be frank we haven't had much luck so far. Both their cars were covered in fingerprints, which complicates things, and there are no matches with any DNA samples we have in our database. We did hold a second interview with Amanda Ranka, the pastor's wife, who was very cooperative. But we found no evidence of any illegal activities, and our attempts to talk to the ladies of your church who supposedly work as church ambassadors haven't led anywhere. Those we spoke to all confirmed that they willingly performed these duties for the ministry, which included raising money from donors. However, they all insist that their methods are legal and above board.'

'But surely what Anaka and I told you must hold some water. We were encouraged – although discreetly – to woo the men to convince them to donate money. One of them even offered to massage my feet!'

'But that's not a crime, Hawa. He didn't force himself on you when you declined the offer, as you yourself confirmed. Unless you wish to press charges now, which is absolutely within your rights.'

'How about Jattu?' Hawa replied, her voice climbing in indignation. 'I passed on what she told us after we visited her in Glasgow. It was she who initially outlined the true role of these church ambassadors.'

'I have attempted to talk to Jattu Sesay twice, and she has been uncooperative. She told me that God had blessed her with a good husband and a healthy child, and it would be better for her to stay in her lane and mind her own business. The way forward, as I see it, is to step up our search for Othella, which is why I called you in today. We've decided to hold a press conference, and I just wanted to see if you would be willing to add your voice to our appeals to the public.'

CHAPTER 22

The briefing was held in the same room as the press conference regarding the deaths of Stella Kowa and Naomi Wreh. Hawa noticed that there were fewer members of the fourth estate present, realising that what some might consider a mere missing person's enquiry would not have the same juice and gravitas as the activities of an apparent serial killer. She had arrived at police headquarters with Anaka in her Mini, both choosing the dark dresses they had worn to Stella Kowa's vigil all those weeks ago.

McKeown met them at the reception, along with a plain-clothes officer she introduced as Detective Ruth Williamson, and led the way into a private side room with a coffee machine and a water cooler.

'This is our base for today, ladies; feel free to ask for anything you need. Hawa, as Othella's main point of contact, you will sit with us as we launch the appeal. Anaka can stay and watch on the screen in here or sit at the back of the briefing room.'

Considering her options, Anaka asked to stay in the room, rising to give Hawa a tight hug and whispering in her ear that she was with her in spirit.

The briefing room was half full when they walked in, a number of the gathered press rising to take pictures as the officers and Hawa took their positions at the table.

'Good morning, and thanks for joining us for today's briefing. My name is Detective Inspector Cynthia McKeown. With me today are Detective Ruth Williamson and Hawa Barrie, and we are here concerning Othella Savage, who went missing from her flat in Baberton some weeks ago.' McKeown raised a missing person's flyer, swivelling it to the various corners of the room as she spoke.

'Without a shadow of doubt, there are suspicious circumstances surrounding the disappearance of Othella Savage, and we will do everything within our power to get to the bottom of the matter. She has been missing for close to five weeks now, and the investigation has been moved from the purview of the local CID to a major investigation team headed by myself.'

Detective McKeown leaned forward and paused to take a sip of water before continuing, her eyes surveying the room as she spoke. 'Our key priority is Othella's wellbeing, and we have a responsibility to explore multiple scenarios: first, the possibility of Othella voluntarily seeking to absent herself from friends and family. We also have to face the fact that Othella may have come to significant harm, with her having been murdered the unfortunate worst-case scenario; or that she has been abducted and is currently being held against her will. If Othella has been harmed or has lost her life, we need to explore how this happened, and who might be involved. We will also explore the possibility that Othella may have deliberately harmed herself. Detective Ruth

Williamson will now provide some background information on Othella.'

Detective Williamson picked up the narrative, her voice steady, a shade quieter than McKeown's. 'Othella Savage is a 26-year-old female who was born in Glasgow but spent her formative years in Sierra Leone, West Africa, where she went through school and university. She returned to the United Kingdom in 2018 to pursue a postgraduate degree at the University of Stirling. Up till her disappearance, she lived in a flat at Baberton in Edinburgh. Othella is described by her friends and family as having a sunny disposition and positive personality. Othella has no known ailments, mental or physical, and is not on any medication. As far as we are aware, she has never deliberately absented herself or gone missing. On the successful completion of her studies, Othella initially made a living working as a hairdresser at Simba's Salon on Gorgie Road, but she recently started operating from her flat in Baberton. There is nothing we are currently aware of that would have led Othella to suddenly flee or leave the area, although our investigations continue in this regard.' Detective Williamson looked up from her script and removed her glasses, indicating that she had finished.

'Our intention at this juncture is to continue to engage with Othella's local community, both in Baberton where she lives, and her friends within the Sierra Leonean and wider African community here in Scotland,' McKeown continued. 'With us here today is Miss Hawa Barrie, Othella's friend from their youth in Sierra Leone — a friendship that has continued to thrive here in Scotland. She would like to say a few words.'

Hawa had been an accomplished speaker in university, frequently participating in panel discussions on the civil war and political corruption. She felt just a hint of nervousness as she spoke; her voice was for the most part calm and measured.

'My friend and sister, Othella Savage, disappeared from her flat five weeks ago, as has been outlined by the detectives. I was with her on the day she was last seen, and she was her usual effervescent and positive self, with no cause for concern or signs of distress or trauma. She hasn't changed much from the picture on the flyer, and she had the same hairstyle when I last saw her. And, Othella, if you are out there, I implore you to make contact in whatever way possible to me directly or to the police. We are here for you and will always be ready to help you deal with whatever situation you are currently facing. We love and miss you and hope to see you soon.'

The rest of the briefing was devoted to questions from the press, who once again were desperate to pursue the serial-killer angle, keen to link Othella's disappearance to the murders of two other Black women from West Africa.

They retreated to the room where they had left Anaka, McKeown praising Hawa for the composure she had shown at the press conference. 'You spoke well. These occasions are difficult for loved ones, and I have to commend you for holding it together.'

Anaka stood to give Hawa a hug. 'She's right, Hawa. You represented very well.'

'We'll be in touch with any further developments,'

Detective Williamson promised, her head tilted at a sympathetic angle.

Under the auspices of Detective McKeown, the search for Othella intensified, although Anaka remained certain that the added momentum was as a direct result of a scathing interview Hawa had given to a couple of newspapers. They were quick to twist her dissatisfaction into a sensationalist accusation of *institutionalised racism*. One of the papers – *The Lothian Courier* – even featured a banner headline next to a picture of Hawa: *Missing Woman's Best Friend Accuses Police Scotland of Racism.*

A couple of days later, McKeown, Williamson and a bevy of officers in uniform descended on Baberton, where they distributed Othella's missing person's flyer to members of the public. There was even a feature on the BBC's *Reporting Scotland*, showing clips of officers searching dustbins and hedges in the neighbourhood park, whilst others trawled the local canal. McKeown herself was interviewed, taking great pains to stress that there was no evidence that Othella Savage's disappearance was directly linked to the deaths of two other women from Africa.

CHAPTER 23

Amanda Ranka came to see Hawa and Anaka over the weekend. She arrived in her Tesla just as the street lights had flickered on in the car park, now an earlier occurrence in the dark of winter.

'At least now you have finished your studies, which gives you more time to work. Studying while working is a delicate balancing act – and I remember it well from my student days,' she explained, as she draped her jacket over a chair. 'I left the comfort of my parents' cosy house here in Edinburgh and insisted on going all the way up to Aberdeen to study. The cold up there is on a whole other level. Shared flats with some questionable people who thought hygiene was optional and worked as a waitress in a grotty café. Tough, but it builds character.'

'Did you meet your husband while studying up in Aberdeen?' Anaka asked.

'No. We met at a fundraising function here in Edinburgh about a decade ago. Before university, I took a couple of gap years and worked for VSO in Zambia. Did plenty of work with HIV orphans and teenage mothers, which piqued my interest in aid and charity. Hearing the pastor speak about the harrowing legacy of civil war in Sierra Leone, and the strides Lion Mountain was taking to make a difference, I was captivated. I had been working as a lawyer for a couple of years, and realised I had a set of skills that could prove useful. And then we fell in love and I came on board. It's been a journey of peaks and valleys since then, but we continue to march forward.'

'And your faith is also so strong, Amanda,' Hawa said innocently. 'I don't mean any offence, but people in the UK don't seem to be that religious.'

'People always need an anchor; something that grounds them and defines their place on this planet and their direction in life. They're often spiritual or superstitious without being overly religious. I chose to be close to Christianity mainly because Lion Mountain preaches giving back and helping the less fortunate. For me, it's about fundamental morality and being kind to our fellow human beings.' Amanda smiled, before continuing, her eyes somehow mesmeric. 'But enough preaching from me, especially as you two are already converted, as it were. Let's get down to business. I'm here to discuss cash, not crucifixes. We usually hold a big charity Christmas dinner here in Edinburgh to celebrate the work of our ambassadors whilst seeking to raise more funds. We didn't have one last year due to a few logistical problems, but we will be resuming this year. They usually take place in the second week of December, after which the pastor and I travel to Sierra Leone for our annual retreat. With Ronald away, however, the organisation and planning falls on my shoulders. I have drawn up a rough programme and would like you, Hawa, to deliver the keynote address, whilst Anaka here could perhaps grace us with a musical performance?'

Mildly honoured, if also a little worried, Hawa leaned forward. 'What would the keynote address involve? I've not long been an ambassador – surely there must be others who are more entrenched in the ministry.'

'True, but not many of them have studied international conflict and cooperation, Miss Hawa. You have the perfect blend of education and faith to be able to place what we do in its proper context.' Amanda flashed her an encouraging smile. 'And so, the keynote address has to be delivered by you. In the past, it has involved providing a brief history of Sierra Leone with an emphasis on her people and culture, while outlining some of the current problems that need addressing. We initially focused on child soldiers from the war and teenage mothers. But the recent Ebola epidemic and the mudslide deaths led to a shift in focus. In any case, all you have to do is put together a presentation that you can talk through on the day.' She paused, draining the final dregs of the fruit tea Hawa had made her. 'Othella delivered the keynote address at the last dinner we held. And while she is not currently with us, we believe that you, Hawa Barrie, are the person most capable of filling her shoes.'

The dinner was to be held at the Dalmahoy Hotel in Kirknewton, an expansive venue of long sprawling driveways and lush greenery just off the A71.

Amanda had sent Hawa the programme via email, and she and Anaka examined it on her laptop after they had finished watching *EastEnders* one evening.

The Lion Mountain Charity Ball is our flagship fundraising event, attended by well-meaning people from all spectrums of society. A glamourous evening of relaxation and revelry for all.

The evening will commence with a drinks reception, after which guests will be invited to take their seats for a three-course meal, with complimentary drinks provided.

Throughout the meal there will be live musical performances, followed by the Pledge and Auction segment of the evening.

Beneath this outline, there were links to sponsorship packages, with gold, silver and bronze options already secured and no longer available. 'Damn! Wonder how much they would have cost,' Anaka exclaimed, the light from the laptop casting a glow over her face.

Hawa continued clicking, opening an 'other opportunities' link, which advertised seating packages for tables for ten people costing between £800 and £2,500. She whistled, turning to Anaka. 'This looks like a big serious occasion, Anaka. If Amanda expects us to stand up in front of this calibre of guest, we have to make sure we are ready.'

Amanda had instructed all the church ambassadors to meet her at the Dalmahoy Hotel the day before the function. Hawa drove her and Anaka over in the decrepit Mini, which looked starkly shabby parked between a sleek Porsche that looked like it had just rolled off a factory assembly line and a BMW with shimmering bodywork straight out of a sci-fi movie.

Amanda was waiting at the top of the stairs at the hotel's

entrance, accompanied by a sharp-looking lady with a clip-board. Smiling, Amanda dished out her customary hugs to Anaka and Hawa, introducing the woman as Susi Davidson, the hotel's head of hospitality. 'Susi and I roomed together at Aberdeen back in the day. But she's clever and studied hospi-tality, whilst I plodded on down the legal route. She's like a sister to me, and she's been organising our events for years.'

Susi Davidson smiled throughout the introduction, then led the way into the hotel and to a side room which featured ornate paintings of Highland cows and stags on the walls. In the centre of the room was a high glass table loaded with an assortment of beverages. 'Help yourself to drinks whilst we wait for the rest of your party to arrive,' Susi Davidson said, her voice light and assuring. 'There's free Wi-Fi, and the toilets are through the door at the far side of the room.'

'Chat amongst yourselves, ladies,' Amanda added. 'I think we're only waiting for three more, and then we can com-mence the briefing. I'll step out with Susi to firm up one or two other arrangements for tomorrow.'

Hawa and Anaka surveyed the room. The other ambas-sadors were scattered across tartan-upholstered low couches and armchairs. She recognised most of the women from the function at Pastor Ranka's house, though a few were new to her.

Most of them were inside their phones, but a couple who were sitting closest to Anaka and Hawa looked up and offered half-smiles in greeting. Hawa recognised Aisha Brewah, the girl who had desperately demanded informa-tion on agencies to work for, which would allow her to make swift money. She had grown slimmer since Hawa had last seen her working as a waitress at Pastor Ranka's house, her cheeks heavily rouged to match her scarlet lipstick. She was chewing gum rhythmically, her eyes not leaving her phone. Hawa continued to survey the other ladies who numbered eleven in total, eight of them Black, whilst two were White and one Asian.

'Hey, isn't that woman in the chair by the door the same one whose passport was in the pastor's study?' Anaka whispered in Hawa's ear. 'Kumba something or other. Remember how her Instagram was private?'

Hawa, marvelling at her friend's ability to remember Kumba Matturi's face, whipped out her phone, swiftly trawling through her pictures until she found the one she was looking for. She looked up at the woman Anaka had pointed out – the resemblance suddenly obvious. She was wearing a white shirt and black jeans, her sleek Ray-Ban glasses hoisted to her forehead beneath a deep red bandana.

As if aware she was being discussed, the woman suddenly looked up, surveyed the room briefly, then tossed a question into it: 'Who is delivering the Othella speech this year?'

'I think that would be me?' Hawa replied uncertainly.

'And who are you? Don't think I've seen you at any ambassador functions before, and now all of a sudden you're going to deliver a big speech tomorrow?'

'My name is Hawa Barrie, and this is my friend Anaka Hart. I'm from Sierra Leone, but Anaka's from America.'

'They call me Kumba,' the woman replied. 'Hawa Barrie? You must be a Fula then. What part of Sierra Leone are you from?'

'I am a Fula indeed. My father comes from Kabala, but I was born and raised in Freetown.'

'My name tells you where I am from. I am Kumba Matturi,' the woman replied, placing her phone face down on the chair in between her legs. 'From Kono. Piece of advice for your big speech tomorrow, Hawa – just keep it short and sharp and please don't do an Othella by overloading it with big book talk. I know she's missing, so I'm trying not to show her disrespect, but her speech two years ago lasted almost fifteen minutes! These men are here tomorrow to relax. If they need information on our country, they can go to a library or throw their heads into the internet. We are here to drink, relax, shake bodies on the dance floor and then go our separate ways.'

'Thanks for your advice,' Hawa replied, her eyes hardening. 'Last time I checked, Amanda was in charge of proceedings. My speech is an opportunity to throw light on the issues we have in our country. Apologies if what I say tomorrow comes in the way of you throwing down on the dance floor and getting happy,' she snapped, Anaka placing her hand on her shoulder as if to moderate her anger.

'You offer people simple advice, and they jump down your throat with palaver business,' Kumba returned, fixing Hawa with a reciprocal hard look. She then leaned forward in her seat, thrusting her face towards her. 'I was a church ambassador long before you turned up, and it is my duty to try to help new sisters who join Lion Mountain. Aisha, sitting over there, is a new ambassador, and Pastor Ranka out of love and light asked that we live together, and that I act like a big sister to her by advising her on faith. And that is the same kind of advice I am giving you for free, Hawa!'

She then removed the red bandana to reveal miniature cascading braids of a deep brown colour, which she pulled to one side. An ugly scar sat just below her left ear.

'This wound is from our war back home. Rebels stormed into my village when I was in primary school and vomited petrol over all our houses. Our people's throats were cut just like how you slaughter sheep for Ramadan Pray Day. A child rebel actually stabbed me, and this is the mark of his knife that I will carry to the grave. If it were not for the grace of God, I would have died!' The whole room was now silent, all the ambassadors focused on Kumba, her voiced tinged with emotion. 'And now we are in beautiful Scotland, which is very cold but has many opportunities and lovely people. I attended Lion Mountain here in Edinburgh in the same way we always attended Lion Mountain back in Sierra Leone. And then Pastor Ranka asked me to work as an ambassador. And through God's blessings, me, who got stabbed in the neck and used to struggle for rice and palm oil to eat, now sits in planes and travels to nice places with donors for our church. Nobody forces anybody to do anything you do not want to do. Last week I was in Sweden and was given this watch as a gift by a very sweet man who donated £10,000 to the church.'

Pausing, Kumba pulled up the sleeve of her white shirt to reveal the watch, hoisting her wrist so all could see it. 'This watch is by a company that I have never heard of called Audemars Piguet. I googled the price, my sisters, and if I tell you how much it costs, your envy will see you praying for something bad to happen to me.' She gave a bitter giggle, her eyes shifting from her audience to home in on Hawa. 'God has opened up strong luck for us to be in this position today, where we can improve our own personal lives whilst also helping our suffering people back home, Hawa. And so tomorrow, keep your speech short and don't talk too much book-book politics like your friend Othella did. Let's just have fun and flow with the luck and goodwill that Lion Mountain has thrown our way!'

CHAPTER 24

Amanda had forbidden Hawa and Anaka from turning up at the charity dinner in the battered Mini, laughing that it *does not conform to the ambience and atmosphere of the evening.* 'Don't worry. Khalil has been hired as one of our carriage riders for the evening. Many of the donors will be staying at the Dalmahoy overnight, though quite a few who live locally might need to be driven home.'

Khalil arrived at the Balerno flat at 6 p.m. as agreed, climbing the stairs to present both Hawa and Anaka with huge bouquets of flowers, with the compliments of Amanda. He was wearing a sleek black tuxedo over a white shirt, at the neck of which nestled a royal blue cravat, and his head carried a new haircut, a neat fade with shaped edges. Giggling, Hawa and Anaka set the flowers in vases on the coffee table, handing the television remote over to Khalil so he could choose something to watch whilst they disappeared into the bathroom to put the finishing touches to their make-up.

A shopping trip to Glasgow had left them both with long dresses from Zara, Anaka settling for a shimmering black piece featuring a provocative slit that travelled halfway up her left leg. Hawa had chosen a high-necked sleeveless green dress and was now using a headtie as a makeshift headband over which her braids cascaded. Their make-up completed, they clouded themselves in perfume before joining Khalil, who led the way down to Amanda's black Tesla, which he had been given responsibility over for the night.

As agreed, they arrived at the Dalmahoy a full hour before any of the guests. Whilst Anaka did a final sound-check for her performance, Hawa and the other ambassadors gathered in the room they had been briefed in the previous evening. Kumba, so hostile the night before, offered her a smile and a wave from across the room.

Returning Kumba's smile, Hawa went over to join her, where she was busy studying a board with the seating arrangements. The ambassadors had been distributed amongst the tables, with instructions to discuss the church's mission with the guests at every opportunity. 'Though not too aggressively,' Amanda had reminded them at the briefing. 'Charm and charisma must always be at the heart of what you do, ladies.'

'I see we are at the same table,' Kumba said when Hawa reached her. 'Table fourteen.' Kumba was wearing a champagne-coloured dress, the expensive watch, the origins of which she had explained to Hawa and the other ambassadors during her rant the previous evening, glinting on her wrist as her finger trailed down the names on the board.

'Sorry for attacking you yesterday, Hawa. Was just a little stressed as I had some red news from back home; my mama had a stroke, and they say her left arm is now dead and refuses to move.'

'No harm done,' Hawa replied, fixing Kumba with a supportive smile. 'Sorry to hear about your mama, and God willing she recovers soon. When were you last back home? Do you have any plans to go and see her in her illness?'

'My papers have only recently been organised. Amanda helped me with my immigration case. Thanks to her, I now have a red book. But you know yourself, Hawa, that you do not go back home clapping empty-handed; you have to carry serious money on your head whilst bringing things for our relatives who are many like fish in the sea. And so for now I just send a little every month to help the family, especially with Mama's sickness.' Dropping her eyes to study a text she had received on her phone, she looked up at Hawa, her smile sad. 'And I guess that's why I take this ambassador business seriously, Hawa. It is easy money when I spend time with these rich White men. And most of the time it is just dinner in posh restaurants and travelling. I left school in form four back home and therefore do not have the education to rub hands with a big and important job in this country. When I first came to Scotland, I worked as a kitchen porter in res- taurants and wiped the backsides of old people in nursing homes. I worked so many shifts for Lesley's Links that I should have been made a shareholder. But having done those difficult jackass jobs for so long, I realised I will never be able to make the money to help my family back home. God, in His wisdom, brought me to this country for a reason, Hawa, and I believe it is to work for Pastor Ranka. My grand- mother used to say that if a cow dropped dead in your yard, you should not question what killed it; instead, you should simply cut the cow into pieces, cook the meat and then eat it. In life, we should not always question the colour of the good luck that God throws our way!'

The guests began to arrive at 6.30 p.m. for the drinks reception, with the dinner scheduled to commence an hour later. Waiting staff in the hotel's sleek uniform flowed amongst the arrivals, checking in coats and jackets, whilst others offered flutes of champagne from gold trays. The guests were almost all White, smiling patrons who mingled with the ambassadors, laughter and warm conversation soon filling the room.

Hawa was deep in conversation with a regal-looking woman who explained that she was a lecturer in politics at Napier University, when she felt Anaka at her shoulder. The American whispered in her ear that Detective Inspector McKeown was amongst the guests. Trying not to attract too much attention, Anaka gestured to where the detective was standing in a group of guests beneath a painting featuring a couple of thick St Bernard dogs. As if prearranged, Anaka picked up the conversation with the lecturer, who was fascinated that the American had attended college in Atlanta, a city she had visited for seminars.

Leaving them deep in conversation, Hawa moved in the direction of McKeown, pausing on the way to deposit her empty cranberry juice glass on a table. McKeown had freed her hair from its customary bun, her blonde hair falling over her shoulders. She was wearing a green dress, which Hawa used to start their conversation.

'Green seems to be a popular colour tonight. I didn't know the police did charity dinners,' she added, flashing the detective with a smile.

'Oh, we do plenty of charity functions. The Police Federation has always endeavoured to get on board with worthwhile initiatives, and apparently, we've been attending this particular function for quite a few years now. Given the current circumstances, I volunteered myself this year,' Detective McKeown said, raising a flute of some clear fizzy drink to her lips.

'And do you feel that something could be found here?'

'I'm just here to get the lay of the land. But it's nearly Christmas and there's nothing wrong with letting one's hair down once in a while. So, I hear you're going to Sierra Leone later this month for your sister's wedding, Hawa? When will you be back? And will we be able to reach you whilst you're away?'

'I have your email address and will definitely stay in touch. That besides, my UK number should still work in Sierra Leone with WhatsApp,' Hawa replied.

'Good to know. And whilst you're here, could I ask you about a member of your church named Jeremiah Holt? I believe he organises walks for church members in the Pentlands?'

'You mean Jam Jerry? Yeah, he lives in Bathgate.'

'Why do you call him Jam Jerry?'

Hawa laughed before replying, picking up a glass of orange juice from the tray of a smiling passing waitress. 'He makes homemade jam, which he sells in church, so everybody calls him Jam Jerry.'

'And was Othella close with Jam Jerry?'

'Reasonably so, I believe. They often went on walks together. Just the two of them at times. Othella told me she went with him to Switzerland and France a few summers ago to follow the Tour de France. Jam Jerry booked it all and went with a little group from the church. Othella was the only woman to go, and she spoke warmly of the experience. Is Jam Jerry a person of interest in your investigations?'

'I couldn't really say for now. We're exploring a whole range of possibilities,' McKeown replied.

Their conversation was interrupted by the voice of Amanda, who was standing at the entrance to the room, a microphone resting in her right hand, an expensive watch glimmering on her wrist. She was wearing a striking burnt-orange dress, her hair hoisted above her head in a neat beehive. Smiling, she thanked them all for attending and briefly explained the format of the evening before inviting them to move through to the Sir Alexander Fleming Suite, where dinner would be served.

Hawa delivered her speech after dessert. She had put together a presentation on her laptop, using Anaka as a test audience. The American had timed her, praising Hawa for its depth and detail, and her awe had led to her spending a couple of evenings watching *Amistad* and *Blood Diamond*, which Hawa had suggested as big Hollywood movies on Sierra Leone.

The speech concluded, the hall broke into applause, Anaka and Amanda joining her on the stage to deliver smiles and hugs. For the rest of the evening, Hawa was constantly fielding guests who, moved by her speech on Sierra Leone, sought more information, keen to make donations to help such a worthwhile charitable initiative.

'Like you said, Miss Hawa, this goes beyond religion. It's about our responsibility to help the less fortunate of this planet,' she was told by a woman in a red dress who said she was a retired geography teacher. 'I covered social problems like these all the time with the pupils – we even went on a trip to Uganda to build houses in a local village. A humbling experience that left me in tears every day!'

Meanwhile, Hawa's eyes were searching for McKeown, whom she wanted to talk to further about Jam Jerry, who now, it seemed, was a person of interest. However, she failed to spot her, telling herself the detective inspector had probably left already.

Anaka sang to close the evening, delivering a new track which she would feature in the event that she was one day able to go solo with her own album. 'It's a bit of an old-school new jack swing kind of number with a minor G-Funk influence,' Anaka had explained to Hawa when she came home from a chambermaiding shift to find that the living room had been converted into a makeshift recording studio.

The song concluded. The hall rose in a standing ovation, guests clustering around Anaka as the night unwound to praise the socially conscious lyrics of her song.

'I must confess to always being very suspicious of rap music, Anaka, but I was blown away,' Amanda exclaimed, on a high from the donations that had poured in during the evening.

'I feel you,' Anaka replied, her eyes mocking and sarcastic. 'Rap's not just about drugs, violence and misogyny. It's just like any other form of music, Amanda – it can deliver whatever message you want it to.'

★

Khalil was on hand to ferry them back to the flat after the dinner. On a high and once more unable to sleep, Hawa went to her phone. She started with Facebook, which was dominated by news of a plane full of cocaine which had mysteriously landed at Lungi Airport in Freetown. It had been abandoned on the runway, with the light-skinned individuals on board escaping in a Jeep that had driven through a gap in the perimeter fence. The chief of police had given a briefing, promising that all efforts would be made to apprehend the traffickers, who sought to bring the good name of Sierra Leone down.

She also visited Songhai Sista, fascinated by Anaka's ability to keep it fresh with new snippets from her experiences in Scotland. She had featured Othella's African icons wall, explaining how essential it was that people took the time to learn more about the history of that great continent. Smiling, Hawa continued her trawl.

She had grown closer to Kumba Matturi during the course of the evening, exchanging phone numbers with her before they left, whilst also friending her on social media, thereby lowering the older woman's privacy barriers. Kumba had already posted a few photos from the evening on Instagram, and Hawa smiled to see herself in some of the pictures.

Kumba's other posts stretched back a year and a half, and predominantly featured her in the company of the same White man, a roundish fellow who looked as if he was in his early fifties. There were posts from trips to Paris, Barcelona, Prague and even Dubai. Other pictures showed her with the young girl, Aisha, some in a relaxed domestic space that Hawa assumed must be the accommodation they shared.

Her tongue untangled by alcohol, Kumba had explained that she was Lion Mountain's top ambassador, the one Pastor Ranka turned to when he wanted to secure heavy donations for the church.

'Next week, Aisha and I are going down to London to meet some businessmen. People in this country do not take the affairs of God seriously, and so Pastor Ranka says it is our divine duty to open their eyes to the power of Christ!' She had then insisted that Hawa visit them soon, a meal in their company being the ideal way for her to better understand the ways of Lion Mountain Church.

Hawa had decided to take up Jam Jerry Holt's offer of a walk to the Pentland Hills. Given Detective McKeown's enquiries at the fundraising dinner, it seemed he was an angle worth exploring in her search for her friend. Othella had always recommended the walks to the Pentlands, explaining it was good exercise and gave her a chance to clear her head. Back then, Hawa had declined, pointing out that African people did not climb hills for pleasure. Anaka expressed a similar sentiment when Hawa suggested that she also come on the walk with Jam Jerry.

'I agree with you, Hawa; Black folk don't climb mountains, ski, swim with sharks or bungee jump,' she giggled, as she lay covered to the chin in her tartan blanket. 'But you go. If it's just the two of you together, Jerry might open up and drop useful information.'

'I think Jerry and Othella were closer than I realised. And McKeown admitted they're looking into him. You've got

McKeown's card, and if I'm not back by six, you know what to do,' Hawa finished, smiling down at Anaka.

'Just be careful, Hawa. I've seen enough movies to know that hills and mountains are good places to hide dead bodies.'

Jam Jerry picked her up just after noon, laughing at how close Hawa was to the Pentlands Hills already. 'You live in bloody Balerno, Hawa, just a few minutes away. You should come down on your own sometime – you're bound to like it.'

Jam Jerry had brought appropriate gear for Hawa, supplying her with a baggy mauve waterproof jacket and matching trousers, which he said belonged to his daughter, Helen. 'Helen loved a walk, so she did. She didn't have the easiest time in school, so I used to bring her up here for a change of scenery. Surely you don't plan on wearing those trainers?' he paused to ask, pointing incredulously at Hawa's running shoes.

'That's all I have. They're comfortable and flexible,' Hawa laughed, lifting her feet for Jam Jerry's closer inspection. Smiling back, he disappeared into the cluttered boot of his car, emerging presently with a pair of scuffed walking boots caked with mud.

'You'll wear these, Hawa. Also Helen's, who was a size seven. Othella wore them on her first few walks with me until she bought her own pair. Will they fit you?'

'I'm a six but I'm wearing thick socks, so they should be fine. Thanks Jerry – much appreciated,' Hawa said as she settled in the passenger seat of his car, her feet on the ground outside as she changed footwear.

It was spitting rain when they started out, Jam Jerry setting a brisk pace which Hawa managed to keep up with, the cold wind buffeting them and flapping away at their waterproofs as they climbed. Jam Jerry explained the area, pointing out remnants of ancient walls, metal railings from the days of the Industrial Revolution, and the shimmering reservoir in the distance, his voice ringing with enthusiasm. They paused at the top of a steep incline whilst he delved into his rucksack, producing a plastic container containing homemade scones. 'Baked these over the weekend. They're a wee bit too sweet but perfect for an energy boost. Here, try them with this blueberry jam I made yesterday.'

Hawa found the scones to be perfect, the jam lifting the flavour, and she nodded her appreciation as she settled on a rock. Jam Jerry paid another visit to the confines of the rucksack, emerging this time with a knocked-in blue flask, from which he poured hot chocolate into a paper cup, the steam rising into the air as he handed it to Hawa. 'Only a snip of sugar in this, Hawa. Should warm you up though, which is the important thing.'

'A lovely experience this, Jerry. Thanks very much. I can see why Othella spoke so highly of these walks.'

'We had some good times, that's for sure.'

'She did enjoy spending time with you.'

'Othella was different. She had an energy and an essence that resonated with me.'

'You mean she did things differently from most women from our country?' Hawa laughed, rising from the rock to stretch.

'I didn't say that, Hawa. She was just different. A pure spirit.'

'It's OK, Jerry. Just teasing. Even at school, we used to laugh at Othella for always defying our expectations. One of the reasons we christened her "Unopposed". So I can understand why she enjoyed hanging out with you. What places did you visit beyond the Pentlands and your trip to see the Tour de France?'

'Just those, really. To be honest, she was a big help to me when things were tough.'

'And you were just friends?' Hawa jabbed out, her voice firm.

'Just friends, Hawa. I know society has always found it hard to comprehend the concept of platonic relationships between people of opposite genders. But Othella and I were just kindred spirits who spent time together puffing up hills and discussing odd tastes in music. We both miss her, Hawa, and hopefully, she'll turn up soon. Have you tried reaching out to Katarina? She might have heard from Othella.'

'Who's Katarina?'

'Katarina Meers. Do you not know her? Katarina's definitely worth a shout. After all, she was you before you arrived in Scotland, Hawa. Othella's best friend. They did everything together, though she only came to church a couple of times. Think she lives up in Ayr now. Othella helped her move up there years ago. And I think she went to visit her once in a while. Did she never mention Katarina to you?'

'Once in a while,' Hawa lied.

They continued their walk for another hour and a half,

Jam Jerry plotting a circuitous route that involved skipping across narrow streams, climbing over a couple of stiles and encountering a flock of sheep not the least bit impressed by their presence.

The rain had abated by the time they made it back to Jam Jerry's car. 'Don't worry about the waterproofs and the boots, Hawa, just dump them in the boot. Cleaning them is frankly pointless and you can use them on our next walk, provided I've not broken you.' He smiled, his face open and rendered red by the elements.

Hawa made her way round to the boot, which Jam Jerry had clicked open. Inside was chaos – an assortment of tools, old clothes, a dented water can, plastic tubs of paint and a few books. One of the books caught her attention. She remembered Othella foisting a copy on her on account of it being quite short and therefore an easy read: *Devil in a Blue Dress* by Walter Mosley. Opening it quickly, she realised that it was indeed Othella's copy. Her friend had numbered it in her usual manner – Unopposed 61 – beneath which was one of her customary hand-written quotations:

> *Always recognise that human individuals are ends, and do not use them as means to your end.*
>   *Immanuel Kant*

Inside the book was a receipt, which she slipped into her pocket, moving around to join Jerry, who had produced a batch of miniature muffins, his smile wide.

CHAPTER 25

Anaka was out on another date with Khalil when Jam Jerry dropped Hawa off. Extracting the receipt she had taken from Othella's copy of *Devil in a Blue Dress*, she went through to the kitchen, which was blessed with brighter lights, to get a better look. It was for a meal at a restaurant in Pitlochry, the Inn on The Tay. The items on the bill suggested dinner for two, including sea bass and sticky toffee pudding, choices she recognised as Othella's favourites. The order for cranberry juice was another telltale sign. Hawa remembered how Othella's fridge never seemed to run out of it.

Unsure what to do with this information, she ran a bath, switching on the television whilst she waited. Following Anaka's example, she went to YouTube and chose a soul playlist. As she waited for the bath to fill, she picked up her phone to answer a message from Anaka, confirming that she was safe and sound at home and there was no need to call McKeown to get a police helicopter to search for her remains on the Pentlands.

Next, she turned her attention to Katarina Meers, whom Jam Jerry had described as *you before you arrived in Scotland*.

Why had Othella never mentioned her? Surely friendships were allowed to overlap, and it was strange that Othella hadn't thought to introduce them.

After her bath, Hawa went to her bedroom to get her laptop. Feeling guilty at Anaka's insistence at making her bed, she had done it herself before she left that morning. The six pillows had been stacked Jenga-style again though, and Hawa couldn't help laughing at Anaka's adherence to routine. Logging on, she went straight to Facebook, which revealed four people with the name Katarina Meers. The second one's info piqued Hawa's interest:

Intro

💼 *Worked at Nationwide Building Society*

🎓 *Studied at University of Pretoria*

🎓 *Studied at Stirling University*

🏠 *Lives in Ayr, Scotland*

📍 *From Pretoria, South Africa*

Katarina's profile picture showed her at a music concert wearing a matching fluorescent T-shirt and baseball cap. Standing next to her was Othella.

Hawa went to visit Kumba and Aisha the following weekend. Since the fundraising dinner, Kumba had taken to deluging her with messages, seeking and providing advice in equal measure on a variety of issues.

'Aisha and I are the only ambassadors who live in an actual

house and not a tight flat,' Kumba had explained to Hawa during a late-night phone call. 'Pastor Ranka allocated me a whole three-bedroom place in Clermiston. I lived there alone for two months. But then one day, Pastor Ranka brought Aisha over, saying that she had newly arrived from London but wanted to grow her faith whilst learning about Lion Mountain. And because I am older and my eyes know the church's business well, I am like a big sister to Aisha, which is the same thing I would like to be to you, Hawa.'

Putting Kumba's address into Google Maps, Hawa drove over, arriving in a tasteful neighbourhood that featured mostly bungalows set in their own gardens. Aisha answered the door, hugging Hawa as she explained that Kumba was taking a shower. She led the way into a living room which hosted a couple of beige-coloured sofas, a giant faux-silver chandelier and a massive television on one of the walls.

'This is where Pastor Ranka allows me to live, Miss Hawa. I remember how I met you at that party when my feet had just newly entered cold Scotland. You were a person with a clean heart who gave me the addresses of places where to work. And I am still so grateful, Miss Hawa.'

'You do not have to call me *Miss Hawa*,' Hawa replied, smiling as she settled on one of the couches. 'Just Hawa is fine.'

'But you are older than me, Miss Hawa, and so I must speak to you with respect,' Aisha replied, taking the couch opposite.

'Not in this country, Aisha. Here, people mostly just use first names, so Hawa is fine.'

They were interrupted by the arrival of Kumba, her smile

reaching across the room, putting Hawa further at ease.

'So happy you came, my sister. I hope Aisha has not been dirtying your ears with empty talk. Have you offered Hawa something to drink, Aisha? Remember the lessons we have been through on hospitality and being a good hostess? Bring Hawa something to drink. And remember not to put the red wine in the fridge like you did the last time, bush girl!'

Smiling, Aisha rose from the room, Kumba continuing the conversation with Hawa in her absence. 'She is still new to the ways of this country and has to be reminded every day. She is a beautiful girl, no doubt, but she needs to understand how to entertain and make men comfortable if she is to grow as a church ambassador. And that is why Pastor Ranka brought her to stay with me.'

'She seems lovely – very polite,' Hawa replied, suddenly uneasy. 'How old is Aisha?'

'How old are you, Aisha?' Kumba bellowed, the girl promptly yelling back that she was nineteen.

'Nineteen,' Kumba said, as though Hawa had not clearly heard Aisha's answer from the kitchen. 'She is nineteen, which means that if she were in the villages where I grew up back home, she would already be married with at least two children by now.'

Aisha returned, balancing bottles of wine and gin and a pitcher of cloudy apple juice on a tray that she then set down on the low coffee table. Flashing a shy smile at Hawa, she asked what she would like to drink.

'Apple juice is fine, Aisha, and once again, please remember that you do not have to call me *Miss Hawa*.'

'Do not remove the habits of respect from her,' Kumba

interjected. 'Back home, we are taught to respect our elders, and if she calls you *Miss Hawa*, then you must accept the title with happy eyes. If somebody raises you up, Hawa, you do not put yourself down! She calls me Aunty Kumba, and even if her brain was removed from her head, she would know not to call me by just my first name!'

Aisha poured Hawa's apple juice, then asked if Kumba would like some gin or Merlot, pronouncing the letter T, drawing a sneering laugh from Kumba.

'Like I said, she is still a bush girl from the village,' Kumba said, wiping her eyes. 'It is pronounced *Merlow*, Aisha. These are the lessons you need to learn if you are to climb high within Lion Mountain. My schooling from back home is very limited, but I have learned the civilised habits of these overseas countries, which means that I can mix with rich men in any restaurant or top hotel. And that's why living here with me will benefit you.'

Giggling in embarrassment, Aisha finished pouring the drinks, then retreated to the kitchen, from where Hawa heard the sound of plates and cutlery being washed up.

'So, has Aisha been out on ambassador trips by herself or do you go with her?'

'She has not been on any trip alone so far, because she is still in training; did you not see how she embarrassed herself just now? How then can she step out on church ambassador business? For now, she comes with me so I can protect and guide her. Have you been on many trips yourself, Hawa? You are also quite new, are you not?'

'Only to Bridge of Allan to see Gerald Carmichael,' Hawa

lied, remembering him from their interaction in Pastor Ranka's study.

'Big Gerald!' Kumba exclaimed. 'Been with him quite a few times. He gives heavy donations to the church, so he is very popular with Pastor Ranka. I have also been to his house in that Bridge of Allan place in Stirling. But he usually comes here to Edinburgh when he wants to be with me. I told him I was African and therefore liked eating meat, so he took me to that Dakota Hotel in Queensferry. We had big steaks to eat. His steak still had blood in it, which was very strange, Hawa. Back home, meat must always be cooked properly. And after the meals, we just stayed in the hotel upstairs. Do you get on well with Gerald?'

'Yes,' Hawa replied, reasoning that Kumba might open up a bit more if she thought they were on the same page when it came to their duties as ambassadors.

'I like Gerald, because of all the donors I have been with, he extends his hands the most with generosity. When I told him my mama's hand was dead after her stroke, he transferred a thousand pounds to my account.'

Their conversation was interrupted by one of Kumba's three mobile phones – all of which she had laid on the coffee table – vibrating angrily. Peering at the screen, she picked it up, explaining to Hawa that it was one of the donors. 'I must take this call, Hawa. This is another man who throws money at me,' she laughed, her eyes dancing. 'I will be just a few minutes.' Rising from the couch, she yelled for Aisha to come back to the living room to keep Hawa company.

★

Before she left, Hawa took Aisha's number. With Kumba away on her phone call, the girl had opened up a bit more, her confidence growing, though she just looked sad and confused when Hawa tried to ask how she was finding life as a church ambassador. Just as she had at the wedding where Hawa had first met her, Aisha reiterated her desire to work hard to make money to help her people back home. 'After my aunty gave me to Pastor Ranka,' she said, 'he brought me from London to live with Kumba. He said living with her in this lovely house was an opportunity to understand the grace of God whilst also learning more about Lion Mountain Church.'

Sighing at the memory as she lay in bed, Hawa entered her phone. Taking Katarina Meers' details from her Facebook page, she had sent her a message, explaining the circumstances of Othella's disappearance and asking if she would be able to meet for a drink to discuss it. There was no reply.

There were more texts from Ramat, as per usual. Her younger sister had always had a disjointed brain, throwing messages in spurts at Hawa in whatever manner they came to her. Today's cache numbered fourteen, ranging from a plea to ask if Hawa had managed to buy sand-coloured shoes to match the bridesmaids' dresses to a report that Pa Lamina, the old carpenter who lived in the single room across the shared yard, had died in a horrible accident whilst travelling to Makeni in the north of the country.

The next day, Anaka emerged from her room in the afternoon, collapsing on the couch whilst Hawa was on her laptop checking flights to Sierra Leone.

'She stirs and walks,' Hawa teased, lowering the lid of the laptop as she smiled at the American. 'How was last night?'

'All good,' Anaka replied, stifling a yawn as she stretched on the couch. 'Went out with big Khalil again. Real sweet dude he is, and no funny business!'

'I've never been to Khalil's house, so lucky you,' Hawa replied.

'His spot's fresh and snug. A one-bedroom place that's clean and smells nice. And then he just talked to me about his mama and the house he's building for her back in Sierra Leone. Said that you guys find blessings in life by doing good things for your parents.' She giggled, then yawned, stretching as her arms lifted her T-shirt, exposing her taut stomach. 'Was going to spend the night, but he said he was working early today. He gave me a ride back. We're going out again on Friday.'

Their conversation was interrupted by Hawa's phone vibrating. Glancing at it, she rose to her feet, Anaka following suit, as if joined to her with string.

The message was from Katarina Meers, who was in Edinburgh for the weekend for a friend's thirtieth birthday celebrations. She would be delighted to meet Hawa. She suggested Café Andaluz on George Street for an early afternoon nibble, since she would already be in the city centre picking out a present.

Remembering the complications that came with finding a place to park in the centre of Edinburgh, Hawa caught the number 44 bus from Lanark Road to meet Katarina Meers.

She got to Princes Street about half an hour early and killed time browsing a few shops.

Katarina Meers was already at Café Andaluz when she arrived. Hawa immediately recognised her from her social media pictures. Explaining to a smiling waitress that she had already seen the person she was here to meet, she made her way towards Katarina, who raised her head from her phone as she approached.

Katarina Meers had deep blondish-brown hair, her skin bearing signs of having recently experienced sun. She was wearing a sky-blue shirt over a pair of black jeans, with black Adidas trainers completing her outfit.

Rising, she moved from behind the table to gather Hawa in an embrace. 'Hawa Barrie in person! Seen so many pictures of you on Othella's phone, not to mention the number of times your name came up in her chronicles of mischief from high school and university back in Sierra Leone! Sit down, sit down and let's get something to drink. How are you?'

'I'm surviving; you know how it is in this country balancing work and book learning. Hopping back home at the end of the month for my sister's wedding. I've had to provide most of the support, if you know what I mean.'

'For your sister's wedding? I take it you're broke then?' Katarina laughed, her eyes warm. 'Trust me, I can relate. I did the overseas sister wedding support routine a few years ago and I'm still repairing the dent in my bank account. So I'm paying for lunch, Hawa, there's no point trying to argue. Now, where has Othella got to? I heard about Naomi and the other woman from your church who lost their lives. And then I heard that Othella has gone missing, which really freaked me out!'

'It's grim and it has me totally at a loss,' Hawa replied, pouring water from a slender carafe into a glass. 'I've been in constant contact with the police, but still, no luck.'

'They haven't turned up anything useful? I tried calling her a few times when I found out she'd gone missing, but no luck!'

'Same here. Still just blanks, Katarina. And so I decided to look into it myself, which is how I found Naomi Wreh dead in the boot of her car.' Hawa helped herself to another sip of water, judging that the weight of her words warranted a pause. She studied Katarina, whose complexion had paled slightly, a worried sheen shrouding her eyes.

'Yeah, Naomi's death seriously shook me up when I heard about it on the news.'

'You knew Naomi?' Hawa asked, her eyes alert.

'Loosely – through Othella. I met her a couple of times over the years. And she did turn up in the odd conversation.'

'I didn't realise they knew each other. I'm actually trying to trace all of Othella's friends and acquaintances here in Scotland. Jam Jerry suggested you as someone who was very close to Othella a while back, which is why I reached out. You say she mentioned me to you frequently; but to be honest, Katarina, she never mentioned you to me.'

'We fell out over your church, Hawa.'

'How, exactly?'

'The ambassadors' programme. Othella really did believe in the humanitarian side of the church and the good it could do for people back in your country. But I just happen to be an atheist, which, let's say, did not sit well with the circles Othella ran in. I went once out of courtesy, but I was just not feeling it. Made the mistake of mentioning to your Pastor Ranka that I really didn't believe in organised religion. Othella was not impressed and said I could have bitten my tongue rather than embarrassing her. I think quite a few people took offence; after all, I was the White girl who turned up to a predominantly Black church to disrespect their religion. The charity drives seemed positive though, so I did help Othella with that side of things.'

'How?'

'Nothing major. I donated some money when Ebola hit Sierra Leone and also attended one of the Christmas benefit dinners. A real serious affair, it was. Very impressive, with plenty of money raised for the church.'

'So, what took you all the way to Ayr?'

'Got a job up there. Graduated from Stirling with Othella and got the offer about a year later. I work in finance, which isn't as chic and glam as it sounds. Pays the bills, though. Met a decent fellow – we just moved in together. I like the pace of Ayr, Hawa, and to be honest, I don't really miss Edinburgh.'

'Did you ever share one of Pastor Ranka's flats with Othella?'

'Stayed with her for a couple of weeks whilst her flatmate Jattu was away on a holiday in Belgium. But that was ages ago, before you came to Scotland. Over Easter, perhaps, when we were finishing our dissertations. Othella said she was lonely, so I moved in temporarily. But I didn't know Ranka was the one who hooked her up with the flat.'

They chatted some more, Katarina convincing Hawa that

slices of cheesecake for dessert was a stellar idea. 'Interesting how you say it was Jam Jerry who suggested you talk to me. I would have said you should get in touch with him,' Katarina said as she delved into her purse, extracting a credit card to settle the bill. 'They did spend a lot of time together, though she swore they were just walking buddies. I didn't want to pry, but there was a light in her eyes whenever she returned from their walks. I did offer to come on a couple of occasions, but I got the feeling that Othella didn't really want me there. So I figured her time with Jerry was kind of sacred and I stepped back. Maybe I wasn't welcome because I wasn't feeling the whole religion thing.'

'Or maybe Jerry wanted time alone with Othella,' Hawa said, rising to put on her jacket.

'With Othella and Naomi both,' Katarina replied.

'Naomi Wreh?'

'Yep. Naomi also went on quite a few solo walks with Jam Jerry, apparently. Othella used to say they were the only two who connected with him on that level, whatever that meant.'

CHAPTER 26

Hawa spent the next couple of days putting the final things in place for her sister's wedding. 'I need to see what else I can get my mouthy sister for her big day. I've already bought the big items and put down a deposit for the souvenir pens and keychains she wanted. I'll pick them up tomorrow.'

'What about her dress?' Anaka asked.

'I already bought her a lovely second-hand wedding dress from a charity shop in Stockbridge. She'll wear it to the church, then we'll all change into Africana *ashobies* made by a local seamstress on the ground in Sierra Leone. Which reminds me, Anaka – we need your measurements.'

'An *ashobie*? What's that?" the American asked, her brow furrowed.

'Special outfits worn at weddings. Both sides take *ashobies* which represent their families. And if you are to come to Sierra Leone with me, you will be part of the bride's party and so you'll have to wear our family's *ashobie*.'

Hawa fetched her laptop and showed her photos from friends' and relatives' weddings on Facebook and general images from the internet.

'Wow – love these!' Anaka gushed. 'Those high headties

are so elegant! *Ashobie* for me, all day, every day. I'll be a true African sister!'

Hawa had been to DHL earlier in the month and brought home one of their bigger boxes, a garish yellow-and-red specimen. Dropping to their knees, they commenced packing, stacking the items inside, pausing frequently to remove and rearrange them, anxious to maximise the available space. Anaka, by virtue of her extensive travels, provided useful advice on how to cram-pack.

'Nice job!' Anaka said as they rose to their feet to survey their handiwork. 'When are you dispatching this?'

'I'll send it off on Wednesday. We leave on the Friday, but Ramat's wedding isn't till the following weekend, which gives us plenty of time. We'll be away for seventeen days.'

'Really, really looking forward to this, Hawa! A chance to actually visit Africa has been on my bucket list for ages. So exciting! You must be gassed to go back and see your folks!'

'For sure. I've missed them a lot. Been looking forward to this. The only stain is the fact that Othella's still missing – not to mention Stella and Naomi, who are no longer with us. McKeown says she'll stay in touch, though, and bring me up to speed with any developments.'

'Ranka's in Sierra Leone. Going to see him out there might help. And you could talk to Othella's mama again. She might be able to give us some useful details.'

On the day before they left for Sierra Leone, Hawa tidied up the flat. Anaka had gone out with Khalil again, a final goodbye date. He had come up to the flat to present her with a massive bouquet of flowers. Whilst Anaka was applying the finishing touches to her look, Hawa had chatted with Khalil over glasses of apple juice. He thanked her profusely for introducing him to Anaka. He foresaw good things with her – she was the calibre of woman one sat down in marriage with. They had left just after eight, Khalil having booked a table at The Boathouse, a restaurant in South Queensferry that had been recommended by one of the DJs at Sing City.

Left to her own devices, Hawa decided to put away Othella's belongings. Since transferring them from the flat in Baberton, she had abandoned them at the bottom of her wardrobe and in those nooks and crannies of her room that had not been taken over by Ramat's wedding things.

She left Othella's clothes in the wardrobe, making space for them on the top shelf. The African icons were still in their cardboard boxes: Nelson Mandela, Patrice Lumumba, Haile Selassie and Kwame Nkrumah among them. Anaka had been most enamoured by the inclusion of Miriam Makeba, spending an evening listening to her songs on YouTube. 'I've always loved her music. Brenda Fassie and Yvonne Chaka Chaka too. South African divas were another big influence on my singing style!' Smiling at the memory, Hawa found space for the box at the bottom of the cupboard that housed the flat's boiler.

Which left her with Othella's books. There was a simple shelf unit in the living room, an off-white structure that had been placed to the left of one of the windows. It was largely empty at the moment, the only occupants being a collection of mint-green vases, a couple of encyclopaedias and her coursebooks on international conflict and cooperation. Her friend's books would definitely spruce up the room, she thought, thinking of how almost every television interview these days seemed to feature a bookcase in the background.

With YouTube again providing mood music, she commenced the shelving of Othella's books, flicking to the title pages to read the proverbs, quotations and wise sayings her friend had hand-written on the title pages.

A Grain of Wheat – No matter the size of a cow, it always ends up as soup. May 2020.

Mission to Kala – A fish has no business with a raincoat. February 2018.

So Long a Letter – Yams hold no secrets for knives. September 2019.

The Poor Christ of Bomba – Handshakes do not last forever. May 2019.

As Hawa raised *The Poor Christ of Bomba* to the shelf, still hearing the epigraph running through her head in Othella's voice, something fell out and slapped onto the floor. Frowning, she bent down to pick it up.

It was Othella's red book. Her British passport.

Sierra Leone

CHAPTER 27

The hot air thumped them as they got off the plane, both women breaking into a heavy sweat. Joining the other passengers, they clambered on to a rattling bus, which ferried them to the main terminal. Joining a winding queue, they were processed by a woman with fried hair in a floral uniform. She barely glanced at Hawa's green Sierra Leonean passport, but her eyes lit up when she realised that Anaka carried an American document. Her demeanour immediately changed, switching from the bored Krio she had used to address Hawa to a clumsy attempt at an American accent. 'The visa is thirty daarlars and you can pay cash, no problem,' she gushed, drawing out every syllable in a manner that made Hawa wince.

They collected their luggage from a winding carousel that appeared through a hole in the wall leading out to the dark airfield, then trundled through passport control and customs. On the wall was a giant mural of the country's president, his eyes menacing as he glowered down on proceedings.

Rolling their suitcases, they made their way to the main concourse, where they were instantly waylaid by a screeching Ramat, who hurtled towards them, throwing herself on Hawa whilst Anaka observed with bewildered laughter. 'You are here, Hawa, my sister! In spite of all the problems of living in a cold country, you climbed high on a plane and have arrived for my wedding!'

Unwrapping herself from her sister, Ramat then jumped on Anaka. 'My American big sister! I have heard so many golden words about you, Anaka Hart. Hawa tells me that the voice in your throat was put there by angels and that you have sung music all over the world with big stars that we only see on television! Welcome to Sierra Leone, big sister Anaka. Allow me to carry your suitcase.'

Before Anaka could protest, Ramat had prised the suitcase from her grasp, passing it on to a smiling man with a shaved dome of a head who stood slightly to one side. 'This is Mustapha, Papa's driver. He will take us over to Freetown.'

'And how is Papa?' Hawa asked, also passing her suitcase on to Mustapha, who deftly wheeled them ahead of him.

'Papa would have come to collect you, but he has a big meeting. The Danish have almost finished building a new power plant to supply electricity to the city, and Papa had to take the president and his ministers round to see the progress.'

'And how about Aunty Theresa? I guess she could not come to meet me either?' Hawa laughed.

Ramat's expression went from unbridled joy to straight-mouthed displeasure when she heard their stepmother's name. 'She's at the Big House – she says she will see you when you get to the city. But you will be staying with me in Tengbeh Town, Hawa. The Big House is filled with Aunty Theresa's family members. The only person there who has our surname is Papa. The rest are all Aunty Theresa's close and faraway relatives who have taken over every room the way cockroaches invade a dark kitchen at night!' She hissed to punctuate her irritation, jumping ahead to help Mustapha load the suitcases into the car, a white Toyota Hilux sheathed in a coat of red dust.

The car loaded, Ramat sat in the front next to Mustapha, Hawa and Anaka taking the back seats. 'We are going to have to use the government ferry to cross over to Freetown,' Ramat explained, pivoting to face them. 'There was an air taxi service which used old Russian helicopters to cross the river. It took only seven minutes. But one of the helicopters crashed last year, killing football people from Niger who had come here to play. And so the government shut it down. In this godforsaken country, if people do not die in a big disaster, nobody takes anything seriously!'

Sighing, Hawa took up the narrative, explaining to Anaka that the country's international airport was located on an island an hour away from the capital city. 'People usually cross over from Lungi to Freetown using the old government ferry service. But it's assumed that people arriving from abroad have money and so they were expected to take the helicopter service or the hovercraft that was running when I was last here.'

After a 25-minute drive down a narrow road, they got to the ferry dock, where an animated fellow wearing fluorescent green overalls that must have been stifling in the sweltering heat waved Mustapha on board, gesticulating wildly to indicate the precise spot on the deck where he wanted him to position the vehicle.

Leaving Mustapha in the Toyota, the women disembarked, Ramat leading the way up some rusty metal stairs to a bar that overlooked the deck below. Once the man in the green overalls had directed all the vehicles onto the ferry, there was a mad rush of foot passengers trying to board – prominent amongst them were market women toting baskets of dried fish, mangoes and groundnuts on their heads as they jockeyed for position.

Ramat chose a table underneath a wall-length painting of a beach lined with palm trees. and asked Hawa and Anaka what they would like to drink, returning soon afterwards with a couple of Cokes and an Apple Sidra for herself. She was up at the bar again once she had set the drinks down, returning with skewers of roast meat.

'Eat those with caution,' Hawa warned Anaka. 'They're coated in a sizzling pepper sauce that will blow your head off if you're not careful.' Anaka raised her eyebrows, smiling uncertainly as she nibbled at a tiny chunk, choking and spluttering almost instantly, water climbing to her eyes. 'Told you!' Hawa said, Ramat leaping to the bar again for a bottle of water that she handed to the grateful American. The fire in her mouth doused, Anaka croaked a thank you, mopping her eyes with a white handkerchief, also provided by Ramat.

'Wow, that meat has some serious heat! Still can't feel my tongue. The chicken we had at that Nando's place you took me to in Edinburgh is tame compared to this stuff,' Anaka said, a rueful half-smile on her face.

Their attention was suddenly taken by three girls in bright matching *dockett and lappa* outfits. Shaking their bodies to a song that boomed out of speakers mounted on pillars around the bar, the girls mimed along, dropping to their knees every time the chorus hit, hands and hips swaying like elephant grass in a storm. They finished to huge applause, whilst a couple of men handed out leaflets, explaining that the trio would be performing at a number of large venues over the Christmas period.

The performance over, the bartender turned the television back on. Advertisements promoting the local Star Beer and Grafton Mineral Water flickered across the screen, but what came next stunned Hawa and Anaka into silence. An elaborate feature advertising a *tenth anniversary religious retreat under the direction of Pastor Ronald Ranka, a gifted prophet recently returned from Scotland in the United Kingdom to continue his mission of faith and charity.* It was to last for an entire week at the National Stadium, with all citizens invited to attend for an opportunity to experience miracles in the presence of true religious royalty over the Christmas period.

The feature was slickly produced, consisting mainly of footage of Pastor Ranka preaching in a variety of venues, narrated by a mellifluous female voice they recognised as belonging to Amanda. There were also shots of Lion Mountain's charitable projects. Hawa and Anaka recognised the orphanage and vocational centre they had seen in the brochure all those months ago. It concluded with Amanda praising her husband's work whilst again inviting everybody to the retreat.

After they had unpacked and got themselves settled in Ramat's two-bedroom flat in Tengbeh Town, it was time to wash. Hawa explained to Anaka that there was currently no hot water or electricity and as such she would have to make do with a bucket of water that had been boiled in a pot.

'I dispatched the things for your wedding, and they should be here soon,' she told Ramat as they changed. They had agreed to share a room, the other having been offered to Anaka. 'I sent them via DHL in Edinburgh last week and they should be here latest on Thursday. Your wedding dress is in my suitcase, so if thunder strikes and brings bad fortune, you will at least have something to wear for your big day.'

Ramat mumbled a happy reply, as she busied herself going through her sister's hand luggage, pausing to squirt herself with every perfume she encountered. 'But did you at least bring my cream for my skin, Hawa? The sun in this country has made my skin dark like charcoal, and I must at least have a copper colour for the wedding. The bleaching creams we buy from Nigeria are no good! But I hear that you have products in Europe that will lift the colour of my skin!'

'Oh, Ramat, step away from this light-skin mentality, my sister,' Hawa replied, zipping her suitcase closed in mild annoyance. 'You have always had perfect skin. You'll look good even if we dress you in random rags for your wedding.'

'But you can say that, Hawa, because you have always had a yellow-rose colour. You do not understand my struggles. All the girls these days want to achieve that first-world colour, but to get it, you need help from special creams, my sister!'

Anaka joined them, a smile on her face as she tried to decipher the conversation in Krio between the siblings, until Hawa broke off to explain their discussion.

'So you get that colourism drama out here in Africa too?' the American asked, the smile dropping from her face. 'You fine as hell, Ramat. Just need to learn to appreciate yourself more.'

When they were ready, Mustapha, who had been patiently waiting, drove them to the Big House. The traffic between Lumley Junction and Goderich was heavy and unforgiving, made worse by serpentine queues outside the two petrol stations they drove past. Ramat explained that an acute fuel shortage had been steadily building to crisis levels, especially as Christmas was just around the corner. 'This country continues to make people beat their heads in pain,' Ramat concluded. 'We are lucky Papa works for the government, which gives him access to free petrol. Otherwise, we would have had to travel in taxis!'

As they crawled along, street hawkers, for the most part children, clustered at the windows, imploring them to buy random items ranging from toothbrushes and peeled oranges to packets of frozen water and black mints, addressing them as 'aunty' as they desperately tried to secure a sale.

'Why are they calling me aunty?' Anaka asked, puzzled.

'It's out of respect,' Ramat assured her, as she waved away a girl of no more than eight who was trying to sell her boiled eggs. 'They call you aunty because they do not know your name, and because you are older than they are. And they assume you have a lot of money because you are being driven in a big car.'

As they neared the Big House, Hawa took time to point out the places where they had played as children to Anaka, her eyes alight with the memories. 'We used to climb that tree right there to pick ripe mangoes! That was until the owner, Mama Sillah, chased us all the way home with a rattan cane and reported us to Papa! And that's the shack where Pa Koroma the local *karankay* shoemaker lived! He used to tell us about this strange place called Tanganyika, where he had apparently been taught how to repair shoes by Arab traders!'

Once they arrived at the Big House, the gate was opened by a round, shirtless man whose stomach extended in front of him like a well-developed pregnancy. He almost genuflected as they climbed out of the vehicle, and Hawa suddenly remembered his name was Dauda, who had minded the gate since she was a child. They exchanged warm greetings, and before long he was jabbering out details concerning his three wives, who had collectively borne him eight children.

By now, the car was surrounded by a horde of people, Hawa wondering if they were Aunty Theresa's faraway relatives whom Ramat had characterised as having overrun the Big House like an infestation of roaches. The house seemed frayed and tired, the unforgiving sun having bleached the paint on the walls since Hawa had last seen it a couple of years ago.

Climbing the stairs, they entered the living room, where Papa was waiting for them, clothed in an electric-blue kaftan that flowed to the ground. He spread his arms wide, and Hawa noticed his smile was missing a tooth that had definitely still been there when he had come with her to the airport as she departed for her overseas studies.

'My girl-child with a big brain has arrived! My heart is

happy to see you, Hawa. God has been good to you, and by His grace, you are standing in front of me today!'

Hawa dropped into his arms before disentangling herself to introduce Anaka. 'Papa, this is Anaka Hart from America, who became my good friend after we met in Edinburgh. She has never been to Africa, so I brought her as a guest for Ramat's wedding!'

'Anaka, my child. It is good to see your eyes and I hope your feet are not too sore from travelling over the water to our little country. I have been to America only once before for a conference – to San Francisco – many years ago. Where are you from, my child?'

'I'm from Atlanta, sir,' Anaka replied, hugging him as he led her over to a wide couch. One of the numerous unidentified people who had surrounded the car now appeared, carrying a tray with soft drinks for the guests.

Aunty Theresa had still not made her presence felt, Papa explaining uneasily that she was cleansing herself. 'She was under the cloud of a slight malaria last week, but she's feeling a bit better now. She will be out soon, and she's delighted you managed to come for your sister's wedding.'

Aunty Theresa emerged twenty minutes later, wearing a garish cotton sleeveless blouse and a matching *lappa*. Hawa rose to greet her, their hug limp and strained. Her stepmother offered a similar hug to Anaka, throwing questions at both of them about life overseas and how things were in a country where ice fell out of the sky and slept on the ground for days. She was smaller than Hawa remembered her – her imposing size had once been the perfect accessory for her rants and fiery commands. 'I have not cooked yet,' she told them, 'as we were not sure when you were arriving. But there are butter biscuits and boiled groundnuts if you want something to chew?'

'We ate a big meal on the plane, Aunty Theresa, and nibbled some meat on the ferry over. Our stomachs are fine,' Hawa replied.

For the rest of the evening they talked of little else but the arrangements for Ramat's wedding, Aunty Theresa expressing deep satisfaction that the ceremony was to take place in a branch of the Lion Mountain Church in Wilberforce.

'Your father claims to be a Muslim, and I have always respected his religion, though I cannot understand it. But luckily for us, a true Christian man has stepped out to marry our Ramat. For her to be married under Pastor Ranka's roof is an honour beyond measure and such an occasion will surely lift the name of our family to the sky!'

It was dark when they finally left to return to Ramat's place. There was another blackout across the city and the generator had to be turned on to supply the house, its loud buzzing making conversation all but impossible.

Before leaving, Hawa handed out the gifts she had brought for Papa and Aunty Theresa, her stepmother's stiff demeanour softening as she posed with the handbag and held the clothes up against her bosom, her face a mask of satisfaction. Papa was also elated, declaring that it would be an honour for him to wear one of the new Marks & Spencer suits to his daughter's wedding.

CHAPTER 28

In bed that night after they had returned from the Big House, Hawa was finally granted time alone with her thoughts, though she had spent much of the flight over to Sierra Leone distilling events in her mind. Two men appeared to be connected to Othella's disappearance: Jerry Holt and Pastor Ronald Ranka. Her friend's passport's sudden appearance in her copy of *The Poor Christ of Bomba* had placed a dark shroud over Hawa's mood, the possibility that Othella had come to some dark demise now hard to ignore. Up to that point, its absence had offered a sliver of hope, allowing her to imagine that Othella had found some convoluted way to leave the country. Hawa had called McKeown after she found the red book, and the detective had arrived in person to pick it up. Although still deeply worried, Hawa had code-switched her mood when they arrived in Sierra Leone, aware that her low thoughts could infect Ramat's wedding.

They rose just after ten, Ramat feeding them a breakfast of black-eyed beans cooked in deep red palm oil and served with boiled cassava. Anaka dissolved into compliments, taking endless pictures of the dishes for her blog.

The meal finished, Anaka went with Ramat on a trip to sample the local beach bars. 'I will also take you to meet my good friend Salifu, who sells me fresh fish,' Ramat told her. 'I want to cook original fried soup with snapper fish for you, Anaka. By the time you leave, I'll have put some flesh on your skinny bones!'

They were laughing as they left with Mustapha in the vehicle Papa had allocated them for the duration of their stay, Ramat posing in a pair of sunglasses Anaka had gifted her. Hawa had already revealed her plan to visit Othella's mother at the university, convincing them that her going alone was the best option.

Strolling down to the junction, Hawa caught a taxi driven by a youth in a Tupac Shakur T-shirt. From Tengbeh Town, the vehicle crawled through Brookfields, travelling along Campbell Street and Circular Road. The taxi was typically overloaded, Hawa squeezed into the back seat with three others, whilst a couple of sixth-form schoolgirls occupied the passenger seat next to the driver.

Getting out at Berry Street, she joined a short queue for the students' union bus, which arrived ten minutes later. The drive up Mount Aureol to the university brought back memories, Hawa recalling as the bus groaned and wheezed up the hill how many an old vehicle had been left abandoned there, defeated by the incline.

She listened to the conversations of the students, several of whom were already in holiday mode, as they moaned about unreasonable lecturers whilst looking forward to the dances that had been arranged by student social clubs. It was all much as she remembered it when the bus arrived on campus, stopping as before at the OAU Wall, where everybody disembarked before scattering in all directions to dorms, seminars and lecture rooms.

Dr Zaydah Savage was wearing a white blouse made from *fenteh* material, the neck embroidered with silver threading that swirled in elegant whorls, along with a pair of trousers made from the same material.

She led Hawa down the corridor to her office, an endearing room that featured a large desk and stuffed metal book-cases. 'I'm giving a lecture in twenty minutes in the Mary Kingsley Auditorium, so I'm on the move. But you can walk down with me, Hawa, and we can talk.' Hoisting a burgundy leather bag to her shoulder, Dr Savage closed the door and headed for the stairs, Hawa in her wake.

Once outside, she seemed to shed her joviality, her voice dropping and becoming serious. 'Thank you for stepping up and trying to find Othella.'

'It has not been easy, Aunty Zaydah, and I think there's something deeper behind Othella's disappearance. I've tried to find her, but my search has seen me butting my head against closed doors in frustration. Whatever happened to Othella is linked to Lion Mountain Church, I think. But she was also close friends with a man called Jerry Holt, whom she seemed to spend a lot of time with.'

'Who is this Jerry Holt character, Hawa? Do you think he is capable of hurting my Othella? You said when we spoke last that her flat had been ransacked, which is worrying.'

'I've had the same worry ever since that night, Aunty Zaydah. I have spoken to Jerry and spent time with him. He was definitely much closer to Othella than I was aware of. I think they spent quite a lot of time alone together. But the police seemed more concerned with Stella Kowa and later Naomi Wreh, who were taken from us, and Othella seemed to be almost an afterthought. At one point, they even said that people deliberately choose to disappear at times, and that it's their right if that's what they want to do.'

'And what do you think, Hawa? I can tell from your eyes that something else is troubling you.'

'I found Othella's passport the day before I travelled, Aunty Zaydah. It was in one of her books. Which makes me think that perhaps she did not leave the UK. I would have stayed to work a bit more with the police, but I had to travel for Ramat's wedding. I'm so sorry, Aunty Zaydah. I left her passport with Detective McKeown.'

They had reached the entrance to the auditorium, Hawa hearing the once familiar hubbub of students chatting as they waited for their lecturer to arrive. Dr Savage stopped, placing a hand on Hawa's shoulder.

'I am not disappointed, by any means. You absolutely had to come for Ramat's wedding, and you must make sure you enjoy your time back home. We are all very proud of your academic achievements in Scotland. Come see me tomorrow at my quarters and we will talk further. And since Pastor Ronald Ranka is here in Sierra Leone at the moment, we will be able to put our eyes on him and see if he can help us find my Othella.'

Hawa returned to see Dr Zaydah Savage the following day, bringing Ramat and Anaka with her. Mustapha dropped them off in the Hilux, his mood soaring when Dr Savage suggested that he did not have to wait for the ladies, as she would drive them home herself. Thinking of the possibilities open to him with a free vehicle in a nationwide fuel shortage, the driver beamed, his smile expanding when Hawa presented him with a thin wad of money with which to buy rice to eat.

Dr Savage lived in lecturer's quarters at the lower faculty, which Hawa remembered well from their days at university when Othella often left the hostels to visit if she was hungry or needed something urgently from her mother. She lived alone, but for a houseboy and a woman named Sallay who prepared her meals. A bubbly brown mongrel named Shelley lived in the yard and came bounding up to the vehicle to wag its tail vigorously at the new arrivals.

Hawa introduced Anaka. Dr Savage offered her a warm greeting, after which she turned her attention to Ramat. 'The last time I saw you, Ramat, you were a little child with snot round your nose,' she teased. 'Now you're a full-grown woman getting married.'

She led the way into her dining room, sitting them down at a long table covered with dull blue plastic sheeting. Dipping into the fridge at the far side of the kitchen, she extracted bottles of soft drinks whilst chatting to her guests and issuing orders to Sallay. A large tray of jollof rice was dished out, with chunks of goat meat and chicken scattered across its surface.

'This is an authentic African experience, Anaka. Since you are joining us from America, today you will eat with your hands whilst dining from a communal tray as is the custom here in Sierra Leone.' As if on cue, Sallay reappeared, carrying a deep calabash of warm soapy water they used to wash their hands. Anaka took picture after picture for her blog, explaining the concept behind Songhai Sista to an amused Dr Savage.

Dr Savage chatted away as they ate, pontificating on how lecturers were considering going on strike in the new year over deplorable working conditions. 'That's why very few people these days want to earn a living in the classroom. There's little incentive when the whole educational system is rotten to the core. But we're the lucky ones, because at least university lecturers are afforded a smattering of respect. Schoolteachers, on the other hand, are treated worse than bush vermin!'

The meal finished, they moved to the living room, whilst Sallay cleared away the tray and cleaned the table. Placing their drinks on low stools next to their chairs, they finally steered the conversation towards Othella.

'Fill me in on what my daughter was up to in Edinburgh. Leave nothing out, Hawa. I want to know how this Pastor Ranka and his church are involved! I visited his compound up in Juba Hills eighteen months ago to discuss a programme geared towards improving education for girls. The university launched the initiative, and our chancellor thought it a good idea that some of the female lecturers put in an appearance. We visited a few schools, vocational institutions and the Lion Mountain facility. Ranka himself showed us around, and I must say that I was rather impressed at what they were doing up there.'

'I have been up to his compound also, Aunty Zaydah,'

Ramat chipped in. 'In my final year at YWCA, we went there for a day to use their sewing machines, which were far better than the broken-down old ones we used. Pastor Ranka spoke to us, and we were fed a lovely meal at the end of the day. Most of the girls on the trip kept saying that they hoped they would one day be able to spend more time at Lion Mountain's compound. Quite a few of them transferred from the Agape Church they worshipped in and started attending Lion Mountain.'

'There is no doubt they do a lot of positive things, even in Scotland where they raise the money to finance many of the programmes you describe,' Hawa said. 'And I think that's what attracted Othella to the church, as you always raised her to be socially conscious and considerate, Aunty Zaydah. But that should not blind us to the darkness that seems to be attached to Pastor Ranka. Don't forget that two young women directly connected to his ministry have lost their lives. I think it's time we paid him a visit.'

CHAPTER 29

Pastor Ranka was on television the next day. They had just eaten a breakfast of oysters fried in nut oil with yams, once more deftly prepared by Ramat. Fascinated, Anaka took down the recipe in the notes section of her phone, buzzing around Ramat as she prepared the meal on a tripod of fire stones at the far end of the communal yard. Leaning over the pots and pans, Anaka took pictures of every stage of the meal, gushing that her Songhai Sista feature on *Foods of the Home Continent* was going to be *epic*.

Anaka was busy complimenting the flavour and texture of the food when the pastor jumped on to the screen. They all fell silent as Ramat increased the volume, bright blue numbers flickering as the sound filled the room.

The report showed Pastor Ranka with Sierra Leone's first lady, who had arrived to inspect the church's orphanage, accompanied by the usual entourage of overenthusiastic security personnel and a bevy of sycophants.

Ranka met her at the entrance, a smile spreading across his face as he led her through the dormitories, where alert children stood next to their tidy beds, the metal trunks housing their clothes resting on the floor beside them. The

feature concluded with snippets of speeches delivered by
Pastor Ranka and the first lady, the former proclaiming that
after years abroad, he had returned home to Sierra Leone
permanently to directly oversee the transformative work his
ministry continued to do.

'When God instructs you, you have no alternative but
to do His bidding! The Almighty came to me in a dream,
stating that it was time for me to return home to continue
His work amongst my own people. And so here I am!' His
comments were drowned out by thunderous applause from
the crowd in the packed compound, the entire neighbourhood having crammed in to catch a glimpse of the powerful
pastor and the first lady.

She spoke next, promising her husband the president's support for the life-changing work of Lion Mountain Ministries,
whilst also making a personal donation of fifty bags of rice
and $10,000. There was more loud applause followed by a
performance of the national anthem by the orphans, their
faces uncertain and nervous as they stared into the camera.

'Of course, he will never say that he returned home because
his church ambassadors were being left for dead in car boots,
and he was under investigation by the police! Religion out
here is the ultimate,' Hawa explained to Anaka. 'If you can
convince people that you are the proxy to a higher power,
you can achieve limitless things. The power Pastor Ranka
has here far outweighs any influence he had in Scotland,
where most people don't give two hoots about religion.'

'And there are elections next year,' Ramat continued,
collecting their plates to wash them outside in the yard in a
bath-pan of soapy water. 'That means all the top politicians

want to be close to big religious people like pastors and imams because they have massive followings. If Pastor Ranka places his hands on a candidate in support, many of his congregation will follow his directions without asking any questions. And that is why the first lady is anxious to pose with him.'

Taking turns to wash in the cramped bathroom, they left just after noon for the Big House, Mustapha having arrived with the Hilux to ferry them over. Ramat fed him a plate of the yams and oysters as he waited for them to get ready, his eyes warm with appreciation. The sun was close to its angriest. Anaka stood in the yard next to the Hilux, her arms spread as she smiled up to the sky. 'After that hard Scottish cold, it's great to catch some sunshine!'

Ramat laughed at her as she climbed into the front seat, saying that you could always tell who the JCs were this time of the year by their fascination with the sun. 'We hide from the heat, but you JCs act like you want to put the sun in your suitcases and take it back to your cold countries with you!'

Hawa then spent the first few minutes of the ride over to the Big House explaining to Anaka who JCs were. 'It stands for *just come*, meaning people who have just arrived or just come back home. JCs show up every Christmas and they're usually expected to have lots of money from working over-seas. They sip cold drinks in beach restaurants with white towels around their shoulders to wipe away the sweat since they can no longer handle the heat of their motherland. So, you and I are JCs!'

★

Later that evening, Hawa and Anaka finally met Ramat's fiancé. Oozing goodwill and charisma, Stephen introduced himself, expressing regret and deep sorrow for not having arrived earlier from his job in the provinces to see them.

'The Chinese engineers we work with are no joke, Miss Hawa. Even when I told them it was to do with my wedding, I was not given permission to leave the plant early to come and receive you at the airport.'

Stephen was an angular fellow with an engaging smile and a precise goatee, his light skin the shade of a new calabash. He spoke and moved in a confident manner, leading Anaka to proclaim that Ramat had indeed chosen a *fine brother* to marry. To make up for lost time, Stephen insisted on driving them all to a new nightclub at Government Wharf in the city centre later that evening.

Hawa, her thoughts still besieged by Othella's disappearance, would have preferred to stay home and plan how she would approach Pastor Ranka. Once again, she had to remind herself of the importance of staying upbeat for Ramat's sake, especially since, as the older sister who had travelled from overseas to attend the wedding, she had been elevated to a high status in her family's hierarchy.

The music in the club was predominantly Afrobeats, patrons leaping to the dance floor whenever a familiar song boomed through the speakers. Struggling with the heat and feeling sweat trickling down her back after some vigorous dancing, Hawa excused herself for a fresh-air break, whispering in Anaka's ear that she would be back in about five minutes.

As she was squeezing through the entrance, she felt a tap

on her shoulder. Turning sharply, she came face to face with a smiling woman of slender build, her hair cropped down to her scalp. The woman was wearing baggy trousers woven from *gara* material and a black blouse, with large wooden earrings and a matching necklace completing her look.

'Tina Kanu?' Hawa smiled in recognition. 'Is that you? Hello, queen! How are you doing?'

'Are those really your eyes, Hawa Barrie? I heard that you were dropping in for your sister's wedding. But I am a queen no more. I was expelled from the group a couple of months ago, Hawa. Did you not notice my removal from the WhatsApp group?' the woman replied.

'Way too busy with drama back in Scotland, so I had little time to read every single message. So sorry to hear, Tina. What happened?'

'I followed the drama in Scotland of which you speak, Hawa. Closely. Heard how two women got murdered and our fellow queen, Othella, is still missing. Remember that I work in the media out here. I'm a newsreader and a freelance journalist for *The Satellite*. But enough about me. Let's go back inside and I'll get you a drink.'

Returning inside, Hawa introduced Tina to Anaka, Stephen and Ramat, the group making a place for her at their table. When the others headed for the dance floor, Hawa continued her conversation with Tina, both of them nursing bottles of Maltina.

'Someone like you, Tina, is exactly who I need to talk to, since your job means you're up to date with Freetown gossip. But more importantly, why were you removed from *The Queens of Sheba*?'

'I published a story about how overseas NGO workers frequently sexually exploit our young girls in their compounds. Unknown to me, quite a few of our queens were dating these NGO men. When my story broke, they said that I had deliberately set out to humiliate fellow club members. I tried explaining that the issue was bigger than them, but they voted to expel me. Therefore, I am a Queen of Sheba no more,' Tina finished, sighing as she took another sip from her brown bottle.

'That's similar to what I'm facing in my search for Othella,' Hawa said, leaning forward. 'The exact same scenario occurred in Scotland with young women working as church ambassadors for Pastor Ranka's church. Some of the girls I spoke to back in Scotland were not happy with me, insisting that their relationships were consensual and held no doubt or darkness.'

'Pastor Ronald Ranka walks on water in this country, Hawa, and if you aim to go after him, you must make sure you have strong connections. I wrote an article about his brother, the government minister Cecil Ranka, concerning misappropriated government funds – I was arrested for libel. Spent a week locked up at Pademba Road Prison. If the Bar Association and my editor had not vehemently opposed my incarceration, I might still be there now.'

Their conversation was interrupted by the return of Anaka. Struggling with the heat, she was using a laminated menu as a makeshift fan as she praised the quality of the music.

They decided to leave after three, Hawa continuing her discussion with Tina as they walked to their vehicles. 'You should find time to come and visit me at *The Satellite*, and we can discuss matters in more detail away from this noise. 'We're on Garrison Street, right opposite the entrance to Victoria Park.'

The offices of *The Satellite* were located between a foreign exchange bureau and a Lebanese supermarket. Hawa had decided to go and see Tina Kanu alone, again leaving Anaka in the hands of Ramat, the latter prattling that she had planned a trip to a chimpanzee sanctuary located in the hills above Freetown.

Hawa took another taxi, enjoying once more the conversation of her fellow travellers, the rotund man sitting next to her on the vehicle's back seat spending the entire journey convincing the other passengers that a sister was preferable to a brother. 'Sisters take care of the entire family, but boy-children waste all their money only on their wives!' he exclaimed in conclusion, eyeing Hawa, expecting agreement for his theory.

Tina Kanu was delighted to see Hawa when she arrived, ushering her into a small room with a leather couch and a couple of computers on a broad table. Shouting at an office messenger to go out and buy them cold soft drinks from a nearby kiosk, Tina moved across to open a window, then settled next to Hawa on the couch.

'This is where I rub hands at the moment. Not a lot of money in the newspaper business, but this is what I enjoy.'

'Tailor-made for you,' Hawa replied, smiling. 'And good to see that you're putting your English degree to good use. I sold out and moved on to studying conflict and why people fight and kill each other.'

'Oh, that's simple, Hawa,' Tina replied, laughing. 'People fight and kill each other for money and power,'

'Always. Always money and power. But thanks for making time for me. I didn't have much luck tracing Othella in Scotland, so now I want to learn a bit more about Lion Mountain's activities out here, since she worked quite closely with them.'

'I followed the dark issues in Scotland and even covered Stella Kowa's death in *The Satellite* when it happened,' Tina replied, rising to receive a couple of bottles of 7 Up from the office messenger. 'But since it happened overseas, nobody really gave the story much attention. Those who read the article at the time seemed more impressed by the fact that Ronald Ranka was influential enough to have a big church ministry in a White man's country. Even the office messengers spent a whole afternoon arguing whether the Ranka brothers are amongst the richest men in the country. Not one mention of Stella Kowa, our sister who had died, in their entire conversation.'

'And what is the church like out here, Tina? How big is Ranka?'

'Immense, Hawa. It's a trifecta of influence: a rich man in this society is powerful; a rich man with political connections is even more powerful. But a rich man with political and religious influence is capable of doing literally anything in this country. I wrote an article about Ranka's church last September, but my editor refused to publish it.'

'What was the article about?' Hawa asked.

'The concept of *Holy Hour*, which Ranka's followers instituted in the Juba Hills area where he lives. They would randomly declare times of the day as *Holy Hour*, during which Ranka or one of his subordinate preachers was said to be convening with God. His followers would go so far as erecting roadblocks in front of his compound, denying vehicles passage until *Holy Hour* had concluded. It got worse when a couple of his gatemen beat up a group of teenage girls with rattan canes for walking by his compound wearing short skirts. They claimed that it was their duty to purge the nation of *loose behaviour and the over-sexualisation of our young girls*. That's a direct quotation, by the way,' Tina added, her faced lined in disapproval. 'What about your end? What is his church like in Scotland?'

'Obviously, he doesn't have the leeway to blatantly abuse people's freedoms like that in the United Kingdom, Tina. But even though we live overseas, we Africans always hold religion up with respect, which still gives Ranka significant power. The women who were killed, and indeed our own Othella, worked as church ambassadors who helped raise funds for the ministry, using very suspect methods. But the women do not see it as exploitation, and instead, having experienced serious suffering whilst living here in Sierra Leone, believe that having access to wealth and privilege is a good thing.'

'The old adage of a rich man being a good man,' Tina said bitterly. 'Remember the proverb that says that in life you sometimes shut your eyes and eat a fat-foot centipede? As women in our society, we are often encouraged to put up with difficult circumstances as long as we benefit from them. I am married to Sullay Mansaray, from our English honours class. He works as a teacher at The Prince of Wales

School and as a part-time lecturer at a teachers' training college in Goderich. People laugh at me, saying my man is a poor teacher with no substance because he has no money. When I was expelled from the Queens, some of them said I had written my article out of envy because they had found successful NGO men whilst I wallowed in hardship with a mere teacher. Human beings in a poor society often become sugar ants who are easily attracted to the sweetness of wealth and privilege.'

'I thought Ranka was big in Scotland, Tina, especially as he owns property and stuff. But since returning, I can see that his influence here is at an astronomical level. But like you said, this influence is definitely hiding some deep darkness.' Hawa paused, taking a swig from her soft drink.

'The journalist in me says you need more evidence. I tried, Hawa, but ended up being thrown in jail. And that is a road I do not want to travel down again. But we could possibly try to talk to someone who has actually lived in Ranka's compound here in Freetown. One of the young ladies who prance around this city wearing his T-shirts, perhaps?'

'But would they not be loyal to Ranka? Would they be willing to open our eyes to the clean truth?' Hawa replied.

'Not all the ladies associated with Lion Mountain have uplifting stories. The youngest daughter of a neighbour used to attend his church and even lived in the compound for a time. But she returned home to her mother's house not that long ago. She now rarely leaves the house, and her mother was saying to me the other day that she is under the grip of a serious illness. Perhaps we could talk to her. I have a few articles to complete for tomorrow's edition. But tell me where you are staying, and I'll come collect you. This can be the next step in finding out if Pastor Ranka's hands are involved in the disappearance of Othella Savage.'

CHAPTER 30

Tina Kanu picked Hawa up just after noon the following day. Stephen had planned a day of sightseeing exclusively for Anaka, pointing out that their big visitor from America needed to experience *the true beauty and glamour of Sierra Leone*. 'Don't worry about her, Miss Hawa,' he had said as they clambered into his high vehicle. 'I will take care of Miss Anaka with both my hands. Just let us know where you are later in the day, and we will come and pick you up! There is a spot up at Hill Station that serves good food and organic palm wine. We could go there for something to eat in the evening.'

Tina had arrived for Hawa in a wheezing Mazda, laughing as she coaxed it up the hills of Tengbeh Town, slaloming to avoid the ruts and rocks that punctuated the road. 'Low cars are not fit for our wretched roads, Hawa. And that is why, in this country, the vehicles of choice are often big four-wheel drives. I read how people in the countries where you live no longer like these big vehicles and call them gas guzzlers. I wrote an article after the government ordered fifty Range Rovers for their ministers, complaining firstly of the cost of the vehicles, but also about the environmental damage they cause. Nobody paid any attention. In this country, the bigger the car you drive, the better you are.'

'I hear you. Back in Scotland, I drive a little Mini that was given to me free. If I were to drive it in this country, people would laugh at me and say that I had no blessings,' Hawa laughed in reply. 'So, where do you live, Tina? I remember you staying up at New England Ville when we were in university.'

'That's where my parents live, and I am still staying with them at the moment. The house my husband Sullay and I lived in burned down. With no electricity in this city, like most other folk, we relied on a Tiger generator. But we could not leave it outside, because thieves would take it. One evening it exploded in the house. Luckily, we were not harmed, although all our things were eaten by the fire. And so, we are with my parents until we are able to stand on our feet again. Where there is life, there is hope.' Smiling, Tina adjusted her mirror, swivelling her head in both directions before joining the seething traffic of a main road. 'The woman we are going to see lives just down the road from where I stay. Her mother is a retired geography teacher. She used to help me with private lessons when I was a child. Her daughter was high up in business with Ranka and wore his T-shirts whenever she came to visit her. But then she fell ill. It will be interesting to see if she can tell us anything.'

Aunty Naffisatu, the retired geography teacher, was expecting them. She lived in a cramped compound dom-inated by a pair of imposing mango trees between which a narrow hammock had been tethered. Seeing Tina's car approaching, she rose out of the hammock, her smile broad. She was a woman who exuded authority, tall in a long green gown and matching headtie. As if on cue, a small boy emerged from the house, carrying a couple of chairs on his head, which he settled next to the hammock.

Hugs exchanged, Aunty Naffisatu invited them to sit on the chairs, her eyes warm. 'You don't come to see me much these days, Tina. Just because you have big books inside your head does not mean you can forget me, the teacher who developed you when you had snot in your nose!' The young boy who had brought out the chairs returned with a low stool and a tray of soft drinks. With movements that suggested he had done it countless times before, the boy used his teeth to open the bottles, then shuffled back into the house.

'It's the pressures of work, Aunty Naffisatu. I think of you always and I'm so happy that you are allowing us to talk to Maseray. This is my friend from university, Hawa Barrie. She now lives in Scotland where she is studying, but she is here for her sister's wedding. She was close to Ronald Ranka's church in Scotland. I don't know if you heard about Stella Kowa who died there, Aunty Naffisatu?'

'Yes, I remember that story vaguely. Was she not the one who was locked in the boot of a car?'

'That was her exactly, Aunty Naffisatu,' Hawa replied, happy that somebody else in Freetown was aware of the circumstances of Stella Kowa's unfortunate demise. 'And a woman from Liberia also died in the same manner,' she added.

'And this business is connected to Ranka's church?' Aunty Naffisatu asked, her earlier good humour now dissipated.

'We think so, although we do not have definite proof. Which is why I wanted to see if we could talk to Maseray, since she was big in Ranka's organisation.'

'Maseray is not well. She had such joy and energy and was a good daughter. Finished college and found a good job at the special court. She even helped me renovate this house and build an extension at the back. But then she left the court to join Lion Mountain. And her fortunes climbed to an even higher level. Even you, Tina, saw how her life luck increased. She was on the television and the radio, always speaking of the good work Lion Mountain did,' Aunty Naffisatu continued, her voice now low. 'And then I did not hear from her for a whole week. I took a taxi up to Ranka's Juba residence, demanding to know where my daughter was. The gatemen would not let me in, saying that I did not have an appointment to see Ranka. For another couple of days, I did not sleep, reading psalms and praying for the safe return of my Maseray. The police laughed in my face, asking what I expected them to do to a powerful man like Ronald Ranka, especially as I had no proof that he had hurt my daughter. And then I got a message on my phone to say that Maseray was at Connaught Hospital.' Aunty Naffisatu paused, the pain of the experience palpable. 'The girl I picked up from that hospital ward was not my daughter. It was as if somebody had thrust their hand down her throat and pulled out her insides and personality. The nurses said that she had been dropped off in a Lion Mountain vehicle and that they were given money to take care of her. But none of the doctors could tell me what was wrong with her. They discharged Maseray after a week and I brought her home. We have been to the clinic with the Indian doctors up at Hastings, but no improvement. I even took her to a traditional medicine man out of desperation, but he also could offer no help. So now she stays inside the house and speaks very little. Only God knows what Ranka's church did to my child. You can speak to her if you want, although she says very little these days.'

Maseray had been placed on a wide bed in a room at the back of her mother's house. The curtains were drawn, leaving the room dark and oppressive, but Hawa and Tina's eyes eventually adjusted to the gloom. A radio had been turned down low, whispered music from some FM station floating through the air. Incense had been lit on a couple of tables on opposite sides of the room, and their smoke spiralled through the air, trailing a pleasant smell.

'Mama Maseray, there are people here to see you,' Aunty Naffisatu said, her voice raised in forced enthusiasm. 'We named her Maseray after my mother, who passed away just before she was born,' she explained, settling next to her daughter on the bed. 'Sit down, Tina and Hawa. Maseray, are you awake?' In reply, Maseray's eyes shot open, swivelling towards the strangers in her space, her face etched with fear and suspicion. 'This is Tina and Hawa. They are here to see you. If you are strong enough, you could come outside and sit with them. They are young ladies like you, Maseray.'

Maseray shook her head. And then she spoke, the words surprisingly strong, belying her physical state. 'Are you from Lion Mountain? Have you also been chosen to do God's work? You are beautiful, like all Lion Mountain women. But you cannot stay forever, because Satan will eat you.'

'What happened to you?' Tina asked quietly.

'Lion Mountain does only good. Lion Mountain helps the women who were hurt during our war. And helps women with jobs. And helps young women who are pregnant with no husbands. And so, if I suffer for Lion Mountain, that is OK. Even our Almighty Saviour suffered on the cross to save us from sin. And that is what has happened to me. And so I will not complain.'

Before Tina could ask another question, Maseray covered her head, then she proceeded to make high keening sounds, like an animal in pain.

Hawa and Tina met up with Ramat, Anaka and Stephen later that evening. As had been promised by Ramat's fiancé, the restaurant up at Hill Station he had recommended served an array of lovely dishes, whilst the heavily advertised organic palm wine was light and refreshing. Hawa was relieved at the distraction. Their visit to see Maseray had left her rattled and hollow. They had spoken little on the drive over, Tina also showing signs of being shaken by the experience. Hawa had insisted that she join them for the meal. 'My treat. You have helped me beyond measure to understand the true nature of Pastor Ranka and his church. The least I can do is break bread with you, my sister. Please accept.'

Anaka's enthusiasm soon lifted the mood, the American sitting between Hawa and Tina to show them the plethora of pictures she had taken on her phone throughout the day. 'Seen quite a few beaches on my travels, but the ones you have here in Sierra Leone are on another level. Such beautiful light sand. And people are so friendly! I even bought a couple of bead necklaces from this cool lady,' Anaka said, lifting her head to display them sitting proudly around her neck.

The restaurant got busier as the evening progressed, a live band arriving on stage to perform a medley of popular songs. They all took turns explaining the lyrics to Anaka, who swung between dancing to the tunes and taking videos.

In bed later, Hawa and Anaka discussed strategy, trying to ignore the giggling of Ramat and Stephen from the next room. 'The plan is to see if I can visit Ranka's house tomorrow,' Hawa explained into the darkness, Anaka a warm hump next to her.

'You're not going alone, Hawa. I was appointed a church ambassador at the same time as you. And we both gave speeches or sang songs at the fundraising gala. I'd say that makes us firm members of his organisation, whether we like it or not.'

'Tina Kanu knows what we're doing, and I've promised to keep her in the loop,' Hawa replied. 'Tomorrow, we'll see if Pastor Ranka can look me in the eye and tell me he knows nothing about Othella's disappearance.'

CHAPTER 31

'If you want to see important people in this country, then the best advice is to descend on their houses during the weekend,' Hawa explained to Anaka when they rose the next morning. 'We shall aim for noon since big men in this society are often late to rise during the weekends, which is when they swallow alcohol and talk big talk.'

Pastor Ronald Ranka's compound was in Juba Hills, overlooking the city. His house was an imposing struc-ture painted yellow and black, with a massive satellite dish positioned on the roof. The residence had been built next to the orphanage, a two-storey building, also yellow and black. High walls topped with barbed wire and shards of glass surrounded the complex, a security feature common to most houses in this part of the city.

Stephen had insisted Hawa take his car. 'You learned how to drive on these streets, Miss Hawa, so you won't be scared of our Freetown traffic. Just remember that you are not in Scotland, and so you must use your horn as often as possible. Driving in this country is like a bitter argument. You must make sure that the car you drive shouts like a lion, otherwise other motorists will bully you!'

The stern black gate of the pastor's compound was manned by a couple of men in faded jeans and white T-shirts which carried Ranka's face and details of the upcoming religious retreat at the National Stadium. Fixing the dusty vehicle with hostile eyes, they asked if Hawa and Anaka had an appointment.

'I am Hawa Barrie, and this is Anaka Hart. We are ambassadors working with Pastor Ranka's church in Scotland. We do not have an appointment, but I am sure he will agree to see us.' Hawa spoke in a stiff English accent, hoping that her tone would cow the men sufficiently to secure them access.

Still uncertain, the two men conferred, until one of them disappeared into the house, emerging onto a high veranda about five minutes later and shouting down to his colleague to open the gate and allow the vehicle through. Once inside, Hawa parked next to a raised concrete stage covered with dozens of plastic chairs in a variety of colours.

The man who had shouted down from the veranda was waiting at a side door, smiling. Following the man, who did not utter a word, they climbed a flight of stairs, the walls festooned with huge crucifixes and Bible verses mounted in massive picture frames. They moved through a living room in which twelve people, all wearing the pastor's T-shirts, were eating from huge trays of fried plantain, rice akara cakes and cassava bread placed on a large coffee table.

Pastor Ranka was waiting for them in the dining room. The room was full, the seats around the ornate table of black glass taken, for the most part, by men who exuded importance and influence, their eyes turning to Hawa and Anaka as they entered. A couple of girls, young enough to still be in high school and wearing tight purple versions of the retreat T-shirt, were suddenly at their side, each carrying a chair which they squeezed in at the head of the table, flanking Pastor Ranka.

He was engrossed in an animated phone conversation, his eyes flickering as the two women walked in. Smiling, he rose from his seat, waving Anaka and Hawa to the newly placed chairs, then strode out onto the veranda to continue the phone call.

As they settled onto the chairs, which were covered with soft suede material, one of the teenage girls spoke. 'The pastor says you should break bread with us since you have arrived during mealtime,' she told them. 'He says you are not allowed to decline and that it is through breaking bread that we stay connected. Indeed, our Lord Jesus' miracles involved turning water into wine and multiplying bread and fish for the worshippers on the mountain; food, therefore, is a major pillar of faith.'

Having not eaten before they left home, Hawa took some cassava bread and fried fish, Anaka asking for a glass of pineapple juice and a small plate of rice akara cakes. The pastor soon joined them, wearing scarlet pyjamas with the top button undone, revealing tufts of chest hair.

'Sisters Hawa and Anaka! Raise your eyes to witness greatness, my people! My Scottish ambassadors are here to see me. God is indeed great. Apologies for having to leave Scotland so suddenly, but affairs of our ministry out here required my urgent attention.' He broke off to address his guests around the table, expanding on Hawa's and Anaka's roles in their church, then returned to his seat, his voice dropping low so only they could hear it.

'I heard how you found yourself in the jaws of hell, and how you discovered Sister Naomi Wreh dead in the boot of her car! But our prayers shrouded you in safety, my sisters, and you are here alive and well with us.' He took Hawa's hands in his, his touch clammy. 'What happened to Sisters Stella and Naomi is clear evidence of the dark times we live in, and why we must continue to pray as a means to shackle the dastardly and diabolical demons of damnation sent to this human plain to afflict and test us!'

Ranka was now on his feet again, seamlessly transitioning into preaching mode as he outlined the forces of darkness his church sought to battle daily, the people around the table listening with rapt attention, totally in his grasp.

'But our work does not end, Sisters Anaka Hart and Hawa Barrie, and it is God's will that you happen to be here in Sierra Leone to witness our tenth anniversary retreat. I am sure you are aware of the positive strides we continue to make, with everything now in place for a unique occasion of healing and power. You will attend the retreat, of course, and spread the word back in Scotland when you return there. Once we conclude the retreat, the plan is to raise positive and inspirational sisters like yourselves, Hawa and Anaka, to positions of high importance within the church.' Pastor Ranka paused, his visible chest hair now shimmering due to the sweat his animated movements had caused.

'Our first appointment will be for the position of chief ambassador for the church here in Sierra Leone, charged with coordinating the affairs of the orphanage and the vocational institute. And that ambassador will be a good friend of yours, who arrived earlier this week and excelled in our interview process.'

A door to the left of the room slid open, and a woman in a Ranka T-shirt and dark jeans came forward to stand next to the pastor. Everyone at the table stood to applaud Othella's appointment.

CHAPTER 32

Othella was immediately swamped by the people around the table, deep warmth dancing in her eyes as they offered congratulations and goodwill. She had lost weight since they had last seen her in Edinburgh on the afternoon she had done Anaka's hair.

Hawa felt her knees buckle slightly, the ongoing applause reduced to a dull, droning sound in her head. Unsteady on her feet, she lowered herself to the chair she had risen from. Anaka's face eventually came into focus, the American now stooping over her. The rest of the guests were oblivious to Hawa and Anaka, all of them clustered around Othella.

Breaking through the group, Othella was suddenly on the other side of Hawa, pulling her to her feet before shrouding her in an embrace. She offered an equally warm hug to Anaka, then volunteered to show them around Lion Mountain's orphanage and the vocational centre for teenage mothers, described by Othella with customary vivacity as *a much-needed space dedicated to opportunity and positive energy for young women.*

Pastor Ranka and his guests remained in proximity as they descended the stairs to the orphanage and vocational centre, which occupied large buildings in the expansive yard behind the main house. Othella gave them an overview of the facilities, her voice measured and steady, though Hawa noticed a slight limp in her friend's gait as they crossed the yard. The orphanage was empty, as it turned out. Othella explained that the children had been taken on a trip to Bunce Island to visit an old slave fort and a reserve for pygmy hippos.

'It was Sister Othella who suggested that we open the minds of the orphans to the history and culture of our nation by taking them on these trips! She has selflessly been pushing this positive agenda behind the scenes, which is why I have raised her to such a high position in our organisation,' Pastor Ranka told them, pride etched on his face.

In the vocational centre, they were shown into a room with a dozen Singer sewing machines, just as Ramat had said. The teenage girls sitting at them, all in Pastor Ranka T-shirts, paused in their endeavours to study the entourage, their eyes alert and uncertain.

The tour over, the other guests returned to the main house, Pastor Ranka refusing to leave Othella's side as she walked Anaka and Hawa to their vehicle. She waved as they drove away, promising to see them again soon.

On their return home, they broke the news of Othella's reappearance to an equally astonished Ramat. 'But to be on the ground in this country all along whilst White police people in Scotland are looking for her is hard to understand!'

Hawa slumped into a low chair. 'Hard to understand is putting it mildly, Ramat. We couldn't throw questions at her because there were over thirty people there.'

'And he wouldn't leave her side!' Anaka added.

'Something just isn't right. We need to corner Othella alone so she can throw light on this whole situation!'

Later that afternoon, Hawa received a text message from Aunty Theresa, asking to come to see her to confidentially discuss certain aspects of the wedding. Anaka had gone for a nap, complaining of a mild headache, and Ramat volunteered to stay behind and keep her company. Again taking Stephen's Jeep, Hawa drove to the Big House, entertaining herself by listening to a radio talk show that was today stridently discussing the acute shortage of fuel in the country, especially so close to Christmas, a time when Sierra Leoneans should be enjoying themselves rather than being bowed down in misery by grinding corruption and the incompetence of politicians.

Dauda was on duty when she arrived at the Big House, the heat having lulled him into a doze, his mouth open in oblivion, chin slumped to his chest. Smiling, Hawa climbed out of the vehicle and squeezed in through the gap between the gates, stepping lightly so as not to rouse him, knowing that he would take at least ten minutes away from her with convoluted narratives concerning the lives of his family.

The front door to the house was closed, so Hawa nipped through to the back yard. The only occupants were a couple of teenage girls who were pounding cassava leaves in a wooden mortar, the pestles in their hands moving in a hypnotic rhythm. Hawa exchanged greetings with them, and they interrupted their pounding to confirm that Aunty Theresa was upstairs.

The living room was deserted, appearing much larger without the customary deluge of hangers-on that seemed to always be around when she visited.

She shouted a greeting along the corridor in the direction of her father's bedroom, and Aunty Theresa replied almost instantly, inviting her to come in. Hawa smiled as she walked past the room she had shared with Ramat when they were children, their double bed now joined by bunk beds that had been squeezed into the corner close to the window.

She was greeted by the strong smell of incense when she entered the bedroom Aunty Theresa shared with her father. The first thing she looked for was the picture of her mother, taken on her wedding day, a bunch of flowers clutched in her hands. Over the years it had held pride of place above a slender mirror, innocence and beauty flowing out of the frame, but it had disappeared, and the walls of the room had been painted sea blue, with no trace of the grey colour from her youth.

Aunty Theresa was sitting on the wide bed with a couple of suitcases open next to her, outfits heaped in neat piles. 'Hawa, my daughter,' she smiled, jabbing at a plastic chair by the mirror as an instruction for her to sit. 'I have been looking at some lovely Africana outfits to give as a gift to your American friend, Anaka. I was chatting to her when last you were here, and she displays a strong desire to inhale and enjoy our Sierra Leonean culture.'

Surprised and wary of this generosity, Hawa thanked Aunty Theresa, saying that it was a lovely idea. They spent a few minutes discussing Ramat's fiancé, Hawa, agreeing that he was a commendable choice who had the requisite character traits to treat Ramat with respect and dignity.

'And he is a Christian man who holds his religion close to his chest,' Aunty Theresa added. 'He too has always attended a branch of Lion Mountain Church. I heard you went to Pastor Ranka's house yesterday, Hawa. And that your friend Othella is alive and well and has been hoisted to a high position of respect in our church? Blessings from the sky continue to rain down on all of us!'

'We went to talk to him about Othella, since we were members of his ministry back in Scotland, and even worked briefly as church ambassadors,' Hawa explained, startled that Aunty Theresa knew about their trip to Juba Hills.

'Pastor Ranka is a chosen prophet who has a rare gift handed down to only a select few mortal men in this world, Hawa. What he continues to do for our Sierra Leonean people spreads blessings to all. Surely you can see this?'

'I hear what you are saying, Aunty Theresa. Our intention was not to complicate the pastor's life, but rather to see if he could help us find Othella. And now that we have seen her eyes again, I guess all is well and good.'

'That is well and good, Hawa, as long as you do not attempt to throw sand into his affairs in the future. Pastor Ranka has even said that he would be willing to officiate the wedding. Can you imagine how that will raise the profile of this family? People from all over the country will chew gossip and be forced to drink envy when they hear that our Ramat's wedding service was conducted by such a powerful man of God!'

'But I am not throwing dirt into his affairs, Aunty Theresa. Two young women very much like myself, who were connected to the pastor's church in Scotland, were killed, with the police still investigating,' Hawa replied, suddenly realising that she was standing up and shouting down at her stepmother.

'There is no need to be upset, Hawa. It is the duty of us older people to guide and direct our children. I did not carry you in my stomach, but your papa appointed me as your mother when he brought me here to sit down with him in marriage.' Her stepmother paused, placing a couple of the outfits from the suitcase in a plastic bag, which she passed on to Hawa.

'Remember that teeth sometimes bite the tongue, which shows that even close relatives exchange words of anger. Please cool down your heart, Hawa. Give these clothes to your friend Anaka, and we will see you later in the week when we put the final touches to the arrangements for the wedding.'

Thanking her, Hawa rose from the chair. She was at the door when Aunty Theresa spoke again, her voice low. 'Your papa and I were wondering if any good men overseas in Scotland or even here have sent sweet words of admiration your way, Hawa? You arrived back home after a year of studying abroad with a female friend. We hear how in these overseas countries two women happily sit down together in marriage, sleep together and even have families. We were therefore just offering prayers that you and Anaka are just ordinary friends and are not involved in behaviour that would rain down shame on the image of our Christian family!'

Without a word, Hawa left the Big House, the drive back to Tengbeh Town a blur.

CHAPTER 33

It was suggested that they all move to the Big House, where they would stay till after the wedding, Aunty Theresa insisting that having the whole family under one roof reflected unity and respect, showing the whole world that the Barrie clan were a people who spoke with one word on all issues.

Hawa was in agreement, on practical grounds, at least, pointing out to a doubtful Ramat that there was no need to worry. 'The Big House was built by our parents before Aunty Theresa arrived in our lives, so we have every right to stay there. It has space, Ramat, which is something we need, especially as your bridesmaids are as many as the grains of sand on the beach. Besides, we can return here after the wedding. Then you'll be going to your husband's house, and Anaka is off back to America whilst I must return soon to Scotland for my graduation in the new year.'

The move proved a sound decision, Ramat's bridesmaids having ample space to try on their dresses and shoes whilst Hawa and Anaka talked them through the cuts and sizes. A hired troupe of gumbay musicians also arrived at the Big House, positioning themselves beneath a wide *baffa* constructed from bamboo sticks and palm thatch. Sweat pouring from their bare arms and torsos, they pounded and blew their instruments, their lead singer hailing the Barrie family and celebrating the fact that a good and proper Christian man had come out to take their daughter away in marriage. Fascinated, Anaka raised her phone to capture it all, her face a mask of appreciation, a smiling Hawa at her side to translate the lyrics.

In the back yard, several temporary tripods of fire stones were erected so the bustling womenfolk could cook food for those who had travelled from afar for the wedding, aromas and sweet smells curling through the air. Hawa was especially cheered by the arrival of her mother's family, who greeted Aunty Theresa stiffly whilst openly declaring that although their late sister was dead, she had still, from the afterlife, guided the lives and fortunes of her two beautiful daughters, who had grown up into very accomplished young ladies. Naturally overjoyed at Ramat's good fortune, they also celebrated Hawa, crowding around her to ask how her studies overseas were progressing, whilst pleading with her to solve all of their individual problems ranging from helping to pay school fees for their kids, to one aunty who wondered if Hawa would be able to buy her a car that she could run as a taxi through the city.

The wedding took place on the Saturday at the branch of Pastor Ranka's church that Aunty Theresa attended in Wilberforce. Ranka was, however, unable to conduct the service – he was consumed with preparations for the week-long retreat, due to commence on the following Monday.

He sent in his place a wiry acolyte who introduced himself as Pastor Joshua, a young brother who held sway over the church's Port Loko branch in the north of the country.

The church was packed, with Ramat resplendent in the beautiful wedding gown Hawa had purchased back in Edinburgh. Papa and Aunty Theresa smiled broadly throughout the ceremony. Her father, true to his word, wore one of the navy-blue suits she had bought for him.

After the ceremony, the new husband and wife went with the whole family to Lumley Beach to take pictures, after which they drove back to the Big House. Hawa, dipping into the money she had saved from cleaning rooms back in Scotland, had hired a 46-seater bus to ferry distant family members between the various locations, including to the evening reception at Brookfields Hotel, for which most of the guests changed into the ornate purple and orange outfits which had been chosen as the *ashobie* for the occasion.

His chest puffed out with pride, Papa delivered a rousing speech, praising the shimmering luck of his daughter, which had seen her secure a man who was strong enough to stand on his own two feet, with a sturdy job that would see him support his new wife and future children with class and dignity.

Hawa, given her elevated status in the family hierarchy, was also compelled to deliver a speech, during which she wished her sister deep luck whilst thanking all who had come from far and wide to celebrate with them.

With ample drink and food for all, the celebrations continued through the night, the highlight coming when Anaka took to the stage to sing a couple of Ramat's favourite songs, all the guests exploding in applause when she finished.

Hawa's filming of Anaka's performance was interrupted by a flashing message, which she ignored, only checking it as she collected a glass of orange juice from the open bar. She didn't recognise the number, but the digits confirmed it was from someone in Sierra Leone.

So happy our little sister Ramat's wedding has gone well! Heard she looks stunning in white! Did not want to disturb you on this special day. Meet me at college tomorrow at twelve at the amphitheatre near the botanical gardens, and we will talk. Othella Unopposed.

The next day was a good time to go and see Othella, with most of the family still recovering from Ramat's wedding. All who attended agreed that it had been a one-of-a-kind occasion that demonstrated the power and status of the Barrie family, who had provided ample amounts of food and drink for everyone, including gatecrashers who had no business being there. The crowning glory had been the distribution of the souvenirs Hawa had procured in Edinburgh on Ramat's orders: small towels, keychains and pens all bearing a smiling image of the bride and groom, the date of their wedding displayed in bright crimson lettering.

Hawa's insomnia had receded since she had arrived back in Sierra Leone, sleep coming to her easily almost every night, although once in a while she was visited by strange and disturbing dreams, often involving her being trapped in the boot of a car. An extreme version of the dream featured Stella Kowa, Naomi Wreh and her together in the boot of a wide red car that drove off the Forth Road Bridge back in Scotland, slowly sinking to the bottom of the oily black river as they screamed hopelessly for help.

Mustapha was already up, agreeing with a smile to drive Hawa up to the university, his mood improving further when she gave him a crisp $10 note, the foreign currency eliciting deep gratitude from the overwhelmed driver.

As they travelled, he tried to engage her with talk of the treacherous and corrupt nature of national politics, which saw honest men like himself continue to struggle. 'Jobs in this country, Aunty Hawa, are like trying to get water from the bottom of a well during high-dry season month of April. If God had not given me a little job to rub hands with, driving your papa around, my wife and children would sleep with air in their stomachs every day! And that is why I hold this job with both hands and do nothing to upset any member of your family, Aunty Hawa!'

Her mind whirring at the prospect of meeting Othella, Hawa's face remained stiff as she absent-mindedly praised Mustapha for his impeccable service, the driver beaming in appreciation at the compliment.

CHAPTER 34

Hawa's memories of the amphitheatre took her back to times when the entire student body had congregated there to debate burning issues. She had been active in student union politics, and amongst other standout meetings, she remembered the anger and incendiary rhetoric that had flowed during a proposed strike to protest against an unreasonable hike in tuition fees. Some radical students had gone so far as to suggest that they waylay members of the college's administration whilst barricading the roads leading up to the campus.

Marinating these memories, she sat at the top of the tiered concrete steps, close to the entrance to the Wilson Theatre, where she had attended many a lecture. She had sent Mustapha on his way, insisting that she would find her way back home. It being a Sunday so close to Christmas, the amphitheatre was deserted, the only people in view a couple of lecturers drinking beer at a table just outside the staff canteen. Checking her phone, she realised she had been there twelve minutes. She decided she'd wait for twenty before heading for Dr Zaydah Savage's quarters to see if Othella was by any chance there with her mother. She had sent her a text message after she discovered Othella alive and well at Ranka's compound; Dr Savage's response had been a terse 'praise God'.

Othella appeared after seventeen minutes, emerging from the botanical gardens. Hawa's elevated position allowed her to study her friend's approach.

Othella was wearing black jeans, a baggy blue-and-black striped T-shirt and a pair of pristine white trainers. Her dreadlocks were concealed beneath a matching blue baseball cap. Spotting Hawa, she waved and smiled, enveloping her in a tight hug when she reached her. She then sat down, kicking off her trainers in the same movement.

'A bit too tight, these are! Bought them at the Gyle Centre back in Edinburgh. They were for a 5K run, which I ended up dropping out of. Twisted my ankle whilst trekking through the Pentlands with Jam Jerry! Talk about drama!'

Hawa realised that Othella was jabbering to mask her nerves, spewing empty talk before confronting what had brought them to the amphitheatre. It was not lost on Hawa how appropriate a location it was for their showdown. The sprawling terraced concrete steps were like quiet observers, silent out of respect for the discussion that was about to unfold. Over the years, Hawa had become accustomed to standing back slightly in the aura of Othella, like an accessory in their friendship. Today, though, she could feel a simmering anger and frustration rise up, her mind reliving the struggles she had been through to find Othella back in Edinburgh.

'Where the hell have you been, Othella? In my mind, I had actually buried you! I thought something bad had happened to you.'

Othella removed the baseball cap and shook her hair free, like a dog shaking off water after swimming in a river.

'I had to leave Scotland, Hawa. Just needed to clear my head and start again.'

'Clear your head? What the hell does that mean? Don't talk to me like someone in a movie! What does *clear your head* even mean?'

'Don't come at me with anger, Hawa. I had to leave after what happened to Stella.'

'But you broke the story like you were dropping empty gossip in my ears, Othella. You sent me dramatic text messages and spoke to Anaka and me about Stella like you were just passing on info you had picked up. And then the very same evening you upped and disappeared?'

'Because it was my fault Stella ended up dead, Hawa.' Othella had by this time placed the baseball cap on the ground between her feet, next to the trainers. 'All my fault!'

'How exactly, Othella?'

'It was my fault because I was the first church ambassador, Hawa. Before you came to Scotland, I worked with Pastor Ranka. When those horrific mudslides killed our people in Regent, I approached him in church to help raise money for the families. He hooked me up with his wife, Amanda, and I was introduced to a couple of men who donated fifteen grand to help. I spoke at a function and provided information on Sierra Leone: our history, our civil war, our political corruption, our malaise. The donations kept flowing. All for a good cause, Hawa. We made a huge difference in just a few years. You saw the orphanage and the vocational institute the other day. The facility for the teenage mothers was all my thinking, Hawa. A chance to make a difference by improving the lot and lives of young girls.'

'And you decided to do this out of the goodness of your heart, Othella, but kept me completely in the dark? Of course, I get it now! Why, oh why would someone like me have an interest in charity and helping the vulnerable in our country?' Hawa's voice had grown louder, her eyes hard. 'I'll answer that for you, Othella, since you think you're talking to a toy doll with an empty plastic head; you did not involve me in your church ambassador drama because you knew it was a disgusting business that involved pimping out sisters to rich White men!'

'I'll let that stupid comment slide because you're angry, Hawa. I shaded you to protect you. You're damn right it was a suspect arrangement with those men. And you were too good for that. Besides, you were in Scotland to study. I always did say that I'd expose you a bit more to Lion Mountain's humanitarian side after your graduated, Hawa. But then things spiralled and got out of hand. Pastor Ranka asked me to recruit more ladies to help with fundraising, and I initially saw it as an opportunity for female empowerment. Black sisters holding their heads high to make a difference. And I know you're dripping major anger, but don't ever suggest I pimped anybody out. They attended functions and were coached by me on what issues to discuss with donors. Quite a lot of them had empty coconut heads and were happy just drifting by whilst working meagre jobs for Lesley's Links in Edinburgh. I wanted to teach them to make a difference, Hawa. I helped some of them apply to study nursing and filled out application forms for a couple to go to Stevenson College to study things like childcare. Not everybody has the mental capacity to enter university like you and I, Hawa.'

'Yeah, I get it, Othella, crystal clear,' Hawa replied. 'This is just like being back in high school. It's all about control for you. Othella Unopposed Savage, who always gets her way by manipulating and scheming! You didn't exploit our sisters, but then your well-meaning church ambassador scheme eventually became a call-girl service, with the very same women you hoped to uplift ending up being used. And now two of them are dead. And instead of helping to clear up the mess, you disappear, and I find you out here holding Ranka's hand whilst you sing Kumbaya!'

Laughter from a group of lecturers settled around a table outside the staff canteen nearby invaded their conversation, easing the tension that had continued to build.

'I spoke to Jattu in Glasgow and to Stella in hospital before she was taken from us. I also found Naomi Wreh dead in her car boot. All whilst looking for a so-called friend who couldn't even send me a message to say they were all right. You couldn't even let your own mother know you were good and safe! You'd only do that if you had something to hide!'

'Because I need to draw something positive out of this mess, Hawa! If I am somebody big in Pastor Ranka's organisation, I can change things from the inside. Judge me all you like. Call me a schemer and a manipulator. Call me worse. But we are not talking student union politics like we used to debate right here where we sit today. Lofty speeches and political theories swallowed from books cannot make a change, Hawa. You need to jump into the mud and get mega-dirty if you want to clean things up! I was threatened too – something wasn't right.'

Another volley of laughter carried across from the canteen. Hawa noticed a waitress now sitting on the lap of a grey-haired lecturer.

'As you know, I lived alone after Jattu got married and moved out,' Othella continued, having also glanced up briefly at the merry academics. 'But I'd come home and find things different in the flat, as if somebody had been there and moved stuff about. I assumed it was Jattu, because she still had a key, but she said it wasn't. And so, I changed the locks without telling anybody. On the day you came by, and I did Anaka's hair, I stepped out to buy a few things from Scotmid, and when I got back, there was somebody in the flat. The door had been forced and I heard things being broken inside. I panicked and caught a train to London. Stayed there a while. And then I saw on social media that Naomi had also been found dead, which really floored me. These were women I had encouraged to get involved with Lion Mountain, Hawa! I had to get out! And so I caught a flight to Guinea and travelled home by road. My mum got me a Sierra Leonean passport a while ago. I'm entitled to one through dual citizenship, but I never really thought I needed one until recently. So, I asked her to DHL it over to me whilst I was laying low in London. I've been staying with her since I arrived. Wanted to keep a low profile, especially after I heard about Stella and Naomi. The guilt of their deaths swamped me for quite a while, Hawa – I would not eat or leave my bedroom in my mum's house for ages. She was very worried, especially as I refused to give her the full details of my association with our murdered sisters and the part I played in them becoming church ambassadors.'

Hawa was startled, a half-formed reply dying on her lips as she remembered her conversations with Othella's mother, when she had expressed strong disdain for Pastor Ranka and the affairs of his church, whilst claiming not to know where her daughter was.

'Now that I am at the very heart of Ranka's ministry, I'm in a position to get more information, Hawa,' Othella continued, her voice gentler now. 'If Ranka is to be made to pay for the horrible things he has done, we need evidence to bring him down. I know for a fact that all the properties he owns in Edinburgh were bought by his brother, the government minister, with public funds meant for our people.'

Hawa snorted in reply, the sound sticking in her throat, her eyes cold and hostile. 'This is hard to believe, Othella! If someone breaks into your flat, surely it would help if you told the police? Perhaps fixing this situation could have involved you staying in Edinburgh whilst helping them figure out who killed Stella and Naomi. I totally see what you are saying about Ranka's connections to government corruption, which is as obvious as the sun shines. But you have to come back to Edinburgh and help find out who murdered two women who were involved in a scheme you started, Othella!'

Othella did not reply, her head bowed as if she was studying some riveting detail of the trainers and baseball cap on the ground between her feet. Hawa stood up, taking a step back from her friend, the silence between them a chasm.

'I had no direct hand in the deaths of Stella Kowa and Naomi Wreh, and my heart breaks for what happened to them. I'd left Edinburgh before either of them was taken from us, Hawa. But I have to keep moving and try to draw some light out of this darkness. And that's why you must come to Pastor Ranka's retreat at the National Stadium. I'll have special passes for the Presidential Pavilion delivered for Anaka, Ramat and yourself. Not everything about the ministry is shrouded in evil and darkness. Ranka sits at the top of a huge organisation that wields massive influence and has done great things for our people, which I myself have been involved in. All the charitable initiatives here in Sierra Leone came from me, Hawa. And the recent focus on uplifting the lives of girls and young women, again came from me. You saw first-hand the work Lion Mountain does when I took you on a tour of the facilities. What we need to do, Hawa, is channel this power and influence in the right direction. I've worked too hard to just let all my efforts just wilt and die. Join us for the last day of the retreat, on New Year's Eve. Ranka will get his comeuppance in good time.'

CHAPTER 35

The blanket coverage for Pastor Ranka's retreat continued to promote it as a unique event – all who attended would receive blessings that would allow them to begin the new year with a clean slate of prosperity and purity. Amanda had now arrived in Sierra Leone, appearing on a popular morning talk show on the African Young Voices channel, flanked either side by two girls whom she introduced as *Sierra Leonean sisters from the church's London branch*, who had also returned home at this special time of the year to give back.

'Our ministry has always stood for women's empowerment,' she told the host. 'Our church ambassadors take the lead in raising funds for the church. Lion Mountain ambassadors are encouraged to look beyond the empty validation of romantic relationships and material wealth. Rather, we urge them to make a difference to the world we live in.'

As promised, Hawa received special passes granting them access to the Presidential Pavilion at the National Stadium, dropped off by a couple of young women in purple retreat T-shirts driving a Prado Land Cruiser.

Anaka, anxious to see what a religious retreat looked

like, implored a reluctant Hawa to attend. 'It's like nothing you've ever seen,' Hawa explained as they ate lunch at a beach restaurant one afternoon. 'When I arrived in Scotland, I was staggered by how many people openly declared that they didn't believe in God. But here, in Africa, everybody believes, be it through Christianity or Islam. As a people, we can also be very superstitious, holding the traditions of our people as deeply sacred,' she added, sipping from a slender bottle of Fanta.

'Definitely a British thing.' Anaka was nursing a bottle of Star Beer. 'I noticed it too. We Americans still like to honour God, and we hold our preachers with deep respect. Black folk claim Jesus helped them get through slavery and Jim Crow.'

'That's so true,' Ramat agreed. 'Whenever I watch American presidents giving speeches on TV, they always finish by saying *God Bless America*, which you never hear from Hawa's British politicians.'

They all laughed at Ramat's classification of *Hawa's British politicians*, chatting away until their meals arrived – foofoo cooked with okra soup, a speciality of the Krios, an ethnic group who lived predominantly in the capital city. 'It's made from fermented cassava, so it has a slightly sour taste,' Ramat told Anaka, knowing that the information would inevitably find its way on to Songhai Sista.

They left for the final day of Pastor Ranka's retreat early in the evening, Mustapha arriving to pick them up in Papa's Hilux. He was wearing an electric-blue full-length gown, looking even smarter than he had for Ramat's wedding. He explained his choice of clothes as they drove along, a light dancing in his eyes.

'Pastor Ranka is a true powerful man of God, which is why I am so happy to be going with you! To own a church in a White man's country overseas is a true sign of blessings from above. I have suffered a lot in this life in this *halakie* country that we call Sierra Leone, and so tonight I will open my heart and pray for good luck and blessings to follow me and my family in the new year!'

They had to park the vehicle in the compound of the Youyi Building, a tall structure nearby that housed several government departments. Vehicular progress beyond that point was impossible due to the throngs descending on the stadium. Walking together, they joined the steady flow of humanity, shuffling towards the venue. Ramat had emphasised on the drive over the importance of remaining vigilant and staying alert, Mustapha nodding in agreement as he threaded the big vehicle through the crowded streets. 'There will be many people there just to snatch bags and finger money from people's pockets. And that is why I suggested we don't carry bags with us today and wear tight-fitting jeans to make it difficult for anyone to slip things out of our pockets!'

Darkness had descended on the city, a customary power cut reducing the buildings on the margins of the streets to shadowy structures, through the windows of which glowed candles and kerosene lamps. The National Stadium had power though, the light from the huge floodlights climbing into the sky, a beacon drawing worshippers in like termites. Booming hymns could be heard through the public address system, interspersed with snatches of Pastor Ranka's familiar voice, outlining the power of true faith to combat the travails and tribulations that afflict mankind.

The crowd slowed to a crawl at the entrance to the stadium, as various cadres of security personnel guided people through the gates: soldiers in camouflage, police in deep blue uniforms, and men in khaki-coloured overalls belonging to Elephant Security, a private firm founded by a retired military general. All of the security men carried automatic weapons, barking at the crowd to be patient and careful, their eyes hostile and suspicious.

Once they were through the tight main gates, movement was much smoother, with the crowds fanning out in all directions once inside. Checking the others were OK, Ramat laughed in relief as they patted their pockets to make sure what they had brought with them was still secure.

'We have passes for the Presidential Pavilion, which should make things a bit more comfortable for us,' Hawa reminded them, passing out the stiff, laminated cards, including one for an enthralled Mustapha, who beamed in appreciation at this special privilege, which would see him sitting with the VIPs at the prayer meeting. Breaking away from the hordes heading for the open stands, Hawa led the way through a set of double doors at the bottom of the stadium's main bowl, pausing for a female church official wearing a purple dress and a headset to examine their passes closely. Smiling, she ushered them through, Mustapha visibly more impressed than the others at being granted access to such luxury.

Another woman, in an identical purple dress, showed them to their seats towards the back of the pavilion, a location

Hawa praised as a convenient spot from which to observe the events that were soon to unfold. Once settled, they looked out at the open stands that stretched in a giant circle around them, thronged with people, their figures reduced to indistinct splotches of colour in the bright stadium lighting.

The organisers had erected a large stage on the pitch, on which they had placed several rows of chairs and three solid-looking lecterns. Hoisted high up above was a huge banner announcing the retreat's theme in block capital letters. The stadium's scoreboard displayed Bible verses interspersed with giant images of Pastor Ranka. From time to time, they played the promotional video for the retreat they had watched on the ferry crossing, the crowd bursting into applause whenever it focused on Lion Mountain's charity initiatives.

From their seats in the Presidential Pavilion, Ramat name-checked the arrival of several dignitaries and top government officials, explaining who they were to Anaka and Hawa, her voice struggling to climb over the booming speakers. 'That's Cecil Ranka, Minister of Trade and Industry – the pastor's brother! He has been appointed to three successive governments. People say he is covered by the blessings of his brother, which grants him special luck.' The minister in question was a bald, rotund man wearing a white safari suit, accompanied by a slender woman in a matching white outfit, whom Ramat identified as his mistress. 'His real wife apparently lives in America with their children. But like a shameless goat who soils the streets with faeces, he now parades around with this side chick who is young enough to be his daughter.'

Next to appear was the choir, a fifty-strong ensemble swathed in the flowing purple and white of the church. Taking their positions on the stage, they broke into songs of praise, the stadium singing along to the lyrics displayed on the scoreboard. After a medley of rousing hymns, the choir retreated to the rows of chairs to the rear, to be replaced almost instantly by Amanda Ranka, her dark hair flowing behind her, dressed once more in a trouser suit, this time in that same ubiquitous shade of purple. Her appearance was met with thunderous applause, after which she spoke briefly, thanking the Sierra Leonean people for accepting her into their hearts, proving that true faith was colour-blind.

Next on stage was Pastor Ranka himself. As if pulled up by an invisible force, the entire stadium rose to their feet, the people standing on the pitch leaping into the air in adulation. The pastor, like his brother, was wearing a pristine white safari suit, a long purple scarf snaking around his neck and reaching to his knees. After a brief opening speech, during which he thanked the crowds for coming to worship with him, he launched into a rousing rant against *the diabolical, demonic and devilish powers of darkness*, and a country that had turned its back on the path of righteousness.

'Seeing our dark ways that transform our young sisters into modern-day Jezebels who dance in nightclubs and spread diseases through fornication and debauchery, God decided to punish this land. To punish it, like He punished the heathens of Sodom and Gomorrah!'

Ranka paused for effect, wiping his damp face with an oversized handkerchief as he took a swig from a bottle of mineral water that rested on his lectern.

'Do you think that the mudslides that killed our people in Regent four years ago was an ordinary natural occurrence? Do you not realise that rain was sent from the sky by the Almighty in the same way He sent rain to flood the world in the time of Noah?'

Hawa remembered the mudslide debacle well. Harrowing videos shared on social media had brought home the sheer horror of the situation, showing dead and broken bodies with mangled limbs being swept down the mountains of Freetown. The desperate need for accommodation in the already teeming city had seen several people erect *pan-body* shacks on the hills of Regent, illegal constructions thrown up without planning permission.

A government attempt to dislodge and destroy these settlements had been met with stiff resistance from the inhabitants. Tensions had risen, and there were running battles between riot police and the people who lived in the shacks, until the government climbed down from its belligerent stance, anxious to prevent the disorder from spreading.

Pastor Ranka had by this time dropped to his knees in apparent pain and regret at his inability to prevent the tragedy that had befallen the people of Regent. His voice rising and falling in a seductive rhythm, he told the crowd how God had given him the unique gift of divine clair-voyance, granting him a vision of the impending mudslide whilst he was living far away in Scotland. He had there-fore asked his congregation there to pray for Sierra Leone through dedicated services and spells of deep fasting.

'I picked up the phone and spoke to the then minister of

culture and religious affairs, asking him to gather men of God to pray for the nation, but I was not listened to! And you saw with your own eyes how Satan swept through Regent, leaving our people dead and devastated!'

The thronged stadium was reduced to total silence by the revelation of the great pastor's gift of clairvoyance and perception, which had made it possible for him to see the mudslide before it occurred. Before long, murmurs of indignation started to ripple through the crowd, as it bemoaned the politicians who had refused to accept the guidance of the great pastor, which would have saved the people of Regent from such stiff suffering and tragedy.

The next part of the programme saw the return of Amanda to the stage, flanked by the two ladies who had been with her during her television interview. Taking turns to speak, they outlined their global fundraising schemes and promised that the church would continue to do everything in its power to improve the circumstances of the afflicted and less fortunate in society, with a particular focus on children.

'A typical case of sugar-coating!' Hawa hissed, gripping Anaka's arm as she spoke. 'They bring these gullible girls from London and parade them as church ambassadors, with no mention of what happens to their sisters in Scotland! It's as if the abduction and murder of two women directly associated with their church does not matter!'

'And even in this country, it is known that the pastor has his hands in corruption. His brother steals government money in the same manner a squirrel steals groundnuts,' Ramat added, picking up her sister's anger.

Mustapha was oblivious to their rants. He had hardly sat down throughout the entire service, his eyes fixed on the stage, his mouth agape.

Pastor Ranka was back now, delivering his closing prayer, speaking of the importance of being close to God when the moon rolled over and a new year showed its face for the first time. He also prayed that the affairs of Sierra Leone should prove clean and prosperous in the months ahead. At the end of his address, the stadium erupted into a standing ovation, as a phalanx of bodyguards in sleek black suits suddenly appeared to escort him off stage and on to the running track, where a convoy of seven vehicles was parked in readiness. Pastor Ranka was ushered into the third vehicle, a Hummer, whilst a collection of church officials and other dignitaries climbed into the other vehicles. A police Land Rover manoeuvred to the head of the convoy, its blue lights revolving eerily in the dark night as the vehicles snaked out of the stadium to the accompaniment of cheers and applause, the choir on their feet again, swaying in time to their closing hymn.

Exiting the stadium was much easier for those seated in the Presidential Pavilion than for the throngs in the open stands, a back entrance depositing Hawa and the others on Syke Street.

They reached the Youyi Building car park after a ten-minute walk. The women waited at the gate whilst Mustapha nipped in to retrieve the Hilux, pausing to hold an animated conversation in Temne with one of the security guards, who apparently hailed from the same village as him.

As they waited for him to return with the vehicle, they

observed the masses heading home, whose loud, excited voices filled the air as they lauded the immense power of Pastor Ranka's preaching.

'Very few of the women are wearing trousers,' Anaka observed, a half-smile on her face.

'Many churches in this country preach that trousers are un-Christian attire for women,' Ramat replied. 'As you can see, most of them are wearing headties. Apparently, us women need to stay covered up in the presence of the Lord.'

'That's why we were getting some funny looks,' added Hawa. 'With our tight jeans and exposed heads, we definitely strayed from the dress code,' she laughed.

Mustapha had by this time arrived with the Hilux, ignoring the angry blaring of horns behind him as he stopped right in the middle of the road for them to climb in. Leaning out of the window, he called the driver behind him a *diseased ground pig*, hissing loudly as he eased the vehicle into traffic, which was, unsurprisingly, moving at a sedate crawl. As they inched along, Hawa pointed out buildings for Anaka, including St Joseph's Convent school, where she had taught for a couple of years, and Phase II Nightclub, the scene of many a long night on the dance floor.

The explosion when it came was massive. Their vehicle shuddered violently as the front windscreen disintegrated, showering them with glass. Howling like a sheep being slaughtered for Ramadan, Hawa unbuckled her seat belt in a haze and crawled out of the vehicle, slumping to the road. She could feel a ringing in her ears, noticing in her confusion that the dark streets were suddenly lit by an orange glow in the night sky. Mustapha was at her side, dragging her out of the street and propping her against the wall of a nearby building. In her daze, she noticed that the left side of his face was covered in blood, a slender shard of glass embedded just above his right eyebrow, reflecting a glint of the bright-orange light in the sky. Undeterred by his injury, Mustapha hurried away, returning soon after with Anaka. He propped her against the wall, her chin slumped on her chest, one of her arms bent at a strange angle.

Staggering to her feet, Hawa tottered back to the vehicle. All around her, people were running in panic, their screams climbing into her muffled ears. Ramat had been sitting in the passenger seat, next to Mustapha. Hawa recalled how she had nagged Ramat on her first day back in Sierra Leone, insisting that her sister should always wear a seat belt. Ramat had laughed, describing them as *posh overseas White people's nonsense*. 'Besides, our public transport is always overloaded anyway, Hawa. You cannot loop a seat belt meant for one person over two or more bodies.'

Opening the door and leaning into the vehicle, Hawa unfastened the belt that her sister had somehow remembered to put on. She dragged her out and they both collapsed onto the road, Ramat's body limp and still. Mustapha was suddenly at her side, scooping Ramat up and leading the way back to the wall, where he lay her next to Anaka, who was uttering soft mewling noises, like a kitten in pain.

Lifting her head, Hawa looked down the street. Several vehicles ahead of them were wreathed in flames that danced in the night air. A knot of people engulfed by fire ran past, their howls harrowing. To their left, a woman, also ablaze, leapt into a nearby gutter where there was no water, writhing in pain, her screams piercing their ears.

The last thing Hawa remembered as she slumped back against the wall was a smell she associated with barbeques – burning meat.

CHAPTER 36

Hawa was locked in a car boot with Anaka and Ramat. But this was a large boot, enabling them all to stretch their feet. Although they could not see each other, they chatted in the dark, Anaka at intervals volunteering to sing to cheer them up.

She opened her eyes to sharp light, a squeaking ceiling fan whirring above. She had been placed underneath a mosquito net, the edges tucked beneath a thick mattress that was covered by a pale-blue bedspread. She remembered how only the more affluent pupils at boarding school had been able to afford mosquito nets, their parents doing everything within their power to keep malaria at bay. Hawa sat up and moved her hands along the sides of the soft material until she found a slit which she parted, sliding her feet out onto the cold floor tiles.

She was in a long hospital ward. The bed opposite her also held a patient who was covered by a mosquito net. Glancing down the ward, she realised the others did not have the same protection. The only signs of life came from a cluster of relatives gathered around a bed towards the far end, the patient sitting up and laughing with them at something on a phone she was holding.

Rising, Hawa walked towards the door at the opposite side of the ward, noticing as she moved that she had been placed in a loose light-green nightdress that reached to her knees. At a desk outside the ward, she found a couple of nurses with their shoes off, their eyes glued to their phones as they discussed a video from which Hawa could hear shouting and sounds of distress.

Looking up, one of the nurses saw her and jumped up and hurried over. 'You should not be out of bed, Ramat. The doctor examined you this morning and said you should rest.'

'My name is Hawa. Ramat is my sister. Is she also here?'

'Sorry, Hawa. You look just like your sister, so we have been mixing up your names,' the nurse replied, smiling nervously.

'Where is Ramat now?'

'Oh, she is fine. Like you, she was also in that fire accident at Old Railway Line. But she is fine.'

'Where is she?'

'She was discharged yesterday and went home with your father and that America woman.'

'You mean Anaka? Was she hurt also?'

'Small injuries, Hawa. They'll be back to see you later. Visiting hours are usually in the evenings,' the nurse said, walking Hawa back to her bed.

'What happened at Old Railway Line?' Hawa asked, choosing to sit on one of the chairs next to her bed rather than return to the claustrophobic confines of the mosquito net.

'Ah ah, my sister Hawa!' the nurse said, sitting down on

the chair next to her. 'Big big accident that killed more than one hundred people!'

'What happened?' Hawa asked again, impatience lacing her voice.

'A tanker full of petrol was banged by a truck carrying iron stones. The tanker fell over, and petrol started to leak out. And then people ran to collect the petrol in containers. Your family said that you are a JC, so you might not know there has been a fuel shortage here for over three months. When people saw free fuel leaking into the street, they thought it was a good opportunity to solve this problem for themselves. There was a man with a kerosene lamp. People were fighting for the petrol and the lamp fell and broke. The fire walked on the fuel and the tanker exploded just like how you see in American movies. Fire everywhere. I've got videos here!'

Before Hawa could protest, the nurse had thrust her phone into her face. The video was taken the morning after the explosion, daylight laying bare the carnage and chaos in its grotesque entirety. A long line of vehicles had been reduced to twisted blackened wrecks, tufts of smoke still wafting up, curious people still ghoulishly stalking the scene, taking pictures and videos on their phones. On the ground lay countless bodies, dark skin burnt away to reveal sickening pink splotches of exposed flesh. A couple of policemen feebly tried to admonish the crowds to move back, their entreaties ignored by people who had come to gawp.

Her stomach now water, Hawa turned her face away from the nurse's phone. So that was the explosion she had heard and seen, the shock wave from the blast having reached their vehicle. She shuddered as she realised how close to death they had come. The nurse was still jabbering away, trawling her phone for more videos to show to Hawa, which she declined.

'Imagine such a big wahala falling on our country on New Year's. The president was on TV last night to declare a week of national mourning.' The nurse paused, her eyes on Hawa. 'They took the dead to Connaught Hospital. You are lucky that your people have money and you could be brought here to a private hospital. I saw another video which showed the bodies piled high in the mortuary at Connaught. Mortal men burnt black like firewood, my sister! The government has started to send big trucks to carry the bodies to Waterloo, where they'll bury them in mass graves like they did after those mudslides in Regent. Waterloo used to be known for good fried fish and cassava bread! But now, it has become the place where we bury our people when they die in big numbers!'

Feeling queasy at the graphic detail and therefore anxious for someone else to talk to, Hawa asked when visiting time was and if there was any way for her to contact her family.

'I can call them for you, no problem, Hawa. Don't worry. God has spared you. That fire explosion just shows that if God has marked your time to die, then nothing can save you.' The nurse paused, once more engrossed with some detail on her phone. 'Even the great Pastor Ronald Ranka, who was at the stadium preaching to everybody, was killed in the fire along with all his close people! And they were driving in expensive cars. It is a clear sign that when God has erased your name from the book of life, no amount of wealth or property can save you! And that is why we should be humble and have simple hearts in this life.'

Her family arrived to see her in the evening, Ramat toting a basket full of acheke and rice pap she had cooked earlier that afternoon. The only sign of trauma from the accident was a plaster just beneath her left eye, Anaka teasing that she looked like a rap star. The American had also got off lightly, the only damage being a sprained wrist that was still swaddled in a tight bandage.

Stephen had driven them to the hospital, having taken leave from his engineering job in Kono the moment he heard about the accident. Papa had also arrived with them, the furrows that adorned his forehead deeper than Hawa remembered as he asked how she was.

'I am fine, Papa. The nurse, the one who talks like a radio, said I banged my head and that I was unconscious.'

'We offer praise that you all survived, Hawa. We thank God — and Mustapha, who pulled you out of the vehicle. Human beings died in that fire like stamped-on cockroaches! Big problem in this country!'

'But why did folk run at that gas tanker? Surely, they should know gas is no joke and can catch fire quickly,' Anaka asked, shaking her head in confusion.

'Poverty strips you of dignity,' Hawa explained. 'People are so desperate, Anaka, that the scene of an accident often becomes an opportunity for them to scavenge something. All they could see was free petrol amidst a national shortage, which they can use themselves or sell to make money.'

'It's illiteracy! This kind of nonsense does not happen in any civilised or straightforward country!' Papa spat, his eyes hard. 'We have big problems here in Sierra Leone, mainly because we have people who are lawless and have no brains in their heads. How can you end up dead just because you wanted to steal petrol? Unbelievable!'

Having avoided the question most on her mind, Hawa eventually asked about Pastor Ranka.

'Remember that his convoy left the stadium first,' Ramat said, her voice low. 'So they were close to the junction where the truck hit the petrol tanker. All seven vehicles were swallowed by the fire, killing all the people in them instantly.'

'Amanda survived, though,' Anaka added. 'Apparently, she stayed behind at the stadium to talk to some important international guests about donating and stuff.'

Hawa returned home the following afternoon, the cut on her head covered by a light bandage as they climbed into Stephen's vehicle. Papa's Hilux had only suffered slight damage in the explosion, with the windscreen and one of the side windows shattered in the blast.

'How is Mustapha? Is he OK?' Hawa asked as they drove through the hospital's gates.

'He's well and fine,' Ramat replied from the passenger seat next to her husband, who was dressed in dark jeans and a Manchester United jersey.

'And how is Aunty Theresa? Did she come and visit me at the hospital, by any chance? Papa did not mention her yesterday.'

'She is in deep mourning at the death of Pastor Ranka

and has not eaten for three days, according to Papa. She has been going to Juba Hills day after day. They sit in Ranka's compound and sing hymns, some of them rolling on the ground in grief.'

Ramat paused to insert a CD. The vehicle's dashboard swallowed it, and soft soukous music flowed out of the speakers. Turning it down, she continued, swivelling to face her sister in the back seat. 'There are live reports from Pastor Ranka's house almost every day on the news. Even the BBC's *Focus on Africa* programme conducted an interview with his Amanda wife!'

'His followers are attributing his death to deep demonic forces,' Stephen said, manoeuvering the vehicle around the deep potholes at Lumley Junction. 'But then, some of them are saying that Pastor Ranka's death was a planned sacrifice to ensure that the fortunes of the country improve. Others insist that he did not die in the fire, that he escaped and travelled to a spiritual place where he is fasting and praying. There is, however, talk of a funeral on the first of February, with the church claiming they need plenty of time to put the affairs of his ministry in order. Rumours in this country have long legs and can travel far!'

'And what about Othella?' Hawa asked, her voice low.

'Your friend has been on TV every day with Amanda, updating people on what Lion Mountain plans to do next,' Anaka replied. 'Looks like she runs things for the whole church ministry now.'

Scotland

CHAPTER 37

Hawa sat cross-legged on the bed, checking her emails on her laptop. There was one from Detective McKeown confirming that Police Scotland had formally closed the search for Othella and that she was no longer classified as a missing person. Hawa had been to see McKeown on her return from Sierra Leone, filling in the gaps for her and explaining Othella's behaviour as best she could. 'A relief no doubt, Hawa, although the deaths of Stella Kowa and Naomi Wreh are still high on our list of priorities,' McKeown had said, her expression pained.

Next, she opened the university portal to find a message asking if she would be attending her graduation in person, and if she would require extra tickets for guests. She had always planned to take Othella, who had raved about the fun she had when she finished her studies. 'After all that sweat and struggle in this cold country away from home, hell yes I attended my graduation!' Othella had explained. 'I bought the highest heels possible and went up to collect my degree scroll like a model on a catwalk. After that there was a ball in the evening, but I organised an alternative party with a few friends. We hired a private room at the golf course just round the corner in Kingsknowe.'

With Othella still in Sierra Leone and Anaka back in the States, Hawa wondered if it was actually worth showing up to the ceremony at all. The American had spent a fortnight in Scotland when they returned from Freetown. Hawa used the time to explore some popular tourist locations with her, including Stirling, Dundee and Glasgow. 'Remember that it's non-negotiable that you come out to Atlanta before the year is over,' Anaka had declared as Hawa drove her to the airport. 'We met in unusual circumstances, for sure, not to mention the Hollywood-level drama that unfolded afterwards. But I will always cherish our friendship, not to mention the opportunity you gave me to visit Sierra Leone!'

Hawa missed her vivacity and spirit. The American had come into her life at the perfect moment, just before Othella disappeared, and now, for the first time since she had arrived in Scotland, Hawa found herself without a close ally or kindred spirit to navigate life with.

After a brief hesitation, remembering the difficult few months she had been through, she typed out a message expressing a desire to attend the graduation ceremony in person. A few clicks through the portal told her that she was automatically entitled to two free tickets for guests, but she had to pay a fee for the use of the academic gown. Settling the payment, she logged off, wondering who she should invite.

Hawa received a text from Kumba Matturi, saying that she would like to discuss something important with her. She had just returned from another shift at the hotel and settled herself in front of the TV when the message thrummed through. Hawa was in the process of replying to the message when the phone started to vibrate, the screen indicating that Kumba was calling her. Smiling, Hawa answered, putting Kumba on speaker and placing the phone face up on the coffee table.

'I knew you would have finished work by now and that's why I called you,' Kumba explained, her voice filling the room with its authority and confidence. 'I thought I should talk to you, my sister, about what happens next with this church ambassador business, especially as you were back home when fire took Pastor Ranka away from us!'

'Very sad indeed, Kumba,' Hawa replied, rising from the couch to draw the living room curtains. 'But I know little about the plans for the church. From what I hear, people have stopped attending on Sundays here in Edinburgh. Amanda is still in Sierra Leone, and there's nobody to coordinate affairs in Scotland.'

'And that is what I want us to discuss, Hawa. I have ideas on a good way forward for us ambassadors, but I need your educated book-learning sense to help me.' Kumba paused, and Hawa wondered if the call had somehow been disconnected. She was about to break the silence when Kumba continued. 'We must keep this church ambassador business running, my sister. There are many ways for us to continue to help our people back home – not everything has to go through the church. I have the contact details of many donors in my phones, and we should see if we can arrange something for them, so they continue to donate. And so, I want to have a small meeting for ambassadors at my house on this Friday coming. I would like you to come, Hawa. If we approach this business with our hands linked together, we will all benefit.'

Hawa struggled to find a place to park when she arrived at Kumba's house on Friday evening, eventually mounting her car on a grass verge halfway down the street.

Aisha opened the door, looking somehow younger than when Hawa had last seen her. 'Let me take your coat, Miss Hawa,' the girl whispered, and Hawa again felt uncomfortable with the girl's fawning attention, wondering if it was due to Kumba's constant reprimands as to what constituted appropriate behaviour for surviving in a White overseas country.

The living room was full when Hawa entered. The women who had not been able to secure chairs were sitting on the lush carpet, giggling in mini clusters of conversation. Kumba, as always, commanded attention, mainly thanks to her snug-fitting scarlet jumpsuit. She was talking to one of the women, her eyes alight as she jabbed a finger at her phone. Raising her head, she saw Hawa smiling as she made her way through the crowd to hug her.

'You came, my sister! It is so good of you, and I am happy to see your eyes. I have not seen you since you returned from Sierra Leone. Your body has gone down, and you are skinny like a dried bonga fish. Did you not eat good cassava leaves and red wallah rice back home? How was your sister's wedding? I saw the pictures you posted on Instagram. Very big occasion with lots of people looking happy. I liked the colour of the *ashobie* your family chose. You have good taste, my sister!'

Hawa thanked Kumba as she was steered towards the kitchen, sharing details of her trip home, the older woman smiling as she listened.

'There is food for you to eat before we start the meeting,' Kumba said, waving her hands over an array of foil trays bearing familiar dishes that brought a smile to Hawa's face. 'Aisha cooked all of this! That girl may not have learned how to entertain men, but she does know how to play with pots! There's jollof rice, foofoo and bitter leaf, acheke with fried snapper fish, and boiled cassava with beans cooked in palm oil. Everything. We spend so much time as ambassadors eating in White people's restaurants that we sometimes forget our own food,' she laughed.

The meeting started half an hour later, the flat by this time stuffed to capacity, with quite a few other women having arrived after Hawa. She recognised most of them from the Christmas fundraising dinner at the Dalmahoy, but there were a few she had not seen before.

'We will first say a prayer for Pastor Ronald Ranka, who brought us together under the banner of Lion Mountain,' Kumba announced, her eyes solemn. 'We pray that God grants him a good and clear road into the next world and that his spirit rests in peace!'

'Amen,' chorused the room.

'Lion Mountain Church here in Edinburgh remains closed, my sisters, but we must remember that we can pray to God in any location and that he will always listen to us. Therefore, we pray that our affairs in this faraway overseas country continue to be bright and good!'

'Amen,' the room said again.

'I called you here today so we can decide how to best continue as church ambassadors,' Kumba continued, her eyes sweeping different sections of her living room as she spoke. 'For although Pastor Ranka is no longer with us, we have a responsibility to push this programme further. And so, I have been going over in my mind how we can all work together with joined hands to organise something.'

'But how can we continue when Pastor Ranka has been taken from us?' asked a smallish woman who had kept her coat on over a nurse's uniform. She was one of the last arrivals, one Hawa had never seen before, and she had the tired eyes of someone who had just finished a long shift. 'Pastor Ranka and Amanda told us what to do and even helped with our paper business to stay in this country,' the woman continued. 'If today I have a red book, it is because of Amanda, who wrote emails to the Home Office and carried my immigration case on her head. We do not have such an influential person as her in your living room here tonight, Kumba,' she added. 'Our ambassador system was to raise money for Lion Mountain, but it also helped us get red books and places to sleep at night.'

The woman's comments were greeted with murmurs of agreement, Hawa finding herself nodding too.

'I hear what you are saying, my sister, but we have to move on,' Kumba countered, the smile on her face having gone from warm to forced. 'You speak clean truth, but we must organise and carry this business forward. Even these places to live you speak of belong to Ranka. What then happens if we are asked to move out now that he is dead? That could happen very soon, especially as we do not know what will be in Amanda's heart when she returns from Sierra Leone! And so, we need to come together and raise money to help ourselves if we are to survive comfortably in this country.'

'What do you want us to do, Kumba?' Hawa replied, her voice low. 'We must remember that not everything with this church ambassador business has been clean and pure. Two women ended up being killed and the police still do not know what happened. Should we not therefore at least wait for them to find their murderer before continuing?'

'That is in the hands of the police and God,' Kumba replied, the smile now completely erased from her face. 'Like I explained to you before at the Dalmahoy, my sisters, I have slept in a bed next to pain and suffering. When that rebel child stabbed my neck in Kono all those years ago, blood poured out of my body like when you open a tap. But I survived that, and today I am able to stand on my own two feet. I cannot go back to washing pots and pans in hotel kitchens or wiping the backsides of old people in nursing homes. Being an ambassador gives me control. People think that this business is about opening your legs to these rich men. But it is more about being able to control them and get what you want from them. A smile, good conversation, a meal in a restaurant, and a kiss can give you plenty of benefits even without sex.' She paused; her eyes were sad.

'I will be setting up a WhatsApp group to coordinate us. I can host fundraising functions no problem, just like Pastor Ranka and Amanda used to do in Broxburn. This house only has three rooms but there is an upstairs and a down-stairs, and it is the best space available, since Pastor Ranka put the rest of you in flats. Sierra Leone belongs to all of us, and we can all explain what's happening there to anybody who wishes to help. We can open a bank account to collect whatever money we make, and then we can decide how to help our people back home. If you are not interested, you can simply remove yourself from the WhatsApp group, and I will know that you have placed your heart somewhere else away from these affairs.'

'According to the government in this country, charities can be set up for relieving poverty, education, religion, health, saving lives, community development, the arts, amateur sport, human rights, religious or racial harmony, the protection of the environment, animal welfare, the efficiency of the armed forces, police, fire or ambulance services,' Hawa explained, reading from the laptop open in front of her. She was sitting at the black glass dining table in Kumba's kitchen, the older woman peering over her shoulder as she read.

They were joined by four of the women who had attended Kumba's first meeting, all sipping glasses of white wine. Kumba had made skewers of roast meat and rice bread, which they ate as they chatted.

'But why do these people set up charities for animals in this country?' one of the women, a lady named Mariama from Glasgow, asked. 'Humans must always be more important, which is how it is back home. There is not enough money to help human beings, and yet people in this country say we should help dogs and cats.'

'Dogs in this country are more important than us human beings,' Kumba added, laughing as she placed an empty wine bottle in a slender silver bin next to her fridge. 'It is in this country that I saw a dog shit, and then the human owner bend down and collect the shit with a plastic bag!'

'It's about responsibility,' Hawa explained, smiling at the other women. 'The dog is incapable of cleaning up after itself and it would be unfair for someone else to step in its business. And so, it makes sense that the human owner deals with it. Anyway, I am sure Kumba's charity will not be for dogs and cats. But you must decide what you want to do with money that you raise.'

'We should help the market women back home,' Kumba suggested, her eyes sad. 'Before I arrived here in Scotland and before the war came, I used to help my mother at the market. But the women had no place to leave their little children. So maybe we can build a day-care centre like they have in this country?'

'How will we raise money for this charity business?' one of the women asked. 'I understand us wanting to help our people back home, but we must remember that we do not have a lot of time. To survive every month in this country, I have to work many shifts for a nursing agency. As ambassadors, we raised money for the church, but we also got money from the donors for ourselves to rub our hands with.'

'We could hold a fashion show and cook our rich food for guests to eat,' Hawa suggested. 'And then we can charge people to attend with special prices for patrons. That's what we did when I was at university back home.'

'I like this idea,' Kumba added. 'We should organise the events that came out of Hawa's mouth. And I am not saying that you should not go out with donors like used to happen during Pastor Ranka's time. If a man sees you and admires you and wants to buy you food in their restaurants or take you for a trip in a plane, then you are allowed to say yes. As long as you stay safe and protect yourself, my sisters.'

CHAPTER 38

Kumba Matturi's first independent fundraising function for church ambassadors was hosted on a Friday, a month after she had summoned the other women to her house for the planning meeting.

Hawa had monitored developments through the WhatsApp group Kumba had set up, witnessing how the ambassadors' enthusiasm grew as the days passed. Kumba had asked Hawa to speak at the function, in the same manner as she had spoken at the Christmas fundraiser at the Dalmahoy. 'I can arrange these men and get them to attend, Hawa, but I do not have the book-learning knowledge to tell them about our problems back home. But you talk their English grammar like drinking water, so you can speak.'

Mainly out of curiosity, Hawa agreed, arriving in the Mini, which she parked in her now usual spot on the grass verge down the street.

In the drive in front of Kumba's house, she saw a thick red BMW 4x4, its number plate announcing it had been manufactured only last year. Assuming it belonged to one of the donors, Hawa rang the bell and waited.

Kumba herself answered, wearing a bottle-green trouser

suit in exactly the same cut and fashion as the ones Amanda Ranka favoured. As if inside Hawa's head, Kumba provided an explanation. 'As you can see, I've decided to dress just like Amanda. This is the way Hillary Clinton and other big women politicians usually dress on the television. This kind of dressing has respect, and so these men will know that what we are doing here is not a soft-play business.'

Kumba had installed a bookshelf in the hall since Hawa's last visit, and she explained her thinking as she led her through. 'Pastor Ranka had a lot of books in his house. I thought I would do the same to give this place some weight. And besides, books in this country are cheap, Hawa! I took a box to the big Tesco store at Corstorphine. A charity was selling them, and I paid £5 for over twenty books,' she laughed.

The living room was half full when Hawa walked in. Most of the women from the last meeting were present, mingling with several guests, all of them men. They were all were holding drinks, the conversation light and jovial.

Steering Hawa into the kitchen, Kumba told her where to find drinks, and asked if she had prepared something to say to the donors. 'It does not need to be a big speech. These are new people who I met on my last trip to St Andrews. They have heard of Pastor Ranka's church but know little about our country and so you can tell them about the war, Ebola and the mudslides.'

Before Hawa could fully process the request, Kumba pushed open the kitchen door, marching to the middle of her living room, a slender glass in one hand, the other raised to draw attention.

'My heart is very glad that you attended this meeting with us today,' she began, her voice full of confidence despite her halting English. 'We are here this evening at the number one function to see if we can continue to raise money for our people back home in Sierra Leone. Our sister, Hawa Barrie, is here tonight and was recently located in Sierra Leone and was there live during that Satan fire that killed Pastor Ranka at Christmas. Lion Mountain did so many good things to improve the country. But now that Pastor Ranka is dead, we are trying to see if we can continue his good work!'

Kumba's comments were met with applause from the room, which then settled back into its previous rhythm, with the women chatting to the guests. Hawa's recent trip back home made her the focus of attention, with several of the men drawn to her. Taking her time, she provided an abridged version of the speech she had delivered at the Christmas function, after which she answered questions on the debacles that had befallen her country and outlined what people could do to help, Kumba's beaming face hovering in the background.

Kumba descended on Hawa once they had bid farewell to the last guest just after 11 p.m., her eyes shining with admiration. 'Ah, my sister Hawa! I used to attack you for the big book-learning talk you used to do, but tonight I see that you are the one who can carry this of our business forward!'

'Happy to help for now, Kumba, but I'm not sure how far I can go with this,' replied Hawa, carrying a tray of empty glasses through to the kitchen, where other women were helping to tidy up. 'If you want these men to donate money to help our people back home, you must set up an official charity.'

'And that's why I brought you here! I have no information on how to set up this charity business, but you can climb into the internet and then phone people who can help us get the papers we need. God brings people together, Hawa, and you were brought into my life to direct and guide me.'

Prattling like an animated pepper bird, Kumba followed Hawa to her car when she left just before midnight. 'Is this what you are driving?' she asked, disbelief dancing in her eyes as she surveyed the dilapidated Mini. 'Ah, Hawa! To come all the way to this rich White country and then allow yourself to drive a rotten, *kpata-kpata* car like this? You should go to Arnold Clark, Hawa – even if your credit is dirty, they will give you a car that fits your status. Raise yourself up, my sister! We work very hard for money in this cold country, and we deserve some enjoyment. Did you not see the BMW in my drive? I got it last week. As long as you can afford the repayments, they will give you any car in this country!'

CHAPTER 39

After climbing the stairs to her flat after another shift at the hotel a couple of days later, Hawa was startled to find Aisha sitting on the floor in front of her door, a couple of bulky suitcases either side of her like protective pillars. The girl was wearing a black overcoat a size too small over a bulky sweatshirt that declared allegiance to some American college sports team. High-heeled shoes completed the ensemble, which seemed disjointed and discordant.

On seeing Hawa, Aisha stumbled to her feet, knocking over one of the suitcases, which she scrambled to erect before facing her.

'I am so sorry, Miss Hawa. I did not know where else to go, so asked around and was told you lived here! I tried to phone you but there was no answer. I told an old man with a dog who was entering the building that you were my sister, and he let me in.' The girl was crying, her tears leaving salt trails down her face.

'But why are you here, Aisha? Is everything OK? Don't cry. Tell me what happened. Are you not living with Kumba anymore?' Hawa had by this time opened the door and started to wheel one of the heavy suitcases into the hall,

Aisha doing the same with the other in her wake. 'Take off that jacket and come sit down.'

Aisha complied, shuffling into the living room after Hawa, who motioned to a chair. 'I was busy at work all day, which is why I missed your calls. So, what's wrong?'

'Kumba said I must leave the house immediately and threw my things into the street.'

'But she cannot do that, Aisha. Did you not say that Amanda and Pastor Ranka gave you permission to live in that house with her?'

'She says she is the chief ambassador and that since Pastor Ranka is dead, she can do what she wants,' sniffed Aisha.

'But you are such a lovely person who never sets any confusion in people's lives. Whenever I saw you with Kumba, you gave her the respect she demanded.'

'She wanted me to go out with one of the donor men who was at the meeting on Friday. Yesterday, she took me to the shops on Princes Street and bought me an outfit. She said that being with the man would help raise money for the benefit of all of us. And so, I got ready, and she helped me paint my face with make-up. But then the man arrived, and we drove away, Hawa. But when we stopped at the traffic lights, he put his hands under my dress. When he did this, I shouted and got out of his car and walked back home.' The girl dissolved into another fit of tears. Hawa, not having any tissues, nipped into the bathroom and returned with a few layers of toilet roll.

'What happened when you got home?' she asked, her voice a level lower.

'Kumba said that I had disgraced her. She said living in

such a lovely house in a White man's country did not come for free. That she had worked hard to be able to afford the lovely furniture in the house and that if I did not want to contribute, then I had to move out. When I argued, she slapped my face, saying that even her youngest sister back home is older than me and so I should speak to her with respect. Then she packed my things and threw them out!'

'Have you been with these donors before, Aisha?'

'Only once, in Pastor Ranka's house. But all I did was sit and talk in a room with a man from Glasgow. But I know nothing about man-business and how to be with them in a bed, Miss Hawa. I just want to be able to work and make clean money in this country to help my people back home.'

'Don't be upset, Aisha. You can live here with me, no problem. Anaka, my American friend, used to stay here with me, but she has gone back home. You can have her room. This is Pastor Ranka's flat also and I do not know what will happen when Amanda returns from Sierra Leone. But for now, we can stay here together. I'll take you to my agency tomorrow, and we can see if we can get you some shifts cleaning hotel bedrooms like me.'

The first thing that Hawa did as she moved through her phone later that evening was to leave Kumba Matturi's WhatsApp group.

Aisha proved to be a most biddable flatmate, Hawa again insisting that the girl drop the 'Miss' when addressing her and simply call her Hawa. 'Age in itself is not an achievement,' she laughed. 'Besides, out in these countries, everybody uses everybody else's first name. So, I am simply Hawa.'

She had taken Aisha to her agency on Morrison Street. Lesley, the proprietor, was delighted to secure a new recruit. Hawa managed to get them shifts together, taking the responsibility for teaching the girl the protocols of the hotel, and they both travelled to work and back in the old Mini.

Despite Hawa's protests, Aisha insisted on regularly cleaning the flat, and her attention to detail was stunning, even for someone with the high standards of cleanliness that came from living under Aunty Theresa's control. And though she had been adamant that Aisha's cleaning shouldn't extend to her room, she had returned home on a couple of occasions to find her bed snugly made, the pillows stacked in the same Jenga pattern that Anaka had favoured. Assuming it was some social media fad, Hawa had just smiled, the arrangement reminding her of her American friend.

Later that evening, after they had shared a meal of boiled yams and pepper soup, Aisha revealed that she had been in her third year of secondary school back in Sierra Leone when she left to move to London. 'My mother's sister filed papers for me to move here, Miss Hawa – I'm sorry, Hawa. But when I got here, she did not put me in school for over six months. Instead, I just stayed in the house to look after her children whilst she worked night shifts in hospitals and nursing homes. Her children's father had left her, so she lived alone. The children liked me a lot, Miss Hawa, but I was getting angry and hot-hearted because I wanted to go to school. Staying in that flat all the time and taking care of my aunt's children meant that my own affairs were not walking forward. And so, I asked my aunty to put me in school. But she shouted and called me ungrateful. And then, the next

Sunday, when we went to church, Aunty complained about me to Pastor Steele. She said that I now had the demon of disobedience in my heart and was not listening to her advice anymore. Pastor Steele called me to the front of the church before the entire congregation and made me kneel down as he prayed on my head. He then advised my aunty that I move to Scotland, where there were more opportunities. Pastor Steele handed me over to Pastor Ranka and I was brought here. And then they said I should live with Miss Kumba, who carried seniority within Lion Mountain and would therefore help grow my faith.' Her mention of Kumba's name seemed to place a shroud of sadness over the girl, the memories of their separation weighing heavy.

'But you are safe and settled now, Aisha. You can try to do the things you want to do,' Hawa said.

'I would like to study nursing. Or work in a school. When I was in London, Pastor Steele said that although I did not have big education at the moment, I could perhaps become a classroom assistant. Or I could work in after-school clubs helping with children. I did well when looking after my aunt's children in London, and therefore I have the patience.'

'All good plans, Aisha,' Hawa laughed, her eyes warm. 'We could look at enrolling you on a college course, perhaps. We could check out a few prospectuses and see if there's something to suit you. Do you have any other ideas?'

'Oh, Miss Hawa, you are so kind and nice! My heart would like to be able to drive a car in this country, just like you!'

Hawa took Aisha out in the Mini three times a week. They

left just after nine each evening when the roads were naturally quieter. 'Driving lessons are very expensive and we are trying to save money. We will go in my car, and I will find a quiet place to teach you. And when your confidence grows, we will book you actual lessons, and then a test.'

Aisha proved to be a quick learner, Hawa talking her through gear changes and manoeuvres as they travelled through Balerno and Currie. At other times, they would take the Long Dalmahoy Road all the way to Kirknewton and down to Ratho and Newbridge, where they parked and ordered food from the McDonald's there, chatting and sharing memories of their respective lives back home in Sierra Leone.

CHAPTER 40

As usual, Hawa had struggled to fall asleep, slipping under at just after three in the morning. And she was woken the next morning by Aisha gently shaking her shoulder, her voice worried and urgent.

'The police are here, Miss Hawa. The woman says she knows you and that she tried phoning you, but there was no reply.'

Her words drained the final dregs of sleep from Hawa's body. Having gone to bed in an oversized T-shirt, she pulled on a pair of tracksuit bottoms and followed Aisha out of the room, stifling a yawn as she did so.

Detective Inspector Cynthia McKeown was waiting for her in the living room.

'Sorry to disturb you, Hawa. I called, but there was no answer, and it couldn't wait. Shall we sit down?'

'Absolutely,' Hawa replied, her mind whirring. What reason could McKeown have to visit her this early? Aisha had retreated to the kitchen, Hawa deducing from the sound of the kettle that she was making tea. The detective took the same seat she had chosen on her last visit, balancing a green binder on which she placed her phone on her lap.

'Sorry to come this early in the morning, Hawa. I was wondering if you know a woman named Kumba Matturi?'

'Yes.'

'In what capacity do you know her?'

'Through Lion Mountain Church.'

'Have you ever been to Kumba Matturi's house?'

'She has plans to set up a charity. After Pastor Ranka's death and the apparent closure of the church, Kumba thought that we should get together to form an organisation to raise money to help with problems back home. And so, she invited us over to discuss strategy. We then held a charity function at her house.'

'How many people were at this function, Hawa?'

'Quite a few. Mostly women from back home and donors invited by Kumba. Is everything OK, detective? Is Kumba OK?'

'Kumba is fine physically, though she's very shaken. There was an incident at her house last night and she phoned the police. Apparently, somebody with a key attempted to enter her property, and the only thing that stopped them was the fact that she had fitted deadbolts to her door. When the person could not gain access, they set fire to her car. We believe the person responsible must be someone she knows since they had a key.' McKeown paused to clean her glasses with a handkerchief that she extracted from the inside pocket of her jacket, her movements neat and precise. 'Kumba says that until recently she lived with one Aisha Brewah, who now lives here? She tells us that they had a serious disagreement, after which Aisha moved out. Is Aisha the woman who let me in just now?'

'Are you thinking that Aisha's a suspect? She's just a child! And she was here all through the night.'

'I hear what you're saying, Hawa, but I would like to ask her a few questions, if possible.'

As if on cue, Aisha entered from the kitchen bearing a tray. She placed it on the table then sat down next to Hawa, facing McKeown.

'Aisha Brewah? I hope you don't mind me asking you a few questions. Your former flatmate, Kumba Matturi, was subjected to a very unpleasant experience last night. Someone attempted to break into her house and then her car was set on fire. When I asked if there was anyone who might have a grudge against her, she mentioned that you'd had a serious falling out in the recent past?'

'She asked me to leave her flat, officer. And so, I put my things in a taxi and came here to stay with Hawa,' Aisha whispered, her eyes to the carpet.

'And you were here right through the night?'

'Yes. I worked a day shift at the hotel, but I was home by six. Hawa and I ate together, and I went to bed after the ten o'clock news. I left Miss Hawa up alone watching television.'

'That's exactly what happened,' Hawa cut in. 'And it's quite a distance from Balerno to Clermiston. I don't think she is the person to travel all that way without a car just to do something so horrible to Kumba.'

Detective McKeown accepted a cup of tea, then asked a few more questions, and when she left, Hawa offered to walk her down to the car park.

'I know that Aisha could not have attacked Kumba herself, but I need to cover all the bases. Kumba saw the perpetrator from the upstairs window, running away as her car burned, and we are pretty certain that it was a man.'

'Do you think this is connected to the deaths of Naomi and Stella?'

'It's too early to say, Hawa. But it is concerning that somebody continues to target women from Sierra Leone, specifically those connected to Lion Mountain. God only knows what would have happened if they had gained access to Kumba's house last night.'

CHAPTER 41

With Othella back home, Hawa was struggling to find a place to get her hair done for her graduation. Remembering how good Jattu's had looked at the birthday party for her son all those months ago, she sent her a text to ask if she could suggest someone. Jattu replied almost immediately, recommending a lady named Anne-Marie, who lived in Glasgow. She added that she was free over the weekend and would happily make an appointment for Hawa, pick her up from Glasgow Central Station, and take her to Anne-Marie's place.

True to her word, she was waiting when Hawa arrived on an early afternoon train from Edinburgh, pulling her into a tight hug that was accompanied by the scent of expensive perfume.

'We must hurry, because I parked in a place I am not supposed to, my sister. Parking in these big cities is no play-play business. You came alone? Has your American friend returned to her home country?' Jattu asked as they nipped across a busy road to where she had abandoned her Range Rover in front of a JS McColl's in a bay marked LOADING ONLY.

'You mean Anaka? Yes, she went back to America. But before she left, she drew the attention of our Khalil, who liked her much,' Hawa laughed as she climbed into the passenger seat of the big vehicle.

'Which Khalil are you talking about, Hawa? You mean big Khalil who dropped out of nursing to be a bodyguard at nightclubs?'

'That Khalil indeed.'

'But he's unserious and has no direction! To come all this way to this overseas country and to then just waste your life on foolishness,' Jattu said, fiddling with the Bluetooth settings as she eased the vehicle into traffic.

'He's a nice and sweet man, Jattu,' Hawa said seriously. 'Always had a good heart and can be trusted. He's sad that Anaka has gone away and says he wants to go visit her in America.'

'A good heart and nice character do not pay the bills, Hawa. My husband is twenty years older than me, and my people used to laugh at me, saying I was dating a silver fox grandfather only for his money. But he is kind to me. And although they say he is old, he produced sperm that jumped into my womb and gave me a child.'

They laughed as they travelled, Jattu joining the bypass before exiting at Junction 1A for Polmadie. 'Anne-Marie lives on the south side, not too far from Hampden Park where they kick football,' she explained. 'I texted her yesterday to say we were coming, and she said no problem. Did you bring your own hair?'

'I took care of Othella's possessions after she disappeared, so I just helped myself to a couple of packets of Brazilian hair. I'm sure she won't mind.'

'I heard how your eyes found Othella alive and well in Sierra Leone, Hawa. If God has not marked somebody's name to be removed from this world, then they will not be removed from this world. I saw videos on WhatsApp of her giving big speeches about Lion Mountain, talking about the importance of not just relying on prayer but also taking steps to develop our country.'

'Othella has decided to walk her own path,' Hawa replied.

As Jattu accelerated away from a pedestrian crossing, her voice dropped to a conspiratorial whisper. 'But between you and me, Hawa, people are saying that they did not find Pastor Ranka's dead body in his car. That such a powerful man of God cannot be taken from this world in an accident! I think he is alive, my sister, and will reappear to preach falsehoods in our country again!'

Anne-Marie lived in a top-floor flat in Shawlands, the limited parking options available forcing Jattu to mount her vehicle onto a pavement nearby.

She opened the door herself, wearing a burgundy dressing gown, her hair rising above her like an untrimmed hedge. 'Haven't been up long,' she explained, although it was almost two in the afternoon, and she had agreed a midday appointment with Jattu. 'I worked a tough agency shift last night, observing a young woman who refuses to eat and harms herself. This country never stops amazing me, my sisters; they have food like sand on the beach and yet people deliberately refuse to eat! In all my years back in Sierra Leone, I never came across this sickness!'

'Eating disorders and self-harm are much more complex than people think, my sister,' Hawa said carefully. 'What they are faced with is very sad.'

The hairdresser had by this time led the way into a tastefully furnished living room whose high windows looked on to the gardens below. A chair stood facing a slender mirror that had been leant against a wall festooned with African carvings in deep brown wood. 'Let me jump in the shower and I will do your hair no problem. Sit down and relax. I'll be five minutes.'

Anne-Marie disappeared from the room, leaving Jattu and Hawa in conversation, returning a few minutes later with her head covered by a bright orange cloth, the rest of her looking stunning in a form-fitting outfit woven from Ghanaian kente cloth. She chatted away as she arranged Hawa's head in neat cornrows in preparation for the long weave. Not one for holding back, she was soon telling them how she had paid for a plane ticket for a man from Sierra Leone to join her here in Scotland, only for him to leave her.

'He said I'm too curvy and that I cook African food all the time,' Anne-Marie laughed, her eyes bitter. 'And then I saw a message on his phone. The rag of a man was texting some straight-cut White girls when I was out at work. I tried to get him a job, but he said that he has a master's degree from back home and so would not wash dishes in kitchens or do care work. And so, I alone in this cold country worked shifts like a mad dog, whilst also doing hair to support us both. He moved out two weeks ago, and I hear he is now living with a skinny Scottish woman in a place called Coatbridge. Nonsense idiot!'

'And that is why I settled for a White man,' Jattu laughed, winking at Hawa, who was also shaking in laughter under Anne-Marie's hands, as her new friend methodically stitched the strips of synthetic hair into the cornrows.

Halfway through, Anne-Marie stopped to offer them food, explaining that she had also taken to making authentic Sierra Leonean dishes to sell. 'I have cassava leaves cooked with nut oil, potato leaves, okra, tola and even crain crain. I store them in my freezer in little plastic tubs – £5 each. Would you like to try some? My cooking is so good, you'll chew off your fingers in appreciation.'

Hungry, Hawa and Jattu accepted her offer, so Anne-Marie went to the kitchen to heat the dishes. She returned shortly, and all three of them settled down to eat, chatting further about the pressures of living as Black women in cold, faraway Scotland.

'And what about this business of our sisters being killed and locked in car boots in that Edinburgh place of yours?' Anne-Marie asked, suddenly serious. 'We escape war and hunger in Sierra Leone, only to come and die in this country? I heard also that Kumba Matturi's car was burned! How is she coping? At least now you have found your friend Othella?' She pronounced Othella's name without the H, coming out as *Otella*.

'The police are looking into who set Kumba's car on fire and who killed Stella and Naomi, but their investigation moves too softly softly for my liking,' Hawa replied in a tired voice.

Anne-Marie finished Hawa's hair about three hours later, leaving her with a stylish light-brown weave that perfectly complemented her Fula skin tone. 'This is brilliant, Anne-Marie. Even Othella would be proud. Thanks so much. How much do I owe you for the hair and also for the food?'

'£100, my sister. The food is a free sample, though, so no charge. You can hopefully scatter my name as far as Edinburgh by telling your people about my cooking skills. I drive and deliver and can cook whole pots if people are interested. Please even tell your White friends and work-mates. Back home, only senior service and money people eat in top restaurants. And so, even when we find ourselves in these overseas places, we instead prefer parties where we fill our stomachs for free and then carry home take-away portions in plastic containers.' She sidled back over to Hawa, smoothing the edge of the newly installed weave and peering closely at it to make sure it was perfect.

'If I had my way, I'd open a restaurant in this country, my sisters,' she continued, finally satisfied with Hawa's hair. 'Indians, Chinese, Italians and even Moroccans have restaur-ants in this Glasgow city. Why then can us Sierra Leoneans not also have a restaurant where we can sell our own food? It is because we never speak with one word, and instead pull each other down with jealousy and two-tongued gossip!'

By the time Hawa got on the train back to Edinburgh later that evening, Anne-Marie and Jattu had managed to solve – in theory, at least – all the problems afflicting African women in Scotland, chief amongst them being lofty plans to open a restaurant in the centre of Glasgow that traded exclu-sively in Sierra Leonean cuisine before the year was out.

CHAPTER 42

Santa arrived in his church suit on the morning of Hawa's graduation ceremony to drive them all to Stirling. He had exchanged the creaking Volkswagen Golf for a similarly suspect Fiat Uno, which he insisted had a brilliant engine because it had belonged to an old disabled woman who seldom drove. 'And since this is a special occasion, I thought it would be good for me to use my new car for the first time. You are the guest of honour, Hawa, and we all know that you will be pouring alcohol in your stomach later on. And therefore, allow me to drive you home,' he chuckled as he opened the back door of the vehicle with a comedic flourish. Elijah Foot-Patrol was absent, however, away in London for a dinner and dance organised by the UK branch of their country's ruling political party.

'For the degree of Master of Science in International Conflict and Cooperation, with Distinction, Ms Hawanatu Barrie,' announced a grey-haired professor draped in an elaborate crimson academic gown. As Hawa strutted across the stage to receive her scroll, she could hear Aisha cheering through the polite applause, bringing a smile to her face.

On the drive back to Edinburgh, Santa praised Hawa's big brain, describing her as a *sense-bird who should thank God always for the gift of intelligence.*

Along with Aisha and Santa, Hawa had also invited Khalil for a graduation meal at Rumbidzai's Room. She had also asked Debbie and Karen-Louise, a couple of girls who worked for her agency and had been especially kind to her when she first arrived in Scotland, helping her to negotiate the complexities of chambermaiding.

Karen-Louise had baked a large lemon drizzle cake, and Debbie was weighed down with giant balloons and a card bearing congratulatory messages for Hawa. When they arrived at the restaurant, Rumbidzai insisted on personally serving them, assisted by the same tight-trousered waiter from Hawa's first visit with Anaka. Santa, delighted at being in the company of so many attractive women, had seated himself between Karen-Louise and Debbie, regaling them with stories of life back in Sierra Leone, whilst they spent their time convincing him that the haggis was *an actual Highland beastie.*

They took pictures throughout the evening, experimenting with filters that contorted and mangled their images, reducing them all to helpless laughter. At the end of the night, Santa insisted on reciting a convoluted prayer celebrating Hawa's accomplishment, thanking *Jehovah Ebeneezer* for covering *his sister* in the Blood of Jesus, whilst pleading that her path into the future remain prosperous and pure.

It was snowing when they left the restaurant, Rumbidzai coming out with them whilst thanking Hawa profusely for her continued support. 'It is always good to see fellow African faces at my place. Come back anytime!'

Khalil had convinced the others to head to Sing City for a karaoke after-party, but Hawa had to decline because she was working an early shift at the hotel the next day. She was adamant that Aisha go along, however. 'Living in this country must also be about enjoying yourself once in a while, Aisha. Khalil will take care of you. I've heard you singing in the shower. Go try something,' she laughed, and further encouragement was provided by Debbie and Karen-Louise as they piled into Khalil's car.

'It's just you and me, my sister,' Santa said as he positioned the remainder of the lemon drizzle cake Karen-Louise had baked for Hawa on his back seat. 'I will drop you off, no problem. I have an early shift tomorrow also and need to embrace my bed as soon as possible.'

Grateful, Hawa gave him a hug, making no attempt to stifle a yawn as she climbed into the passenger seat, which had been pulled a little too close to the dashboard. Reaching down, she adjusted the lever, easing herself back to create space for her long legs. Having never really been fans of high heels, her toes had started to throb, and she wiggled her feet out of her graduation shoes.

The snow thickened as they travelled, Santa's wipers squeaking as they battled to keep the white flakes at bay. 'It will be gone by the morning though,' he laughed. 'When I was back home, we used to watch movies in the video store down at the local junction, and I thought it snowed all the time in White people's countries. But I have been here for about four years now, and I have only really seen snow two times and it is never very heavy. What scares me is that black ice that covers the road and makes our cars skate!'

Hawa mumbled a reply about how real drastic snow happened in countries like Russia and Canada, the falling whiteness leaving her calm and at peace. They arrived at the Balerno flat, and she struggled back into her shoes, stepping gingerly out of the car for fear of slipping over. True to Santa's predictions, the snow had not settled on the ground, reduced instead to slimy mush.

Santa came up to the flat with her, carrying the cake and the bunch of celebratory balloons, which swayed in the wind as they crossed the car park. Once inside, Hawa sliced off a narrow chunk of the cake, which she placed on a saucer in the fridge. She gave the rest to Santa, his wide grin conveying his pleasure.

'Thanks for a lovely evening, Hawa, my sister, and for treating me to a lovely meal. You have always been a clean-hearted person who treats people with respect and dignity. Like I said in my prayers, your affairs will stay away from darkness, and you will never encounter a situation in life that will cause you to beat your head in pain.'

'I should be thanking you, Santa! For all the money you spend on petrol ferrying us around and for being a lovely flatmate before I moved out. I'll call you tomorrow. Stay safe and enjoy the cake.' After another hug, he was gone, Hawa following the glow of his headlights as he drove out of the car park, his tyres leaving narrow furrows through the slush.

Alone, she showered, playing soft Spotify music on her phone. She then brushed her teeth and rubbed camphor cream over her face, arms and legs. In bed, she went to her phone as per usual to gauge the flow of social media.

There was a flood of congratulations waiting for her on *The Queens of Sheba* group, almost all of her former classmates sending messages of elation and praise. Just after the ceremony in Stirling, Aisha had taken several pictures of Hawa hoisting her degree certificate to her chest. Hawa had posted them on Facebook and Instagram during dinner, and the likes on her post had already climbed to over 260.

Smiling, she moved on to messages from Ramat, who in her usual scatterbrained manner had offered Hawa only a short note of congratulations, before going on to lament the fact that her husband's family had already begun to pressure her to get pregnant.

There was also a message from Tina Kanu, along with a video of a Lion Mountain pastor in Kailahun, in the east of the country. Tina had secretly recorded a conversation with him, during which he confirmed that he sucked the breasts of women in his congregation because *the spirit lies in the breast of a lady, and that even when babies are young, they suckle the breasts to get fulfilment of the Lord*. The pastor had then gone on to explain this bizarre ritual as a most appropriate way of removing sin from the bodies of women. Tina had published the story online and in the print edition of *The Satellite* to unsurprising ambivalence from most of the country.

Shaking her head in disbelief, Hawa connected the phone to its charger and laid it on the bedside table. She closed her eyes.

★

The relief and pleasure of graduation left her in a light sleep from which she was woken by movement in the living room. Her eyes half open, she pulled her phone towards her to check the time. Guessing that it must be Aisha back from karaoke, she closed her eyes again, hoping to settle back into the sleep from which she had been jolted. She half listened to the faint noise outside her room, wondering if Aisha would visit the microwave as usual to make the hot chocolate she was fond of.

The sounds, however, did not migrate into the kitchen, and Hawa drowsily assumed that Aisha was going straight to her room. Then there was movement at her door. Someone was easing it open, the glow from the orange street light casting a thin line across her bed.

'You back already, Aisha?' she said in a low voice, lifting her head.

'It's not Aisha. It's me, my sister. Santa.'

Now fully alert, Hawa sat up in the bed, sleep jumping away from her as she switched on the bedside lamp. Santa was standing just inside her room, a half-smile on his face.

'I thought you left, Santa. Did you forget something? I must have left the door open. Silly me!'

'No, you locked the door, Hawa. I have had your spare keys since you first moved in. In fact, I have keys for all of Pastor Ranka's flats.'

'But why would you have our keys, Santa? I know we shared the flat in Longstone, but I live here now with Aisha.' As she spoke, she snaked her hand across to her phone, pulling it free of the charger, her eyes not leaving Santa.

'I've come to take you away, Hawa. You have always

extended kindness and respect to me, and so I plan to take you with soft hands.'

Her heart now thumping, she raised the phone to call 999. She remembered how last summer they had spent some time at the beach near Portobello, playing volleyball with a group of strangers. They had all laughed at Santa, who had struggled to keep up and move his bulk around, often collapsing onto the sand as the ball sailed over his head. She knew there was no way he could reach her before she dialled.

In a blur that defied his size, Santa was on the bed in a flash, smashing the phone out of her hand. It flew across the room, ricocheting off the wall before slithering out of sight under the bed.

'I said that I plan on taking you away with soft hands, Hawa, so don't behave in a manner that will make my heart hot!' Santa spat, his eyes like those of a snake.

Jumping off the bed, Hawa dashed for the door, Santa coming after her with a roar of frustration. She knew that there was no way she could make it out the front door, and so instead headed for the living room, with the intention of putting the big couch between them. She was just out of the bedroom when she heard something swish past her ear and explode onto her left shoulder, driving her to the floor. The pain bit into her, wrenching a howl of anguish from her throat, as she curled into a foetal position. Santa was by this time standing over her, holding a piece of wood that in the half-light of the living room looked like the leg of a table.

'I had planned to let you put on some proper clothes to cover you up before I took you away, Hawa. But if you decide to jump about like a stray rat, you'll have to come as you are!'

She had gone to bed in a loose extra-large football jersey she had bought in one of the sports shops in the Livingston Centre. Kneeling beside her, Santa spoke into her face, his voice having dropped to its usual cadence, as if he were just asking her for something to eat, or suggesting a movie for them to watch as was often the case when they had lived together in Longstone. 'The car is downstairs, Hawa. And if you do not want me to use this wood on you again, you will come quietly.'

He then allowed her to put on a dressing gown, her hands shaking as she pulled the garment around her. Then he stood over her as she chose a pair of trainers that she used for the occasional jog, the table leg swinging in his hand, his eyes never leaving her.

At the door, he paused to look at the wall on which they had placed the pictures of the African icons, his eyes bitter. 'And one day, by God's power, Hawa, people will hang pictures of Pastor Ronald Ranka up on the wall as a great man from Africa who walked a holy path in this world! It is only people like you who do not have eyes to realise true greatness!'

Locking the flat, Santa posted the key through the letter box. 'I guess I do not need your keys anymore. Pastor Ranka gave me keys to all the flats where his ambassadors stayed and asked me to monitor them. I have been coming and going often when you and Aisha are away. I do not do anything unholy whilst here, Hawa. I just walk around and admire how brand new everything is, whilst wondering at the power that was placed on the head of the pastor to allow him to make sure that us Black people exist in this society with dignity and respect. You do not even make your bed, Hawa, even though the good book states that cleanliness is next to godliness. And so, I have to come once in a while to tidy and make your bed and arrange your pillows. You women, who are just like Eve and Jezebel and Delilah and Salome in the Bible, brought evil into the church. You decided to open your legs for donors, and therefore trouble was brought to the door of Pastor Ranka. And so, he had to go back home, where fire carried him away from us! But a man like him cannot really die, and a dream entered my head, informing me that he is alive and will come back to us soon! The light of the sun might be hidden by dark clouds, Hawa, but it always returns to shine bright!'

They were by this time descending the stairs, Hawa forced to lead the way, thinking of perhaps trying to run. As if inside her head, Santa spoke from a couple of steps behind her, his voice laced with grit and menace. 'I am fat, Hawa, but I have big arms that can throw things. You would not want me to throw this wood at your head, my sister. If you think of running or screaming, this wood will make you regret it!'

The car park was deserted, the snow from earlier having picked up again, the cold biting at Hawa's exposed legs as they walked. Santa had left his new vehicle in a bay in the shadow of a clutch of storage units that blocked the glow from the orange street lights.

'This is not actually my car, Hawa. I just borrowed it for today. It belongs to Nancy. You know Nancy? The old busybody lady who lives in the flat next door. The one who complained sometimes that I always play loud gospel music. As if you can put a volume on the music of the Lord? She's away on holiday. But I know where she leaves her spare key for her cleaning lady. And so I went in and took her car keys. I needed a special car just for you, Hawa; to take you to graduation and also for you to sleep in! This is just like that movie *Django* that I watched with you last year. You remember when that slave girl misbehaved and ran away, and how they caught her and put her in that hot box in the sun? You have also misbehaved by opening your mouth on television, putting Pastor Ranka's business in the street. And so, you must also go in a box.'

He had reached the car, thrusting the key into the lock. Her heart jumping, Hawa spun and ran, heading for the dark path that led to the canal. Santa let out a bellow of rage and came after her, throwing his table leg at her retreating back. It glanced off her head, causing her to stagger, her feet unsteady on the melted snow. Off balance, she fell flat on her stomach, a sob of fear and frustration jumping out of her. She clambered to her feet and tried to run again, hampered by a twisted ankle. She had taken about five more steps when Santa's bulk hit her, the weight of his body driving her to the ground, and her head slammed into the squelchy grass underfoot.

As somebody who had always struggled to sleep, Hawa found the boot of the car relaxing, the red glow of the lights and the purring engine calming her like a lullaby. The pain in her shoulder and ankle were now subliminal throbs, present but not to the point of severe discomfort. Her head hurt the most, and she could taste blood and dirt in her mouth. She could feel a thick blanket at the bottom of the boot, and she wondered if it had always been there, or if Santa had placed it there out of consideration for her comfort.

After a while they stopped, the pain in her head having also reduced to a dull ache. She heard a car door slam, and then the jingling of keys. Holding her breath, she listened out, trying to discern where they were. She heard another car door, quite close by, open and close, and then somebody opened the back door of the car she was in, placing something on the seat.

They were moving again, loud gospel music thumping out of the car's speakers. She attempted to read their movements, feeling the car stopping occasionally at what she guessed were traffic lights. She tried to shout whenever this happened, her voice sounding hoarse, the din of Santa's music drowning it out. At some point they seemed to drive much faster, and Hawa guessed they must be on a bypass or motorway. She thought of Stella Kowa, who had been taken from Granton only to be discovered all the way in Dalgety Bay. Perhaps Santa was doing the same with her, seeking a faraway place to abandon her.

A little later, she felt the car's tyres bumping over some slight gaps in the road and wondered if they were going over a bridge. Raising her hands, she pushed hard against the boot's lid, the surface cold and unyielding. She tried kicking, the toes of her trainers pounding against metal, the sound once again swallowed by Santa's music. Out of breath, she gave up, tears of frustration running down her face, as she slipped into what felt like another light sleep.

She was woken by the cold air. She opened her eyes to the black sky above, Santa's hulking silhouette towering over her. She could make out the table leg in his hand, and a wide carton underneath his armpit.

'We have arrived, Hawa. I will leave you here to learn a lesson. The intention is never to kill you church ambassadors, which is why I leave you in places where people can find you. Stella Kowa was found as I intended, but God decided to take her from this world. I left Naomi right in front of her house and to this day I cannot understand why nobody found her, Hawa. We are in very ungodly times and we must not allow people who do not believe in God to destroy all the good progress our church brings to our lives. You ambassadors brought satanic behaviour into a holy space, and our good church became a place of shame and sacrilege. Pastor Ranka introduced you to donors to raise money. But then you started sleeping with them and the newspapers and the television said that our church is no good and is an escort service! And after Pastor Ranka died, you satanic women decided to set up your own organisation, showing no respect for all the great things the church did for you!'

Dropping the table leg, he emptied the carton over Hawa, a shower of tree-shaped air fresheners cascading onto her. 'This will make you understand that I am not a monster, my sister. The sweet smell will give you courage and help you understand that your punishment is not about performing pointless wickedness on your body. God bless you, Hawa, and if it is not your time to leave this earth, then people will locate you.'

The boot slammed shut, the dark sky above disappearing from view. Giving in, she closed her eyes, relieved that the insomnia that she had for so long detested had chosen to stay away.

Again, the cold woke her. Hawa tried to stretch, hoping that the movement would drive out the numbness that had consumed her legs. The blanket beneath her felt wet, and she wasn't sure if the liquid was from the ice and snow outside or from inside her body. The dull aches in her shoulder, head and ankle had returned, all three competing for attention. Swivelling awkwardly, she turned from her side on to her back, her knees facing upwards and touching the boot's lid. Raising her hands, she pushed upwards, using the little strength she had, willing it to rise. She tried shouting again, her voice sounding like it belonged to a stranger. She continued to yell, realising in her head that she wasn't calling out in English, but in Krio with the odd Fula phrase she could remember. But she wasn't in Sierra Leone, she reminded herself, and therefore had to yell for help in English. But distress knows no language, a part of her brain reminded her. Just make a sound, Hawa. Anyone out there would surely respond to shouting from a car boot.

Then she realised that the voice she was hearing was no longer her own but was coming from outside the vehicle. Someone shouting her name. She tried to speak, her mouth open as she croaked out a response.

There was a wrenching noise, as if someone was attacking

the car. And then the boot swung open, and she could see the sky above, which had transformed from the deep blue-black of when Santa had locked her in, to the slate grey of early morning.

There was a shadow standing above her. The shadow had something in its hand. Santa must have returned to hit her with the table leg again, she thought, clumsily raising her hands to protect herself. No blows rained down on her. Instead, she felt herself being half dragged and half lifted out of the boot. There was a person on either side of her, each hoisting one of her arms over a shoulder. Her feet had stiffened, refusing to collaborate with the instructions from her brain that willed them to carry her. In the dim morning light, Aisha's face came into view. She also recognised Jam Jerry, who was holding something long and metal in his hands.

Twisting her neck, which remained stiff and sore, she studied the person on the other side of her, the faint smell of Othella's familiar perfume applying a salve to her distress.

CHAPTER 43

Hawa was on a high bed, similar to the one Stella Kowa had been placed in when they went to visit her at the Royal Infirmary. On a chair next to her, fast asleep with her knees hoisted to her chest, was Aisha, her braids hanging over her face.

Aisha stirred awake, as if aware that Hawa was watching her, letting out a squeal of joy when she saw Hawa's eyes.

'You're awake, Miss Hawa! That demon locked you in the boot, but we found you! By God, we found you, Hawa!' Aisha's voice was choked off by emotion as the enclosure was suddenly occupied by a couple of nurses in pale green uniforms. Behind them, Hawa recognised Detective McKeown, who didn't look quite right in a baggy sweater and a pair of faded jeans, her hair trapped in a tight bobble, her eyes serious behind her glasses.

Easing Aisha out of the way, the nurses descended on Hawa, checking her vitals and gently plying her with questions. Satisfied that she was fine, they slowly raised the bed, hoisting her into a sitting position.

'You can only stay with her for a brief while, detective. She needs to rest. She's still quite weak, as I am sure you can understand,' one of the nurses said, speaking with the authority of one who was used to handing down edicts. She smiled at Hawa before shuffling out of the enclosed area, the other nurses following suit. Cynthia McKeown pulled a chair up to the bed, bringing her eyes level with Hawa's.

'How are you, Hawa? Do you remember what happened?'

Hawa spoke, the words falling out of her mouth. 'Santa took me. Tried to run but fell. He put me in the boot.'

'That's correct, Hawa. He took you over the bridge to Dunfermline and left you at a train station there. But Aisha and Othella found you,' the detective explained.

'I came back from the karaoke and couldn't find you. I called your phone and heard it vibrating under your bed. And so, I phoned Khalil, who had just dropped me off, but he wouldn't answer. But Othella was in the car park. Said she had flown from Sierra Leone to surprise you and attend your graduation. Her plane was delayed due to airport strikes back home, so she got here late. Mr Jam Jerry picked her up from the airport.' Aisha took a deep breath before continuing. 'We phoned Santa because he had driven you home. But the Satan demon wouldn't pick up his phone, and so Mr Jerry drove us to his place in Longstone. We saw him taking a box out of his old car and putting it in the back of the car he took us to your graduation in. We got out and walked towards him, but he looked us in the eyes and just drove off! Mr Jerry drove after him, but we lost him when he went over that long bridge.' Aisha paused, her eyes hard and bitter.

'And then Aisha called me, explaining that they had seen Santa driving over the Forth Road Bridge out of Edinburgh,'

Detective McKeown continued. 'I put out an alert immediately, instructing officers to be on the lookout and to
search industrial estates and train stations over the Forth
Road Bridge from North Queensferry and Rosyth as far as
Kirkcaldy. Luckily, Aisha, Jerry and Othella found you in
Dunfermline just before our officers arrived. It was a huge
advantage that Aisha had seen the car Santa was driving
earlier in the evening, so we knew the exact vehicle to look
out for.'

The detective smiled sadly. 'Your friend, Othella Savage,
is currently with our officers, as we believe she can help us
get to the bottom of this whole disturbing affair. But we
arrested Santa back at his flat in Longstone, Hawa, so you
have nothing to worry about. He was sitting on the couch
watching television when we arrived and came with us
without resisting. He sang hymns and chanted Bible verses
all the way to the station. In fact, he still hadn't stopped by
the time I left!'

Hawa was the third item on the six o'clock BBC news and
the first feature on *Reporting Scotland*. The story was still
developing, with reporters explaining that the so-called Car
Boot Killer had finally been apprehended after abducting
another woman, who was rescued from the boot of a car
in Dunfermline. The *Reporting Scotland* item was much
more extensive, a svelte female reporter with curly dark
hair and searching eyes informing viewers that the woman
who had been abducted was also from Sierra Leone, with
reports suggesting that she too had been a member of the
Lion Mountain Church. The reporter was on location at

Dunfermline Station, blue-and-white police cordon tape visible in the background around the car Hawa had been taken away in.

'The man who abducted Hawa Barrie, a young woman from Sierra Leone, is yet to be named, although unconfirmed reports suggest that he was widely known by the nickname of Santa within his local community. He is currently in police custody, helping them with their enquiries.' The camera then cut to Detective McKeown, looking pristine and professional in a deep charcoal suit, a marked difference from when Hawa had last seen her at her bedside earlier that morning. She stated that the police continued to gather evidence, not only on Hawa's abduction but also on the circumstances around the abduction of two other women who had tragically lost their lives after being subjected to similar trauma.

Hawa had struggled to convince the hospital staff that she was OK watching the news coverage of her abduction. An angular, dark-haired woman, who had introduced herself as Dr Norma Handyside, had been to see Hawa earlier in the day to check on her mental state and ask how she was coping. She had advised against engaging with anything that might cause Hawa to relive the experience, whilst also suggesting that she stay away from social media.

'At a time like this, it is vitally important that you have a support network in place. Families, in particular, are invaluable in this regard.' Here, Dr Handyside had paused to consult her clipboard. 'Your notes, however, say that you are in Scotland studying, with your entire family back in Africa, which is a slight concern in terms of your recovery.'

Smiling, Hawa had assured her that she was fine, pointing

out that she had Othella, Aisha and Jattu, who had driven down from Glasgow with her husband, Callum. Jattu had been inconsolable all afternoon, her husband struggling to soothe her, stressing that the outcome was positive since Hawa was fine and the despicable Santa had been arrested.

The doctors were also monitoring Hawa's physical injuries, the shoulder Santa had hit with the table leg displaying an angry bruise beneath light swelling. She had twisted her ankle in the car park, the diagnosis being a slight sprain rather than a break, and cracked a couple of ribs when Santa's bulk had floored her as she tried to run away. As a precaution, they checked her for concussion, with her motor skills, reactions and speech all holding up.

Aisha, Othella and Jattu watched the news with Hawa, sitting around her bed like diligent sentries. Othella had been led away by McKeown when she arrived at the hospital with Hawa, the detective openly suspicious of her part in the abductions and murders.

On her return hours later with Jam Jerry, Othella had dripped out details of her spell in custody, assuring the other ladies that all was well. 'McKeown was rightly concerned about my role in the church and the fact that I fled the country and disappeared for months. I told her about finding my flat door forced open and someone inside. To think it was Santa who came for me! From all accounts, though, it would appear that he was a deranged lone wolf, abducting women because he thought they had besmirched Lion Mountain's reputation whilst compromising all the good work Pastor Ranka was supposedly doing. But enough about me; my concern is Hawa's recovery.'

Jattu had brought jollof rice for Hawa, convinced that hospital food would impede her recovery. 'I remember well from when I was in to deliver Tyler. They do not put a single grain of salt in the food, and it tastes bland and empty. You need to feel the taste of Maggi cubes and big peppers in your mouth if you are to get better soon!'

Hawa was released from the Royal Infirmary a week later, Jattu insisting that she and Aisha come stay with her in Glasgow. 'You have all been to my house and you know I have the space. My heart will not sit down in peace if you go back to that Balerno flat where you were almost killed! Othella, you can come also if you have nowhere to stay just now.' Othella had declined on the grounds that she was staying in Bathgate with Jam Jerry. But Hawa and Aisha, seeing sense in Jattu's logic, had taken up her offer.

Piling into Jattu and Jam Jerry's cars, they had driven back to the Balerno flat to collect Hawa and Aisha's belongings, which were relatively meagre since the pastor had let the flat fully furnished. Othella stared wistfully at her African icons pictures on the wall, before asking if Hawa would mind if she took them back with her to Sierra Leone to display in the orphanage's dining hall. During their time in the flat together, Aisha and Hawa had added to the collection. Hawa showed Aisha how to access and print pictures, and where to buy cheap frames, though the younger woman's idea of icons had proved to largely be pop stars who were currently popular.

'Thanks so much for looking after my belongings, Hawa – especially my books,' Othella said, her eyes still fixed on the icons display. 'Jerry says he'll send them over to Sierra Leone along with the rest of my things in the near future.' She fell silent, then went over to Hawa and covered her in a hug.

Hawa was very grateful to Jattu for putting them up. 'You allowing us to put our heads on pillows in your house fits my situation perfectly. It will give me a chance to assess my life and decide where I want to live for the foreseeable future.'

They had told McKeown about their new living arrangements, and the detective had confirmed that she already knew Jattu and Jerry's addresses and would keep them in the loop regarding the case. 'It should be quite straightforward, really. Santa – or Gibril Massie, which is his real name – has openly admitted to the abduction of all three women, claiming that the will of God will never be subservient to man-made laws. He also admitted to attempting to break into Kumba Matturi's house in Clermiston. He said his plan was to punish her flesh for undermining the good work of Pastor Ranka by setting up her own church ambassador scheme. When he could not gain access to the house, he set her car on fire instead. Needless to say, he is quite unhinged, and I can see him being committed to a psychiatric facility rather than a conventional prison.'

Elijah Foot-Patrol had returned from London to learn of the horrendous crimes perpetrated by his flatmate. The police had detained him and subjected him to intense questioning, working on the assumption that he was privy to Santa's activities and was, in all likelihood, complicit. He had wept his innocence, before taking time on his eventual release to visit the ladies in Glasgow to plead the same.

A couple of weeks later, the story had almost disappeared

from the newspapers and social media, with only brief residual mentions of the dark affairs that had seen three Black women from West Africa abducted and locked in car boots, two of them dying in the process.

CHAPTER 44

Hawa was scheduled to meet Jam Jerry Holt for another walk in the Pentlands at ten. She and Aisha had recently moved out of Jattu's house in Glasgow, having secured a small flat to rent. Jattu had watched them go with worry in her eyes, insisting that she had the space to accommodate them both, whilst expressing ongoing concern for their welfare.

'We Africans never live alone, my sister! Back home, you never ever see one person living in a house by themselves! Our people surround themselves with neighbours, friends and relatives. In life, every human being needs another human being to knock on their bedroom door every morning to make sure they have survived sleep. It is because our sisters lived alone in this country that they disappeared and were locked in their car boots for days without anybody knowing their location or their situation. And that is why it is good that you will be living with Aisha, and both of you have the other to knock on your doors in the morning.'

Laughing, Hawa had convinced Jattu that they would be OK, promising to text and phone her regularly to assure her she was safe and well. Jattu's husband, Callum, had insisted they go out for a meal the night before they left, before driving them to their new home the following afternoon. The flat, which was located in Kirknewton, was sparsely furnished but cosy, and Hawa had kept it minimalist, her only addition being a slender bookcase she found on Gumtree.

The night before the walk, Hawa had trawled her phone as usual. Anaka Hart had sent her the rough version of the first song from her proposed album, a sultry track that combined the American's seductive vocals with a hard-hitting rap bridge. Anaka's voice was like a warm embrace around Hawa, and the lyrics on positivity and the power of the human spirit brought a smile to her face.

All Hawa's social media feeds were deluged by slickly produced short videos and eye-catching graphics promoting a campaign that had caught the imagination back home: *Othella 'Unopposed' Savage for Mayor of Freetown.* Hawa had followed the news closely from Scotland, and the whole city agreed that Othella's bid was a *sure-ball scheme.* Her opponent was a slug of a man in his seventies, an ex-minister who had served in several corrupt regimes and was currently under investigation for procuring a fleet of decrepit second-hand buses, several of which had broken down within a couple of months of their arrival.

After the death of Pastor Ranka, Othella had assumed command of the ministry in Sierra Leone. Reports from the home country detailed the positive strides she continued to make, the latest being a scholarship scheme for fifteen young ladies who were entering university.

Eventually, she had been convinced to redirect her influence and charisma and turn her hand to politics. Steering clear of the dominant political parties, Othella had decided to run as an independent candidate, building a groundswell of support and goodwill through the charitable projects she continued to lead.

There had also been a change of national government, the new administration replacing the entire cabinet, including Cecil Ranka, the pastor's brother. The anti-corruption council had then instituted a rigorous commission of enquiry, designed *to recover and recoup the copious and illicit funds siphoned off by corrupt politicians, which were rightly the property of the people of Sierra Leone.*

The commission had been able to draw links between Cecil Ranka's embezzled funds and the properties his brother, the pastor, had bought in and around Edinburgh. A joint operation with the British government had seen them all seized, whilst Ranka's overseas accounts were frozen with immediate effect.

Tina Kanu's newspaper, *The Satellite*, had been at the forefront of exposing the corruption, with Hawa regularly phoning and texting her to keep abreast of developments. Discussions with the former church ambassadors had revealed where all of the properties located across Edinburgh and the Lothians were, and Hawa had travelled to each of them in turn to take pictures to send to Tina for publication in *The Satellite*.

After her surprise visit for the graduation ceremony, Othella had implored Hawa to leave Scotland and return home to work by her side where they could make a difference to the lives of their people. Hawa had been granted indefinite leave to remain in the United Kingdom, and wasn't certain she wanted to return to Sierra Leone, as reports of unemployment and general hardship there were still reaching her ears.

Amanda had chosen to return to Scotland. Jam Jerry explained to Hawa that the church remained closed, however, and that the pastor's wife had gone back to practising law at a firm that provided pro bono services to immigrants and asylum seekers.

'I now attend Rhema Church in Dean Village. Mainly, I show up for the music,' Jerry explained as they ate some of his homemade muffins whilst resting halfway up a steep hill. 'I've always enjoyed gospel music, and playing in the band on Sundays makes a nice change from my boring job during the week. Never really been all that religious, anyway. For me, it's enough to be moral and decent to fellow human beings.'

Walks with Jam Jerry Holt had become a fortnightly ritual that Hawa had grown to enjoy. She had even driven to the Regatta shop in Livingston, where an enthusiastic and efficient store assistant had advised her on appropriate walking boots and waterproof clothing for the Scottish climate. Her gear had impressed Jam Jerry, drawing from him one of the mantras of hillwalking: 'No such thing as the wrong weather, Hawa, only the wrong clothes!'

ACKNOWLEDGEMENTS

A popular Sierra Leonean proverb states that *the dreams of dogs stay in their stomachs*, based on the premise that the faithful creatures' inability to speak means that we don't know what they're thinking. Not necessarily true of course. However, thanks to some very special people, these words have not *stayed in my stomach*, but have found their way onto these pages and into the world.

This book is dedicated to the memory of my parents, who are no longer with us. My dad, Foday Snr, who loaned me his name whilst always stressing that education would not necessarily make me rich but would open doors. True. And my mother, Josephine Agnes, who taught me humility and humour. Your strength amidst darkness will always be with me.

Thank you to my three special ladies – Cynthia Rumbidzai, Tanaka Natalie and Mandipa Aisha. Your love and support have been stellar, not to mention the fact that living with you provided authentic context and material for the novel. None of this would have been possible without you.

I would like also to thank my phenomenal agent – Elise Dillsworth – who, during the darkness and drudgery of lockdown, provided a sliver of hope by offering me a Zoom call and giving me invaluable advice and guidance, which continues to this day. Thanks for your kindness, for having my back and for always championing our stories.

The Mo Siewcharran Prize provided the platform for my novel to stand on, and I am very grateful to all who worked on the initiative, especially John Seaton, who represents such positive and noble ideals.

I would also like to extend the deepest appreciation to the brilliant team at Quercus Books; it has been a pleasure and an honour working with you: to my superb editor, Paul Engles, my point man, whose advice and measured insight have been priceless. Thanks also to Stef Bierwerth, Katherine Burdon and Cassie Browne, who read sections of the manuscript, providing invaluable editorial advice. Appreciation to my publicist Myrto Kalavreozou for continuing to open doors. Thanks also to Ross Dickinson, Alex Haywood, Andrew Smith, Jasmine Palmer and Tara Hodgson.

My brilliant copyeditor, Vimbai Shire, deserves special mention. Your observations and comments added lustre and depth to the novel.

As does Nathan Burton – your cover designs are so good they should be illegal; thanks for finding the time.

Then we have Mubanga Kalimamukwento, Stacey Thomas and Zaydah Rassin Kamara, authors with whom I have exchanged writing pieces through the years, bandying ideas whilst moulding stories. All of you are absolute gems.

And my good friend Miatta Gebeh, for constantly bombarding me with books; my shelves would be much emptier without you. Much appreciation also to Adama 'Unopposed'

Rogers for helping me with ideas while allowing me to use your unique nickname. Love always.

I owe a huge thanks to my siblings: Sheik, Gibril, Ahmed, Ishmael, Idriss, Musu. Clan Mannah thrives indeed. To older brother, Sullay Mannah, a special shout-out. I walk in your footsteps and the love and joy of literature was passed down from you. We've come a long way from reading *Mr. Men* books and watching *The Super Friends* on Saturday mornings.

And to certain special special friends who are always available to provide support: Zubairu Wai, Sahr Baryoh, Solomon Caulker, Ibrahim Sesay, Murtada Tunis, Max Gorvie, Dura Bockarie and Moses Zombo.

I must also thank my classmate/comrade from back in the day, Mohamed 'Boozeable' Massaquoi, whose promotion of the novel in the press back in Sierra Leone left me humbled and grateful. I stand on all of your shoulders.

And let's not forget Graeme O'Hara, a special friend, who graciously helped me with manuscript edits and author photographs, not to mention his idea of shooting brilliant videos to promote the book. Absolute works of art they are; deeply appreciated, sir.

Finally, allow me to finish with a standing ovation for the very special human beings who are English teachers; mutants with special powers who delight in reading and revelling in books. I've had the pleasure of working with some extraordinary members of this genre including the following: Kirsty McKeown, Norma Malcolm, Charlie Holt, Sheila Wells, Lesley Gripton, Barbara Jack, Christine Ball, Susi Davidson, Ruth Williamson, Paul Brady, Helen

Marshall, Paul Rooney, Suzie Handyside, Barbara van der Meulen, Karen Borthwick, Shek Toyo Kamara and Anne Hart (my book festival partner). Special thanks to Stephen Toman for reading the manuscript in its early stages and providing the first ever online review. I've stolen some of your names for characters, so please don't sue me.